THE FOX IN THE FIELD

Other Books by Maynard Allington

THE GREY WOLF (1986)

THE FOX IN THE FIELD

A WWII NOVEL
OF INDIA

MAYNARD ALLINGTON

BRASSEY'S (US)
A Maxwell Macmillan Company

Washington • New York • London

Brassey's (US)

Editorial Offices	*Order Department*
Brassey's (US)	Brassey's Book Orders
8000 Westpark Drive	c/o Macmillan Publishing Co.
First Floor	100 Front Street, Box 500
McLean, Virginia 22102	Riverside, New Jersey 08075

Brassey's (US) is a Maxwell Macmillan Company. Brassey's books are available at special discounts for bulk purchases for sales promotions, premiums, fund-raising, or educational use through the Special Sales Director, Macmillan Publishing Company, 866 Third Avenue, New York, New York 10022.

Library of Congress Cataloging-in-Publication Data

Allington, Maynard.
  The fox in the field : a WWII novel of India/Maynard Allington.
    p. cm.
  ISBN 0-02-881085-6
  1. World War, 1939–1945—Fiction. I. Title.
PS3551.L449F68 1994   93-17964
813'.54—dc20   CIP

Designed by Carla Bolte

10 9 8 7 6 5 4 3 2 1

Printed in the United States of America

So he went out and caught three hundred foxes and tied their tails together in pairs, with a torch between each pair. Then he lit the torches and let the foxes run through the fields of the Philistines, burning the grain to the ground along with all the sheaves and shocks of grain, and destroying the olive trees. . . .

—SAMSON
THE BOOK OF JUDGES

HISTORICAL FOREWORD

The *Fox in the Field* is based upon certain real events that occurred between 1941 and 1944. Historical figures such as Churchill, Admiral Canaris, and Field Marshal Rommel, who step on stage in this novel, are well known to readers and need no billing. Less familiar is Subhas Bose, though he remains, alongside Gandhi and Nehru, one of the major architects of Indian independence. For reasons that are not altogether clear, Western scholars have neglected his role—perhaps because it was a militant one in wartime. News of his activities had to be suppressed for purposes of security, and so he tended to slip incognito out of history.

In 1941, awaiting trial for sedition, Bose escaped from house arrest in Calcutta. He crossed the frontier on foot, posing as a deaf mute, and made his way from Kabul to Berlin. There he remained for two years, broadcasting anti-British propaganda to the subcontinent, and creating the first Indian Legion from Indian prisoners captured in North Africa.

Early in 1943, the Germans sent him out of Kiel by U-boat to Singapore. Once more, from Indian prisoners of war, he raised an army of 60,000 and joined the Japanese in the invasion of India. What happened then is part of this story.

Another event the author has described in some detail is the cataclysmic explosion and conflagration on the docks of Bombay in April of 1944. British censors withheld the news for more than a month. Not until late May did the first graphic accounts appear in *Time* and *Life* magazines. Sappers demolished hundreds of buildings to check the fires, which were not brought under control until the fifth day. The official count listed 360 dead, 1,815 injured, and

50,000 homeless, though the actual toll would never be known. Investigators could never rule out sabotage.

All historical characters in *The Fox in the Field* have been depicted as accurately as possible in terms of physical appearance, dress, speech, and the locales in which they appear. If war is a theater of improvisation, they were surely the key actors, and the production had a long run before the show closed. But history has always been an empty stage, full of sound and fury—too often signifying nothing.

Merritt Island, FL
18 March 1993

PROLOGUE

The staff car left London on Sunday morning and drove north in steel-heavy rain to Chequers. General Sir Hastings Ismay, chief of staff to Churchill, rubbed fog from the beaded pane and peered out at the wet, racing country. Another black day, in a black year, and from Storey's Gate—black news, too. Already, the general brooded how best to break it to the prime minister.

Ahead, the chimneys and gables of the manor house took shape in the splinters of falling rain above the stone wall and beechwoods. The sedan slowed for the checkpoint, then splashed round the drive to the entrance.

The driver opened the car door and a black umbrella bloomed in his hand. The general waved it aside and bounded up the steps in the rain.

A male secretary led him past the gray light of mullioned windows. Under a glass case lay Cromwell's empty gloves. They were large—tailored for a heavier hand than Churchill's—though Winston would take the measure of Cromwell in pure brass.

The general found Churchill sitting up in a bed strewn with working papers and cigar ash. Plump and resplendent in his mandarin dressing gown, the PM glanced up over the glasses tilted forward on his nose.

"You needn't tremble." The spoiled Cherub's face had a trace of humor curled into the underlip. "We don't shoot the messenger."

"You may have second thoughts," Ismay replied, "after you've read through these briefs." The general unstrapped his briefcase and laid a sheaf of papers on the bed.

"I presume," Churchill said, "the news is tainted by the usual polecat's musk?"

The chief of staff cleared a gout of nervous phlegm from his throat. "It seems that Subhas Bose escaped from house arrest in Calcutta," he said. "Two months ago, as a matter of fact."

The humor went out of the chubby underlip, and the eyes glowered. "Why wasn't I told?"

"It was my decision." Ismay shrugged. "I thought you had quite enough to worry about at the time. Besides, we were sure he'd be caught straightway."

"Which means he wasn't," Churchill growled.

"The sod's turned up in Berlin. Ribbentrop gave him a cracking welcome."

"I'll wager he did," the PM snapped. "What could suit Hitler more than an armed revolt in India?"

"I rather expect Goebbels will put him on the wireless. It's bloody luck, of course—though I should think Gandhi is the bigger threat."

"Gandhi will only die for his beliefs," Churchill grumbled. "Bose will kill for his. Once you appreciate the distinction, it makes Bose more dangerous in the short run."

"Still," the general insisted, "I doubt he can do much harm from Berlin."

The PM stripped a new cigar and lit it. The frown had deepened into a chasm of reflective thought, and the pale gaze seemed to ransack the bending sinews of smoke for an answer. At last his stare lifted to the chief of staff, who saw at once the cold contempt circumscribed into the pupils.

"And what makes you suppose Bose will stay put in Berlin?"

ESTORIL, NEAR LISBON
1943

1

The sea fell away as the man climbed the path in the pines and, once, he stopped in the shade to glance down the coast where the breakers unfurled in lazy scrolls against the bluffs and beaches. The black hair at his tanned neck needed cutting, and the planed features were scorched dark by a Mediterranean sun. Only the eyes were pale, like the light drowsing in the sea pools below, and the broad mouth looked as if some irreverent humor were about to break from it.

A breeze stirred the pine needles where the sea sparkled against the sunny distances of the day, and the man craned his head back on his wide shoulders and gazed uphill. The cemetery lay higher up near the crown of the hill, and he climbed toward it.

His shirt was streaked with sweat by the time he got to the iron gate in the low wall, and he wiped the moisture from his face. A few wildflowers threw ciphers of windblown color against the sun-bleached headstones and cenotaphs. It seemed less than hospitable to find only the rotting stalks of a dead bouquet at the base of the newest marker. Cut into the marble was a last name—VALADON.

For a long time the man stood before the grave while the wind took scraps of cloud across the sky above his head. If paradise existed, Valadon would already have bluffed his way into it. For an artist who had spent his life painting and selling fake works of the masters, a soul without stain would be easy enough to counterfeit, and it would amuse him to swindle the Devil out of eternity.

The man dropped to one knee and ran his fingers over the grooved letters. He might have been authenticating one of Valadon's own forgeries. Finally he murmured, "*Au revoir*, Emile," and stood up. Once more he squinted at the coast curving into the horizon. He did not see the motorcar in the clump of palms and mimosa on the road out of Estoril. Nor was he aware of the two Englishmen who stood in the deep shade of the trees. One was young and balding, the other burly and squat with a round, tough brawler's face, and the binoculars gripped in his blunt hands were trained on the cemetery.

"Is it Carr?" the younger man asked.

"He's tall enough," the other replied. "Who else could it be—at Valadon's grave?"

"About bloody time. I was beginning to think he wouldn't turn up."

The burly man lowered the binoculars and said, "I knew he'd be back."

A few hours later Derek Carr sat at a table on the open terrace of a restaurant that looked out over the red-tiled roofs and gardens of Estoril to the sea running in against the beach. A cool salt breeze blew off the water, and he ate a meal of *pescada* cooked in butter and lemon juice, and afterward smoked a cigarette and watched the dusk fall and the lights come on in the town and the benches fill in the park across the square.

A balding young man in British tweeds walked past the terrace and out of sight and came back into view crossing into the park. He had a newspaper folded under his arm. After a minute, he strolled out from under the leaves, sat down on the ring of the stone fountain in the square, and opened the newspaper. The street lamp did not cast enough light to read by, but the man sat, reading.

Carr smiled around the cigarette in his mouth and thought, *They're sending out amateurs these days.*

He called for the check, paid it, and went down into the street. In the square, the Englishman had left the fountain, and the water splashed down in a clear sheen from the stone dish. Carr got into a cab and told the driver to take him to the casino.

In the gaming rooms, under the glitter of chandeliers, a noisy crowd teemed—a mix of refugees, diplomats, journalists, and spies. A few refugees had managed to smuggle out their wealth. In front of Germans they gambled with an air of contempt. Others who had only a little money left would risk all of it in one last attempt to win passage fare to South America. For them, the roulette wheel was a fickle deity, and the croupier's rake was its instrument of damnation.

Carr moved among the tables. The white dinner jacket, open on the dark cummerbund, barely accommodated his shoulders, which had the wide slope of an oarsman's. Above the bow tie, the heavy mouth in the brown, flat-cheekboned face was faintly stretched, as if to contain some indifferent humor.

"Always dress the part," Valadon had said. "Be generous when you tip the dealers, and do not win too much. After you have won, lose a little back, then quit."

At one of the dice tables, the pretender to the Spanish throne had drawn a crowd. Squeezed next to him was a girl Carr recognized. Her dark hair was massed atop her head and banded with pearls, and a long evening gown of some gleaming fabric looked as if it had been poured over her figure. She worked for the German ambassador as an informant, and her usual targets were British clipper pilots and foreign correspondents, not royalty; though around the casino, ex-kings were as commonplace as petty crooks. Suddenly, she caught sight of Carr, and her chin lifted antagonistically. An image of a straining naked body floated up in Carr's mind—one of her white breasts had been smaller than the other—and he remembered that he had said he would call her and had not. Now he could feel the resentful heat of her gaze as he moved off into the crowd.

Near the cashier's cage, Carr spotted one more familiar face. It belonged to a stout Greek with Vaselined curls who sold forged visas, and tickets on steamships that would never reach Lisbon because they did not exist. He was holding a lady's brooch up to the light while the lady's husband stood watching. The lady herself sat on one of the deep sofas nearby, a bloom of color on her cheeks. The Greek shook his head and handed the pin back to the husband, who began to protest. They were arguing over the value.

Carr took a chair at the kidney-shaped baccarat table facing the mirrored wall. He nodded at the *Chef de Jeu* perched high above the three croupiers, and put down several large notes on the baize top. The croupier took them and shunted back a stack of checks on the flat of his *palette*. The shoe passed to a new banker.

At the end of an hour, after a run of cards, Carr was ahead forty thousand escudos. Twice, in the panel of glass behind the *Chef de Jeu*, he caught sight of the balding young Englishman moving among the crowded reflections.

A casino waiter named Luis, who peddled information, brought a drink that Carr had not ordered. The hairline moustache in the oily face hovered close as the waiter murmured, "An Englishman was here making inquiries about you."

"When?"

"Two nights ago."

"Is he here now?"

"I do not see him," the waiter said, wiping the cocktail tray with his napkin.

So there are two of them, Carr thought. He dropped a folded bill on the tray. "Thank you, Luis."

The stiff jacket creaked as Luis bowed and straightened against the glimmer of cut glass and the gold cornices of the high-ceilinged room. "*Muito obrigado*," he replied.

Carr tipped the croupier and slipped away from the baccarat table. Leaving the salon, he had a glimpse of the Greek forger in conversation once more with the man who had the brooch. The wife was nowhere in sight. The husband's indignation had given way to an air of quiet despair now as he handed over the pin.

Outside, in a taxi, Carr opened Valadon's silver case and lit one of the custom-rolled Turkish cigarettes. He glanced back through the rear glass of the Citroen and saw the Englishman hurry to a second taxi.

As his own cab snaked uphill, gearing down for each loop of the road, Carr watched the headlights of his pursuer sweeping the terra cotta walls of villas out of the darkness below. Half a kilometer back, the vehicle climbed at the same even pace, making no effort to overtake Carr's.

Near the crown of the hill, the Citroen braked to a stop. Carr got out, paid the driver, and watched him back slowly down the road into some pines on the shoulder where he could turn around. There was no sign of the second cab, but he knew it must be parked not far below, its headlights out.

Beyond a latch gate, stone steps lifted steeply from the road, through dark foliage on the slope, to Valadon's villa. A curved terrace looked down over the tops of the trees to Estoril lit against the sea.

Carr slipped onto the terrace, where a lattice roof, overgrown with tropical vines and flowers, ground its shadow into the stone below. A moon blazed across the row of French windows, bathing the room in its pale radiance. Carr at once caught sight of a stocky figure only half-concealed behind a Japanese screen, one of Valadon's favorite pieces, which he had acquired in Yokohama in a shameless swindle.

Carr circled the house, let himself in at the entrance, and slid the locking bolt into its iron catch. He moved unhurriedly across the room, away from the paper screen, the ivory sheen of his dinner jacket melting its reflection onto the glaze of the Italian marble floor.

The liquor cabinet had a false bottom that opened to the touch of a panel spring. He picked up the 9-mm Beretta pistol, switched on a lamp, and turned with the weapon leveled. Behind the etching of lovers erotically entwined, the larval shadow of the man was almost obscene.

"That's a sixteenth-century screen," Carr said. "All of Yokohama will be enraged if I have to put a bullet through it."

2

A voice behind the screen said, "It's Neville Gage, and I don't fancy any flying lead in my backside, old boy."

The man stepping into view was short, like a figure clumsily cut from a granite block, and his face bore the blunt damage of a blow from a lead pipe across the bridge of the nose.

"Aren't you a long way off your patch?" Carr said. "This is Portugal, not Soho."

"I'm not with the Yard these days," Gage said. "The intelligence boys put me into uniform in thirty-nine."

"Your friend outside in the garden, too?"

"You needn't worry about him. He's only there to keep watch."

"Have a word with him, will you? He nearly spoiled a coup at the baccarat table."

"You'd only win it back," Gage said. "I've seen you turn a knave into a nine. Remember?"

"Spot of luck," Carr said.

"Luck," Gage snorted.

"The first rule of luck," Carr said, "is never to slur the good name of someone holding a pistol on you."

"You can put it up. I'm not here to arrest you."

"I see. You just popped in to say hello."

"I came to offer you *honest* work for a change."

"Why would you do that?" Carr slipped the Beretta into the side pocket of his dinner jacket. "I thought I was a contemptible rat in your book?"

"I never said rats weren't resourceful creatures," Gage replied. "In fact, they are intelligent and cunning."

"Like Scotland Yard detectives?"

"If I were still a detective, I'd want to know where you'd been for the last two years."

"Palma," Carr said.

"Why Palma? There aren't any casinos."

"It's as quiet a place as any to sit out the war," Carr said. "You can live like a rajah on less than bird dung."

"I would have thought you might like to mix in the war."

"What gave you that idiotic idea?"

"Your father was British."

A memory flashed of a man with the shine of black blood down one side of his face, and the eye gone from the draining hollow of one socket.

"To his regret," Carr said.

"You're still half British, and England is at war."

"I carry a Swedish passport, and Sweden is at peace."

"You've carried quite a few passports." Below the smashed nose, a smile found its way into the stone-heavy mouth. "Not as many as your pal, Valadon, of course."

"He doesn't need one now."

"How did you get word of his death?" Gage asked.

"How did you?" Carr answered.

"We came to Estoril looking for you. He'd been in the grave a fortnight. You were his only beneficiary. I was sure you'd turn up before long. You've inherited quite a gallery."

The intelligence officer moved along the wall where the lamp cast its glow across a dozen paintings and pastel drawings on the whitewashed stucco. He paused before a nude, discreetly posed, the warm flesh tones strikingly alive on the canvas.

"My mother." Carr lit a cigarette. "They were lovers."

"I always wondered," Gage said, "about the accuracy of my files."

"What did they say?"

"That she was Swedish. That she left India and went back to Stockholm after your father . . ."

"Shot himself?" Carr said. "There's the old school tie for you. It didn't matter that the evidence was false, only that it was strong enough to convict him. He didn't want his family to face the scandal of a public trial. He confused stupidity with nobility. My mother never forgave the British government."

"There was a formal apology. His name was cleared. That should have meant something."

"Should it?"

"Valadon was a different sort. What attracted her to him?"

"Maybe it was because he didn't play by the rules."

"They never married?"

"No, but it was monogamous, even without benefit of clergy. She died quite early. He never recovered from it." Carr glanced once more at the painting. "The odd part is, he might have been an important artist if he'd tried."

"Why didn't he?"

"Emile had a weakness for the soft life. So he applied his talent to a more profitable enterprise."

"Fraud, you mean."

"He always had the conviction that one day his forgeries would be more valuable than the artists he copied. He had no obligation to look out for me after her death, but he did."

"I dare say." Gage nodded. "Like a Fagin with the proper manners. Did he teach you about dice and cards, too?"

"I was born with a memory for cards. It seemed a pity to waste the gift. All we did was collaborate on our skills."

"You made quite a few contacts for him in the grand casinos. Monte Carlo, London, South America . . ."

"When you meet people who can afford to drop a thousand quid on a spin of roulette, it isn't hard to convince them to gamble on a Matisse or a Modigliani."

Gage shook his head and said, "You weren't selling fake art when you went to Ethiopia in thirty-six."

"That was a different form of gambling."

"What does running guns have in common with cheating at cards?"

"An effortless profit. The Ethiopians had just discovered that their spears had a limited success against Italian tanks."

"You took the guns in at a considerable risk."

"A risk I was paid for."

"We thought you might have had a nobler motive."

"Worse mistakes in judgment have been made," Carr said, "but not many."

"Where did you get the weapons?"

"A Turkish arms merchant. He had a passion for betting high at *chemin de fer*, and no luck. When it came time to dissolve the partnership, Valadon fobbed off a very nice Matisse on him."

"I wouldn't know a Matisse from a packet of Woodbines."

"Did you come all this way to display the gaps in your education?"

"As I've said, old boy, I came to enlist you."

Carr stared at him across the bending plume of the cigarette and said, "Are you unwell?"

"Shall we step outside for a breath of air—just in case?"

They slipped out through the French doors onto the terrace. Down the coast, under a moon, the breakers flashed in against the beach.

"Lisbon is crawling with British spies," Carr said. "Why make the confusion worse by adding another one?"

"Not Lisbon," Gage replied. "We want to whip you off to Bombay."

"Bombay," Carr said. He repeated the word soundlessly, then tipped back his head and laughed, the cords standing out in his brown throat.

"It amuses you," Gage said.

"Hardly."

"Does the name *Subhas Bose* have a familiar ring?"

"The Indian nationalist? The last I heard, he was in Berlin."

"The Germans packed him off to Singapore early this year. He's announced a provisional government and looks to be raising an army to stir up trouble on the mainland."

"That's gratitude for you," Carr said, "after all you've done for him."

"Not long after Bose was put into Singapore, the Jerries landed a chap named Kordt and some others on the Bombay coast. Kordt's a captain in German intelligence."

"How did you get wind of it?"

"A source in the Abwehr—close enough to Canaris to fetch him coffee."

"That's always convenient."

"He went silent," Gage said.

"You mean he was caught and shot, don't you?"

"Probably. In any case, one of his last reports out of Berlin identified Kordt with an operation code-named China Blue."

"That sounds like a tea service."

"The best guess is that Kordt and China Blue are linked some-how to Bose's activities in Singapore. So far, all we've been able to do is identify a possible contact of Kordt's in Bombay—one of Bose's old political allies in the Congress Party."

"Why don't you pick him up?"

"*Her*, not him. At this point, we want answers, not people. What the devil is China Blue, and what does it have to do with Bose?" The intelligence officer was silent, gazing down at the lights of Estoril clumped against the sea. Then, as if everything were set-tled, he said, "It shouldn't be hard for you to work your way into their confidence. No more difficult than palming off another— what's the bloody artist's name?"

"Matisse," Carr said. "Sad to report, Matisse and I aren't inter-ested."

"German intelligence will check your background," Gage said. "First off, there's the businesss of your father, You've every reason to resent the British. On top of that, you've run guns into Ethiopia. You have connections in the arms trade. Put the two together, and you're a prize asset to them."

Carr sat on the marble railing, ablaze in moonlight, and shook his head. "Gage, you slow-witted lout. Is there a history of insanity in your family? What made you think I'd do it?"

"Two reasons," the other said. "First off, you'll be paid."

"Sorry," Carr said.

Gage went on as if he didn't hear. "The second reason you'll do it is because I've had a look round your new digs. It took some doing to get into that basement vault. As I say, you've fallen heir to quite a gallery. Did you know there were nearly sixty paintings? Damned fine, too, from the look of them. Fool most of the experts, I should think. I'll see you get them back, of course, when the job in Bombay is finished—assuming I have your word you won't flog them in U.K. after the war."

"The Portuguese police," Carr said, "call that grand theft."

"I call it seizing evidence. Would you like to confer with the authorities to see which one of us is right? Then, of course, there's your Scotland Yard file. I expect that the big casinos will be grate-ful to get a copy. They may even post your photo at the *salle d'entrée*. You'll be famous, old boy. Don't worry. We'll see to it."

Carr stared down the coast at the surf flaring in against the white strip of beach. All the while, his mind worked over the problem while Gage looked on with the smug confidence of a gambler holding cards.

"I'm at the Palacio," the SIS officer said. "Ring me up in the morning. I'll stand you to a lunch. We can chat about your trip."

3

While the talk about China Blue was taking place in Estoril, the first phase of the operation was unfolding on a bridge over a gorge in the mountains east of Bombay.

It was an old bridge, the pile posts lashed together and anchored to bedrock on either side of the stream, and the water showing through the gaps between the oil-soaked planks made a dark gleam in the shade far below.

Near the center span, where the support timbers flared to a V-notch, a man wearing the uniform of a British major leaned on the handrail and looked through a pair of field glasses at the white road looping up through the pass. He was of medium height and solidly built, his legs brown in the short trousers and sturdy, the calf muscles bulging against knee-length stockings. A Webley .455 revolver hung from a Sam Browne pistol belt, and on either side of the diagonal shoulder strap his khaki shirt was streaked with sweat, the sleeves rolled up above his tanned forearms. Under the glint of blonde hair the features were impassively cool, as if some fatalistic calm had been cut into them, and apart from a trace of melancholy, other emotions were rationed in the face.

The binoculars picked up a convoy of six Bedford lorries and a jeep climbing out of the jungle valley. The vehicles moved silently in the crosspiece hairs, and the major could see the convoy officer in the lead jeep, and a rifleman next to the driver in the cab of each truck, and dust lifting from the wheels, and the wet shine of boulders in the stream below the road where spray blew. The canvas had been stripped from the last lorry, and six Indian troops sat back-to-back in the bed, their .303 Enfield rifles upright between their knees.

The officer on the bridge lowered the binoculars, and the convoy shrank back to toy size beside the flash of the stream. But his eyes, which were pale and unflinching and rimmed with the dust of the country, held fast to the slowly climbing trucks.

"Ten minutes," he called out to the others.

There were twelve under his command: two Sten guns in the scrub above the road where the trucks would halt after rolling across the bridge; a Bren light machine gun higher up in the rocks; the rifleman who had taken the guard's place at the sentry box; and the demolitions man waiting with his plunger at the end of the wire to set off the charge. Minutes earlier, two others had roared off on motorbikes in opposite directions. They would set up roadblocks, above and below the bridge, to turn back any traffic and isolate the convoy.

Around the base of the piling, a five-man crew of turbaned Sikhs worked with picks and shovels in a pretense of making repairs. Each carried a double-edged *khanda*, the religious knife of the sect, but they would not be used unless the fight went to close quarters.

Thirty meters downstream, the body of the sentry who had been posted at the bridge lay in a clump of jungle ferns, a wire-thin garrote twisted into the flesh around his neck. The major squinted hard at the site, but the leafy growth, shaded by overhanging rock, hid the corpse. Satisfied, the officer strolled to the end of the bridge to wait for the trucks, still some distance below, trailing a plume of dust against the jungle.

A bend took them out of sight, but finally they rounded a curve into view, motors whining in low gear, close enough for the major to make out the sunburnt features of the young lieutenant behind the windshield of the jeep. In the back seat, a lance corporal cradled a Sten Mark 1 machine carbine.

The major raised his hand and the jeep ground to a halt. The lieutenant jumped out, saluted, and gave his name and battalion.

The major returned the salute and said, "Major Locke, Royal Engineers. Where are you bound?"

"The armory at Poona, sir. We've just come up from Prince's Dock."

"What's your cargo?"

"Brens and three-oh-threes, mostly. One lorry of ammunition. Trouble with the bridge, sir?"

The clank of picks and shovels rose faintly over the sound of falling water from the cool shade beneath the timbers.

"Weren't you informed?" The major frowned. "A signal went out to Battalion yesterday. The last monsoon weakened the piling. It needs shoring up."

"We crossed it twenty-four hours ago on the way down from Poona. It seemed stout enough then."

"Your lorries were empty. It's a question of weight, isn't it?" The major might have been a schoolmaster chiding a slow pupil. "The order specified that any military traffic a ton or more was to be diverted. I don't understand why your headquarter company didn't get hold of you in Bombay. Were you out on the town?"

The lieutenant reddened. He glanced at the senior officer, who was soft-spoken and whose manner had the imprimatur of privilege stamped over it. The cadences of quiet arrogance in his speech were pure Cambridge—*the sod.*

The lieutenant gazed back over his shoulder at the lorries, then looked at his watch. "Bloody luck," he murmured. "We'll be mucking about on back roads half the night if we have to turn around."

Some of the stern indifference in the major's stare gave way to a flicker of sympathy.

"I shouldn't want to inflict that ordeal," he said, "if we can avoid it. Let's have a look at your load."

They went back to the first truck and the lieutenant opened the flap above the tailgate where the canvas hood was lashed down over the bows. The banded crates of arms were stacked high and roped to the cargo rings.

"Right," the major said. "I think we can get you across. Drop the second man out of the cab. Only one lorry and driver at a time on the bridge. The troops can cross on foot once the vehicles are over. Be sure each lorry comes dead slow."

"Dead slow, sir," the lieutenant said. "I don't fancy pulling a bloody Bedford out of the river."

The major smiled and said, "Nor do I."

The lieutenant grinned back, thinking the major wasn't such a bad sort after all.

The major leaned over the guardrail and called out in Marathi to the work crew. He was ordering them out from under the bridge until the convoy was across.

"I'll go to the other end," he told the lieutenant. "Tell your drivers to watch for my signal."

"Very good, sir." The lieutenant saluted again and turned away.

The jeep came over first, and the driver parked a short way up the road to make room for the lorries. The lance corporal laid his machine carbine on the back seat, took the driver's canteen and his own from their harnesses, and left the jeep.

"Where are you off to?" the major called to him.

"Refill these, sir." The soldier lifted the water bottles into the air.

"Double quick, then," the major said, "and keep clear of the bridge."

The lance corporal slid out of sight down the embankment of loose shale. After a bit, he came into view at the edge of the stream—no more than ten meters, the major calculated, from the sentry's body in the ferns.

The trucks rolled across one at a time, the planks rumbling under the wheels, and parked in the sun on the wide shoulder beyond the sentry box. The drivers stood, talking and smoking, in a patch of shade.

At the stream, the lance corporal screwed the caps onto the canteens, which he had dipped into the cold water to fill, and stood up. Something on the ground caught his attention as he stepped away from the bank. Squatting, he picked up a small object and looked at it.

Perhaps a button from the dead man's tunic, the major thought, and shifted closer to the guardrail.

The lance corporal rose and started for the road, his head down. The major waved another lorry onto the bridge. He glanced over the guardrail again. Now the lance corporal had stopped and was staring up into the shadowy gloom where the support timbers joined the piling.

New possibilities worked into the major's nerves. Could the soldier have spotted the explosive? Or the detcord running down from it? Whatever it was had drawn a puzzled frown. The lance corporal motioned to one of the Sikhs to come over, and passed out of sight into the shadow under the bridge.

The major eased to a spot where he could see down through the gaps between the creosoted planks. The upturned face of the soldier made a pale oval in the shade beside the dark sheen of water. There was a quick, darting movement behind him, and his outcry was muffled behind the hand clamped over his mouth. The major saw the flash of a Sikh knife, and the soldier's throat spilled open under the blade. His arms flew straight out, then clawed at the hand covering his mouth and nostrils, his body straining convulsively. The strength melted out of him. One by one, his arms dropped. Still locked together, the two figures sank out of sight.

When the last lorry had crept across, the major called through cupped hands to the lieutenant, "Bring your lads over. Single line to either side of the bridge."

Now it was time to clear himself. Probably the jeep driver must be wondering about the lance corporal. The Sikh crew had slipped back to the cover of big rocks below the road. The lorry drivers still chatted and joked in the shade near the trucks. The major angled past the group, out of the cross fire of the Sten guns trained down on them from the jungle scrub.

Approaching the jeep, he looked back and saw that the troops were strung out on the bridge. They moved in route march, the boards thumping hollowly under their boots, rifles slung over their shoulders. Without breaking stride, the major opened the flap of his holster and tugged on his left ear. Both Sten guns erupted in rapid fire, the 9-mm slugs spurting dust into the air as they chewed up the ground where the drivers sprawled.

The jeep driver twisted around for the machine carbine on the back seat and the major fired twice at close range, the revolver jumping from the recoil, and he saw a splash of red on the soldier's neck and the jerk of his body from the impact of each bullet. The officer dove for cover and felt the shock wave of the explosion from the bridge as he hit the ground. The center span lurched upward on the edge of his vision, and bits of timber and flying debris, sucked high by the blast, hung in the air a full moment before spinning and tumbling down.

A stench of burnt cordite drifted on the smoke from the wreckage. Only two of the troops remained on the bridge. The crushed body of one showed in the tangle of posts and rubble hanging down over the water. On the span behind him, the second man struggled to his feet and tried to run, bent low, gripping a blood-soaked leg with both hands and stumbling.

High in the rocks, the Bren light machine gun opened up, the echo from each short burst hammering back into the gorge. The running figure pitched forward on the ramp and lay still, and there was only the sound of the wind soughing in the leaves and the water dropping through the gorge.

Still gripping the revolver, the major pushed to his feet. Already his men were sliding downhill in the leafy dappling of jungle scrub, their Sten guns at the ready. The machine gunner came too, dislodging a few loose rocks on the way, the bandoliers of ammunition banging against his chest. The Sikhs clambered up from the stream. They would drive the lorries out. No one spoke. Each man knew his assignment. The group had rehearsed the postattack drill as thoroughly as the attack itself.

The major moved down the line of trucks. The drivers who had been cut down by the opening bursts from the Sten guns were crumpled in awkward postures on the ground. One had tried crawling to cover and lay, still alive, near the front axle of a truck, his eyes not quite focused in a bewildered stare. The major rolled him onto his side. Part of his jaw was shot away. The eyes swiveled up with an effort and the lips pulled back from his bloodied teeth in what could have been either a smile or a grimace. A plea for life? Or for a humane death? Either way, the major thought, it was a hollow concession. He stepped behind the dying man, cocked the revolver, and murmured in German, "I am sorry."

The soldier was still smiling vacantly when the officer shot him behind the ear.

BOMBAY
1944

4

Outside his room, on the whitewashed gallery of the Malabar Arms Hotel in Bombay, Derek Carr tipped his shoulder against a stone arch and gazed across the slate roofs of the district to the curve of the bay, beyond the plume of his cigarette, where the sun was drowning on the water. *Time to go.* Surely a moment of high drama, he thought, and half expected the strains of "God Save the King" to break out of the quiet distances. But no heroic fanfare blew in his behalf, and he put his shoe on the cigarette and went down into the street.

A Victorian office building, its top tier still bathed in the lemon glow of the dying day, loomed above an island square where taxis were parked. Carr climbed into one and told the driver, "Mahalakshmi Temple."

They drove through the glut of traffic out the sea road, and in a little while the taxi rolled to a stop on a rocky littoral where the Arabian Sea spent itself in quiet flashes of twilight. Higher up, the dome of Mahalakshmi swelled on the clear evening. Carr paid the driver and the cab rattled off.

He did not climb the lane past the hawkers of coconuts and sweets and garlands of flowers to the temple but, instead, followed a footpath above the sea to a low bluff shaded by trees. A sedan gleamed in the dusk under the slumping leaves. A young British officer stepped out from behind the wheel, his features not quite distinct in the leafy speckling, and called out, "This way, sir. The colonel's waiting."

As Carr came up, a face leaned into view at the open window of the back seat and said, "Sterns. Intelligence service. Are you always late for appointments?"

"Habitually," Carr said, and had an impression, as he looked down, of quick ferret eyes beneath flattened quills of graying hair, a mouth clamped into a thin line, and pocked skin like plaster of Paris.

The door opened and the colonel said, "Get in. We haven't much time."

Carr climbed in beside the senior officer, who was short and wiry and had the look of a Sandhurst professional rather than a wartime conscript.

"I may as well tell you, straightway," Sterns said, "that I opposed your being sent here."

"Splendid," Carr said. "That puts us in the same camp."

"For quite different reasons, I should think."

"But no doubt the basis of our instant rapport. Is this chap in the front seat one of your cowed subordinates?"

"Lieutenant Paine," Sterns said, "will be your permanent contact with us. I thought the two of you ought to have a look at each other."

"Be honest with me, Paine. What grave blunder did you commit to get handed this particular job?"

"Luck of the draw, sir," Paine said.

"You should know about that," Sterns said to Carr, "from what I've been told."

"Handling cards is just another combat art," Carr said. "Like soldiering."

"Is it really?" Sterns said. "Six weeks ago we lost twenty men in the mountains east of here. Six lorries and a jeep were stolen, and a bridge blown up. The lorries carried arms and ammunition."

"When you gamble," Carr said, "somebody has to win the pot."

"He took it all," Sterns said. "It was a near perfect execution."

"*Near* perfect?"

"One sepoy survived the explosion on the bridge. He gave a description of the chap who led the assault. There's not much doubt it was Kordt, impersonating a British officer. His English was fluent. He spoke Marathi, and his physical characteristics fit Kordt, what little we know about him. I expect you've been briefed?"

"Only that he and some others were landed by submarine to support an operation called China Blue. You people are supposed to put me in touch with a suspected contact of his—a woman."

For the first time, Paine broke in. "She is *that*," he said. Paine still carried some baby fat on his frame, and his chubby face had a flushed energy, as if a varsity cheer had just come from it.

"She's an Anglo-Indian doctor," Sterns said, "who gave up the practice of medicine for the practice of sedition. Her father was Colin Farrar. *Sir* Colin . . ."

"Should I know him?"

"Textiles," Sterns replied. "He made a pile of money on cheap wog labor."

"Why would a lady who's half English work for the Germans?"

"Because she's half Indian, and the Indian half is anticolonial. But that's another story. She took the sari when she took her husband. A Parsi. One of the wealthiest in Bombay."

"And oldest," Paine added, as if this were a factor.

The colonel gave the younger officer a sharp glance, his lips vise-tight in his lower face where the skin was dead white like a shell-marked terrain. A little tin soldier, Carr decided, intolerant of any view that did not conform to his own regimented vision of the world.

"I thought the Parsis kept to themselves in matters of money and matrimony."

"Quite so." Sterns nodded. "I expect you can draw your own conclusions about that. The marriage didn't change her politics. She was active in the radical wing of the Indian National Congress under Bose. At one time she was also a flaming Marxist, if our files have it right."

"A Marxist, married to a Parsi, and taking orders from a fascist." Carr nodded soberly. "Of course. It only makes good sense, doesn't it?"

"You can decide that for yourself. You'll be meeting her Sunday at the polo field."

"Is she playing a chukker?"

"She and her husband sponsor an annual match for charity. Proceeds go for the relief of Indian prisoners of war in Singapore and Burma. You'll be attending with a handsome contribution. That should get you an introduction. The rest is up to you. Express some anti-British sentiments. Shouldn't be difficult for you in view of . . . things." He had groped for the last word, *things*, and now he added, "Oh yes, Paine will be along to arrest you."

"For what?"

"Questioning. You're a known arms smuggler of unsavory reputation. We want to find out what your business is in Bombay."

"You might take a swing at me, sir," Paine said cheerfully. "It would add realism. Don't worry, I've done a bit of boxing. I can roll with it."

Carr chuckled and said to Sterns, "What's the lady's name?"

"Ashley Vora."

"And suppose your scheme doesn't work with her?"

"It's your job to make it work," Sterns said. "If it were up to me, I wouldn't let you touch it. You're quite out of your class with a chap like Kordt." The British officer gazed reflectively at the dead twilight hanging in a far-off smudge of dusk where the sea curved into the horizon. "His sort is rare. He's a scholar. A soldier with intellectual gifts. Whereas"—the resentful stare shifted back to Carr—"you're only a cheat—without a game."

Carr managed to be suitably grave, despite the smile working into his long mouth. "You're right," he said. "It's unfair."

5

After the third chukker, half the spectators left their seats and milled on the green, tamping down the turf torn up by the horse's hooves. Off the field, in the leafy dappling of shade trees, barefooted grooms, holding each bridle close to the bit, walked the ponies that would be ridden when play resumed.

Carr stayed in his seat in the stands and smoked a cigarette, the coat of his white linen suit folded over his arm. He was watching the small group under the striped awning of the reviewing stand. None of them, including Ashley Vora, had left their folding chairs to go down onto the field.

From that distance, Carr could see she was tall, with long legs, and her black hair had the gleam of printer's ink against the white, unflawed skin that seemed to belong still to the mists and moors of the English north, not the sunburnt stretches of India.

An Indian gripping a loud hailer ran along the sideline, calling the spectators off the green. Two mounted umpires cantered onto the turf and reined in. Then came the players, their breeches flared above tall riding boots, pith helmets strapped on, sticks resting high on the shoulders of their red and gold jerseys.

They played four more chukkers, the riders sweating in the heat, shouting to each other and sometimes swearing as they converged in a scrimmage. Then one would break from the pack and take the ball down the field, his weight forward in the saddle, stick lifted high before each shot, the crack of the mallet loud and wooden, and the others would pursue at a gallop, leather creaking under the strain, hooves thudding heavily on the green.

The timekeeper blew a whistle to signal the end of the match, and the riders brought their ponies into line before the reviewing stand. The ponies were blowing hard, their sides heaving, and the captain of the winning team dismounted. Carr's gaze held fast to Ashley Vora, who had come down from the reviewing stand to present the winner's trophy. The pale lavender of her sari did little to conceal the provocative curve of her hips or the heavy swell of her breasts as she moved unhurriedly with the silver cup. The captain took it from her and bowed, and the crowd rose in the stands to applaud.

Later, Carr joined the throng under the archipelago of canvas awnings stretched for shade over the grass. Pennants drooped on banners in the heat, and hand-lettered signs pointed the way to teas, ices, and cakes. He had stopped by a table where a rotund man was taking donations for Indian war relief. The flab around his middle had been buttoned with some difficulty into his frock coat, and his fat neck bulged over the tight, high collar that had a slot cut into it at the throat like a priest's cassock. His face was very black and the sweat gave it a bituminous shine.

"A bank draft for Mrs. Vora," Carr had said. "Will you see she gets it?"

"I am most certainly seeing to this matter absolutely," the Indian replied, as if he had been accused of embezzlement.

A minute later, he had hurried from the table, knocking his chair over in his haste to get up. He had evidently seen the amount of the draft, one thousand pounds, for the whites of his eyes were popping. Carr could feel himself being pointed out to the patroness in the pale lavender sari—could feel her stare in the crowd.

Now, the plump figure in the frock coat bounded up in front of him, bowed hastily, and joined his palms together. "Mrs. Vora is wishing to thank you personally," he said.

Carr followed the man through the crowd. Ashley Vora was standing with her back to them, her black hair banded behind her neck with a pearl clasp and flashing down almost to the curve of her hips. She turned before they reached her and Carr saw that the almond-shaped eyes were stunningly large, as if they needed space to accommodate the violent force in the dark pupils where the emotions were suppressed into a cold purpose. Large oval earrings left a gold gleam on her skin, and her tone, even as she thanked him, held on to some cool reserve, as if the gratitude were only being put into escrow.

He shrugged and replied, "It's all in a patriotic cause."

"For India," she said, "not Britain."

"That hardly matters," he said, "since I'm not British."

"I rather thought you were," Ashley said.

"Why?"

"Your check is written on a London bank."

"Before the war, I traveled about Europe a good deal of the time. A foreign account was always convenient." He smiled and added, "In any case, pounds have no politics. Their character is sterling, not British."

"I'm afraid you can't exchange cynicism for shillings in Bombay," she said.

"I thought cynicism was the official currency of the British in India."

"People who express that belief are usually locked up in British gaols."

"It seems to be your own belief," Carr said.

"I'm a realist," Ashley said. "Not a cynic."

"What's the difference between the two?"

Her mouth, overripe in its fullness, threw away a faint smile as if it were a needless accessory. "The difference between a fox and a fool," she replied.

Carr tipped back his head and laughed softly. "Mrs. Vora, you have a wily nature."

"That's not a virtue of fools," she said.

"Do fools have virtue?"

"Only trust."

"In the British?"

"In British promises," she said.

"Promises are just a cheap form of diplomacy," Carr said. "Nobody takes them seriously, these days."

"Perhaps you're right. Wolves promise nothing to their victims. The politicians in Whitehall are like wolves who run in a pack."

"Didn't Gandhi preach that independence is a collective state of mind?"

"Gandhi is a saint," she said. "Saints are usually part fool."

"I don't plan to be canonized on either count."

This time the trapped amusement lingered on her mouth.

"If you've come to Bombay on business," she said, "perhaps my husband could be helpful. He has many contacts."

"I've come to scatter my father's ashes," Carr said, "while it's still possible."

"Why did you choose India for that?"

"My father was on the governor's staff when the First War broke out. He loved India. Not all wolves run in a pack."

"He was English?"

"There was a scandal over missing funds. Quite a large sum. False evidence got introduced at the inquiry. My father shot himself. Five years after the suicide, he was cleared. The government gave back his honor, like a deposit."

"His dignity, too?"

"That's not refundable. Anyway, what use is dignity to the dead? He was fond of a spot in the mountains out of Igatpuri. I'll take the ashes up there this week."

A khaki sedan had pulled up beyond the checkered shade of the awnings and Carr saw Lieutenant Paine and the driver get out. Paine's square chin was lifted into the sun, the upper half of his face lost in the shadow from the visor of his peaked cap as he stared at the crowd. He spotted Carr and moved toward him. The driver, a corporal, trailed close behind.

The plump Indian in the frock coat popped out of the throng and said excitedly to Ashley, "I think there is coming now mischief and roguery to these peaceful proceedings. . . ."

Paine strode up and gave Ashley a casual military salute. "Good day, Mrs. Vora. I should like a word with this chap, if you don't mind."

The fullness of her upper lip, Carr thought, was nicely engineered for the arrogant contempt that passed across her smile.

"You mean to have it," she said, "whether I mind or not."

"Orders, I'm afraid." Paine turned to Carr. "May I see your passport, sir?"

"I left it in my hotel room."

"Would that be the *Taj*, sir?"

"The Malabar Arms," Carr said.

"Didn't they caution you at customs to keep it in your possession at all times?"

"I can't recall if any deadly consequences were attached to not having it."

"According to your customs declaration, you've come from Lisbon," Paine said, "on a Swedish passport."

"That's an accurate summary of how I got here." Carr nodded.

"What's your business in Bombay?"

"I don't have any firm plans."

Paine said, "I'm afraid that's not a very satisfactory answer."

"It wasn't a very satisfactory question," Carr said.

Paine flushed and said, "I'll have to ask you to come along with me, sir."

"Don't be a bloody nuisance," Carr said.

Paine grasped Carr's sleeve above the elbow and said, "Come along. Let's not have any public unpleasantness. . . ."

Carr's fist caught Paine flush on the nose, and the officer's legs went out from under him. A woman screamed. The corporal threw his arms around Carr from behind.

Paine was sitting down on the grass, his hand cupped over his nose. His fingers came away blood-smeared. An alarmed murmur went up from the crowd as the officer lifted the flap of his holster, but he did not draw his service pistol.

Ashley glanced sharply at Carr, and the black heat in her stare gave way to mild concern.

"All right," Carr said to Paine. "But I can get to the sedan without any help from the king's own."

The officer nodded to the corporal, who dropped his arms. The crowd stepped away from the two men as they walked toward the vehicle. Paine stood up, pressing a handkerchief to his nose.

"Why have you arrested him?" Ashley said.

"You might take some care choosing new friends," Paine said. "That chap is a known arms smuggler, among other things. I was told to bring him in for questioning, that's all. Now he'll be lucky to keep his visa."

In the sedan, Carr looked back at the crowd shrinking in the rear window and said to Paine, "Sorry about the punch. I thought you were going to roll with it."

"So did I," Paine said. He looked down at the blood-spattered linen of the handkerchief. His upper lip was swelling, and he was breathing through his mouth.

"You'd better have that nose looked after."

"Not to worry. It was convincing. That's what matters."

"I'm not sure." Carr shook his head, frowning.

"Oh yes. I saw the look she gave you. It's worth a bloodied nose. You can trust me on it. You'll be hearing from her. . . ."

6

The Indian standing in the lobby of the Malabar Arms was the same comic figure in the frock coat Carr remembered from the polo field. Today he wore a duster and gripped a chauffeur's cap and goggles in one hand as he passed a note with the other.

Carr stepped over to an alcove where dusty sunlight streamed through a window onto an artificial palm, and opened the envelope.

> *Please consider my driver at your disposal should you wish*
> *to undertake the trip to Igatpuri with your father's ashes.*
> *On your way back, perhaps you would be kind enough to*
> *join my husband and me for tea.*

Carr raised his head and said, "Is Mrs. Vora in the city?"

"The *memsahib* is being now domiciled with her husband at their residence on Malabar Hill," the plump Indian replied. "After I have driven your grieving presence to Igatpuri, I taking you to her."

Carr went upstairs for his coat and the urn of ashes and came down again, and they set off in the big Rolls touring car for Igatpuri.

Above Thana, they crossed the bridge to the mainland. The road climbed toward the green mountains vaulting back against the sky, and from unseen valleys a few clouds puffed upward like uncorked genies.

It was midafternoon before they reached the river above Igatpuri, and Carr tapped on the glass, signaling the driver to pull off the road. Below, the stream made a cool, rushing sound on the hot day. Carr left his coat on the back seat, and with the brass urn tramped downhill through the trees to the green water that ran smooth and fast beyond the overhanging leaves. Once, he glanced up and saw the Indian, his goggles lifted above the brim of his cap, staring down from the road.

He was not even sure this was the place. The memory was like a reel of film left too long in a cannister. It lay now behind his stare—a few spliced frames: his mother in a long white dress with ruffled cuffs and brocaded lace, the aloof man (his father?) wearing a high starched Edwardian collar, the green slump of leaves, sky reflections on sunny rips of water.

But the authenticity of the place no more mattered than the authenticity of the memory. The urn contained only the incinerated remains of an English bulldog named Jiggs who had been a pet in the household of a Lisbon diplomat. In Estoril, Gage had described the animal as "flatulent and dribbling slobber."

An irreverent epitaph, but at least the mastiff's death would serve a cause, Carr thought. His own father's death had served nothing.

He overturned the urn and watched Jiggs spread like a stain in the current and disappear. Probably the driver would report what he had seen to Mrs. Vora. Carr lingered in the leafy shade by the stream for another ten minutes to accord the rite its proper solemnity, then climbed the hill to the road.

Ashley was waiting for him on the veranda of the house, its white Victorian contours half-hidden in the flowers and dark foliage. Her gold sari gleamed in the cool shade of the portico arch, and he could feel the centrifugal pull of her black eyes as he stepped from the Rolls in the drive and climbed toward her.

"I would like you to meet my husband," she said. "He is recovering from a stroke and has difficulty with speech, but his mind is clear."

The figure in the wheelchair at the far end of the veranda took little notice of their approach. The paralyzed muscles on the right side of his face had left an eyelid drooping and the mouth slackly fallen, and one arm was useless. Age had tracked deep fissures into the brown skin, and under the loose white muslin of his trousers and shirt, his limbs appeared brittle and bony.

Carr sipped the tea that the servant had brought. Ashley sat forward in the wicker chair, one arm resting on her crossed legs. For most of the conversation, the old man stared down in dull vacancy, only the white gleam of his clothing visible in the deep shadows. When at last he spoke, a ribbon of saliva spilled from the corner of his mouth. Ashley touched the shining wetness with a napkin, and Carr saw that she was gentle, as though caring for a child. She leaned close to the disabled figure, murmuring into his ear, and her eyes brimmed with what seemed genuine pity.

"My husband tires very easily," she said. "You must excuse him now."

A servant appeared and wheeled the invalid into the house.

"We have a tea plantation in the mountains near Pratapgarh. the nights are much cooler. I plan to take him there soon, but he hates to leave his gardens. They are quite lovely. Would you care to see?"

They strolled out under the trees, behind the house, where the last light was fading to wind-stirred embers in the upper leaves. Water lilies floated in the shadows drowning on a reflecting pond, and a gravel path twisted back among the flower beds and the half-gloom of hedgerows. Part of a lattice pavilion showed in the trees, its shell overgrown with foliage and steeped in the shades of the dying day.

As they drew near it, Ashley suddenly stopped and turned to Carr. "Tell me what happened after your arrest."

"I was questioned," he said, "and let go."

"Did they take your visa?"

"There was some talk of lifting it, but I managed to convince them I wasn't here for sinister purposes."

"You have a convincing manner," she said, and Carr could imagine some cynicism on the edge of the remark. Probably it was only a reflection of his own.

"So do cheats and liars," he said.

"People in the arms trade, too?"

"Why ask me?" Carr said, and wondered if they were being watched.

"The officer who came to arrest you seemed to think you might know."

"I hope you upbraided him while defending my reputation."

"I decided to wait and find out if it were true."

Carr lit a cigarette and said, "Would it make any difference if it were?"

"That would depend on your reasons for doing it."

"You could say that it was undertaken for a proper incentive."

"A political motive?"

"Nothing so crass." Above the cigarette's wreathing, the amusement creased back from his eyes. "Profit and greed were the prime considerations. They're always more reliable when you engage in a dangerous form of commerce."

The gloss of paint on her lips gave up a faint smile of disbelief. "People driven by greed don't usually give large sums to Indian war relief."

"Consider that a burial tax," Carr said, "for my father."

"You said he loved India," she replied. "India belongs to those who love her."

Carr thought about her husband in the wheelchair, and wondered what she could know about love. He said, "Tell that to the British. Maybe they'll get out."

"The British won't go," she said, "until they're driven out."

"You're half British yourself," Carr said. "Where does that leave you?"

A breath of air touched the wings of dark hair at her temples, and the moment hovered silently in the reflected gleam of her earrings and the unmoving glitter of the thin gold bands below the white curve of her forearm.

"India is my country," she said. "The difference in our situation is that you honored your father, whereas I had only contempt for mine."

But she was wrong. His memory of his father did not extend to honor. It could not reach past the face with the wet mash of sclera draining down from the bloody socket where the bullet had gone in.

"And your mother?" he said.

"She was beyond contempt in her feelings."

"So was mine. She hated the Crown and blamed it for the suicide. I suppose she tried to instill that in me." He had dealt the remark like a card in a marked deck, and now he waited for her to play it.

"Did she succeed?" Ashley stared at him.

"Only to the degree," Carr replied, "that the fortunes of the British Empire don't interest me."

"It's a pity your father couldn't have shared that view."

"People do what they have to do." Carr shrugged.

"Your friends in the arms trade, too?"

He grinned around the cigarette and replied, "For them it's a moral justification."

"Tell me," Ashley said, "do you still have contacts?"

"That's what the people who arrested me wanted to know."

She smiled and said, "Don't worry, I won't arrest you."

It seemed to Carr the talk had suddenly taken on a tone of negotiation. The slight tension in his nerves had to do with expectancy, not uncertainty.

"Would you be willing to talk with someone," Ashley went on, "who believes in a free India?"

"That would depend on the topic."

"Rifles and bullets, perhaps."

"I'm not in the ballistics business, anymore."

"You know sources who are."

Again he sensed a third presence and glanced along the hedgerow where the dappled gloom melted into the leaves. "It's nearly dark, Mrs. Vora," he said. "I should be off."

Her manner lost none of its cool composure. She might have been talking about another invitation to tea. "Will you consider it?"

"For what?" he replied. "Profit and greed?"

"For India," she said.

Nothing stirred except the leaf shadows on her upturned face, but all the while her dark stare ransacked his expression.

"I'll let you know," he said.

"It will have to be soon," she said. "We've very little time."

After Carr had left, Ashley walked back into the dusky silence of the garden. A figure was seated in the shadows of the lattice pavilion. She could see only his crossed legs, and the smoke drifting from his cigarette.

The German rose, and the gleam of his blonde hair came into view along with the loose smile on his mouth and the shine of his tanned features.

"You heard the conversation?" Ashley said.

"Most of it," Kordt said.

"And you've had a look at him," she said. "What are your feelings?"

"I agree he could be useful," Kordt said, "if he is what he claims to be, and nothing else."

"Then you don't trust him?"

He did not reply at once, but she could see the flash of a cold intelligence at work behind the melancholy stare.

"We'll press on with him," he said, "but I want him checked by our people in Lisbon and London. A complete background report. His father's case, as well. If there was a suicide, I should like to trace the disposition of the remains. It's a bit too tidy—the whole story—isn't it?"

"I believe him," Ashley said. "They wouldn't concoct something that could be so easily disproven. His turning up just now is blind luck, that's all."

"Perhaps," the German said. "I've sent Ram Singh along to have a look at his hotel room."

"I doubt you'll find anything," she said.

Kordt smiled and replied, "Sometimes it's what you don't find that matters. In any case, we'll see what stuff he's made of. . . ."

7

Rutger Kordt came from a Junker family with estates in Würt-
temberg and his earliest memories were of the stone manor
house where, on warm summer nights, laughter drifted up
from grand supper parties in a dining hall lit by branched candle-
sticks, and sometimes the men, still in their formal clothes,
tramped into the forest to hunt. Servants with torches had run
ahead, dragging streamers of shadow over the ground and throwing the glint of fire into the undersides of leaves, and beaters had
struck sticks against skillets and pans to flush the game. The
women in their formal gowns would follow a short way from the
house and call out "Good hunting!" to the huntsman as he gal-
loped past on his horse, kicking up spouts of black loam, a hunting
horn on a leather loop banging up and down against his chest.
Then the pounding thud of hooves would fade into the forest as
Kordt and his sister, Anna, watched from an upstairs window.

Later, they would hear the rifles, and the far-off shouts of the
hunters, and the long mournful note from the huntsman's horn,
signaling a kill. Then the torches would flicker back into view, the
forest leaves streaming through the fiery glint, and finally the stag
would be carried in, lashed by its hooves to a pole in the luminous
glow of burning pikes, head and antlers dangling, and the shine of
blood on its neck where the throat had been cut.

Not long after the peace at Versailles, the Weimar government
appointed his father to a diplomatic post in London. For the next
six years the family resided in apartments in Mayfair, and Kordt
was given over to a British public school. There, after his nose was
twice bloodied in the hedgerows behind the cricket green, he

learned to box, studied Chaucer, Milton, and Kipling, became fluent in English, and developed a romantic fascination for India. On his return to Germany, he entered Heidelberg University to study archaeology and history.

In one of the lecture halls, he found himself next to a burly youth named Heisler who came from Ulm and was the son of a tavern owner. Heisler was half again as broad as Kordt and had a tough, street-brawler's face with a smirking mouth to match the cruel merriment in the eyes, and a thick neck encrusted on the back with boils. He belonged to the fencing club, and his brute size made him a leader of sorts, so that a group generally attached to him like pilot fish. Once, coming away from a lecture, he said to Kordt, "We never see you at the beer halls."

Kordt smiled and said, "I have other things to do."

"What things?" Heisler winked at his companions. "Wait. I know. You're seeing a girl."

"No," Kordt said.

Heisler affected an air of wounded surprise and said, "Too good for the rest of us, then?"

"Why would you think that?"

"What else should we think? The diplomat's son who won't drink with his comrades . . ."

"It's not true."

"You'd better come round, then. Listen. The tavern keeper's old lady serves the beer on Saturday night, and that's not all. I'm letting you in on this, see? Her name's Hilda, and she specializes in cases like yours. She'll show you how it's done. Why neglect such an important aspect of your education?"

To break it off, Kordt said, "Maybe you're right."

But on Saturday evening he did not go to the beer hall, and on Monday Heisler and the others fell into step beside him as the students spilled out of the lecture hall.

"What happened the other night? Hilda was expecting you. She wants to know why you didn't show up."

"I had some reading to do."

"You disappointed the old cow."

"She'll get over it."

"Even in her grief, she sent you a message. She said not to be nervous. She'll get you up."

The others laughed, and Kordt smiled. They were walking in the open on the sun-drenched stones of the common, the green mountainside soaring beyond the town.

"Of course, maybe you don't like girls," Heisler went on. "You're not a queer, are you?"

Kordt stopped walking and stared off at the sun-baked walls of the old castle on the hill above the river. Then he shifted his gaze to Heisler, whose own stare did not flinch away from its smirking humor.

From that day, the baiting grew worse, as if Heisler were deliberately provoking him into a quarrel. It was not that the youth from Ulm limited his bullying to Kordt—others took their share— but only that the bantering seemed more intense in Kordt's case, as if it stemmed from some genuine grievance. Kordt did not understand the resentment, though he imagined it had to do with his own privileged background and class.

Now and then, whispered within earshot, were references to the tavern keeper's wife.

Poor Hilda . . .

Nonsense! It's what the old cow deserves.

For what?

Wasting her affections on a queer.

Another time, on Heisler's cue, they bowed to him and said in unison, *"Guten Tag, Fräulein,"* straining to keep serious faces.

On Saturday evening a taxi stopped on the lighted street outside one of the tavern halls, and the driver went in. Tobacco smoke hung on the air that was heavy with the malt smell of beer drawn from casks above the bar. An accordionist in short trousers and feathered alpine hat played a Bavarian drinking song, the leather straps of the accordion shiny across the shoulders of his Tyrolean shirt, and couples were dancing on the stone floor below the platform where he stood.

"Look for the biggest and loudest fellow there," Kordt had said.

The driver spotted his man straight off in a rowdy crowd at a long plank table and went over. "Herr Heisler?" He had to shout to be heard above the noise.

The upturned face in the smoky light was broad and flat and sported a chipped tooth. "That's me."

"A young gentleman asked me to deliver this, and wait for a reply."

Heisler tore open the wax-sealed flap of the envelope, and his bloodshot gaze held fast to the note handwritten on stationary imprinted at the top with a coat of arms:

> *I am waiting for you at the old castle wall. The only condition I impose is that you come alone.*
>
> K.

From the shadow of the high crumbling wall Kordt watched the lights of the taxi on the road lifting out of the town onto the hill where the castle squatted under a full moon. For awhile there was no sound except the wind shifting the grass on the hill below the ruin, and then the motor of the far-off taxi could be heard as it ground nearer. Later, it stopped in a line of trees on the road, well below the castle, and the headlamps blinked out. Kordt heard a door slam, and the voices of two men, and then the driver stepped into view. He was pointing uphill to the wall.

A second figure came out from under the leafy speckling and climbed toward Kordt. There was no mistaking the blacksmith's brawn smelted into the heavy torso and stocky legs. The roofs of the town swayed against his pitching shape, and the lights of a coal barge sliding downriver seemed to grow smaller as the man, climbing up through the bending grass, swelled all too quickly to size.

Kordt, who had been standing with his shoulder tipped against the wall, stepped out of the shadows. Twenty feet below, Heisler stopped, too, unable to keep the smirking pleasure from his upturned face.

Kordt said, "I see you accepted my terms and came alone."

"You shouldn't have worried. I don't need help."

"The business I have with you is private."

"It's proper form to bring along seconds."

"We won't need them."

"No?" Heisler laughed. "Who's going to take care of you after I finish with you?"

"I'll strike a bargain with you. The loser walks back to town."

"What makes you suppose he'll be able to walk?"

"If you can't," Kordt said, "I'll send the taxi back for you."

The distant barge had melted down to a yellow blaze on the black water. Kordt motioned to Heisler to follow him and stepped through the gap in the wall into a flat, open court. The floor had long ago crumbled, the space now choked with grass that had a glint of the moon's silver, and the shell of the wall was dark against the night. On a heap of stony rubble lay crossed *Schläger*, dueling swords with wide blades and blunted tips.

"Choose," Kordt said.

Heisler picked up one, and Kordt gripped the other. The two men faced each other, and Heisler said, "Standard rules of engagement?"

"Whatever you prefer."

Under standard rules the duel would be fought with the antagonists standing in place, separated by the distance of their weapons, and only blows at the cheeks permitted.

Both men raised their *Schläger* in a salute, then dropped into a fighting stance, left fist curled behind the hip. Heisler attacked at once, and Kordt parried, making no attempt at a riposte. Again, Heisler pressed the fight, this time in a false attack, probing for a weakness in Kordt's technique. Kordt parried as if he had known the moves beforehand. Twice more he parried swift attacks, the blades ringing across the starry silence of the ruined court, and Heisler drew back, breathing from the exertion.

Heisler was the stronger of the two, but slower, relying on brute power to wear down and overwhelm his opponent. Kordt had the superior mental reflexes, and his technique clearly came from early years of training under a fencing master at a *salle d'armes*. It left Heisler frowning in surprise.

Still, Kordt did not press an attack. He was content to parry, and only once feinted a riposte which drew the other man off balance. Kordt could easily have scored a cheek cut and ended the fight, but did not. He preferred to extend the ritual of combat, as if he would exact satisfaction in small installments of humiliation that Heisler paid in the currency of failure. The debt accumulated interest each time Kordt disdained to mount an offense. Even Heisler had begun to guess the strategy. His features had lost their sneering overconfidence to a puzzled scowl.

The hollow clang of steel on steel had slowed. Now, stung to rage, Heisler threw himself into a savage onslaught, the pack of muscle along his neck and shoulders swollen hard. The ringing clash of blades comprised the longest *phrase d'armes* yet during which Kordt chose not to present an offense, and when it was over, he had broken Heisler's will.

Now it was Heisler, his face dripping sweat, who waited to defend.

Kordt smiled, and said, "Would you prefer the left cheek, or the right?"

Heisler did not reply, his chest rising and falling. Kordt feinted, attacking on a slow cadence to draw the riposte, then, quickening the pace off a *beat quarte*, he lunged to the counter riposte, slashing Heisler's right cheek. The blade made a whipsaw sound in the air before it struck, and Heisler clamped a hand to the cut, the ribbons of blood streaming through his fingers.

He glared at Kordt and murmured hoarsely, "Has honor been satisfied?"

"No." Kordt tossed his weapon to one side. "I hope you can use your fists better than a dueling sword."

The *Schläger* dropped from Heisler's grasp, and his hand came away from the cut that gaped open to the bone.

"You Junker bastard, I'll kill you," he breathed, and swung at Kordt's head.

Kordt blocked the punch, drove a fist into the heavy belly, and heard the wind go out of Heisler in a sick grunt. Heisler's hands dropped, and Kordt's right came over them and smashed into the other man's jaw. Heisler winced, his head skewered to one side by the blow. He stumbled back, trying to push Kordt off, but Kordt ducked inside, hitting him under the heart and in the flank. Heisler recovered his balance and swung hard. This time his big fist landed high on Kordt's head, and the power of muscle and sheer bulk behind it buckled Kordt's knees and sent a flash of light to the back of his skull. He grabbed with both arms and held on until Heisler threw him off. The two men circled, Heisler touching the gash on his cheek and glancing at the blood that had by now run down his neck and soaked the front of his shirt.

They fought for twenty minutes, the crack of fists coming in flurries, and at the end of that time both of Heisler's eyes were nearly swollen shut. From a bobbing half crouch Kordt feinted to draw a last punch, and came up swinging hard. Heisler staggered backward and half turned away, his arms thrown up across the red mash of his face. Kordt slammed both fists into his kidney and Heisler sank to one knee, letting out a delayed roar of pain. The punishment he had absorbed seemed to take its toll all at once, and he crashed to the ground, hands still crossed in front of his face.

Kordt stood over him and said, "I hope you have a pleasant walk home."

He retrieved the dueling swords and ducked through the gap in the wall. The grass still shifted in the night wind as he slipped downhill through its silver rippling to the taxi in the trees on the road.

After Heidelberg, Kordt spent two years at Cambridge in graduate study, then sailed to India to undertake the field work for his thesis. It was his intention to trek from Darjeeling, at the foot of the Himalayas, south through Bengal, and up into the Khasi Hills of Assam, searching out ancient ruins and recording the religious history.

His steamship reached Bombay in October and lay at anchor in the harbor through the afternoon, waiting for a berth. Kordt stayed on deck, leaning against the rail and staring across the blue channel at the city beyond the docks. Already, his nerves were overcharged, like those of a young boy handed a present and told not to open it. By the time the vessel had tied up at Apollo Bunder, and he had passed through customs and taken a taxi to a small hotel in Chowpatty, the sun had melted into the sea and the last light lay drowning on the horizon.

He did not wait to unpack but went down into the crowd spilling off the promenade, by the sea wall, down the wide steps onto the tawny expanse of Chowpatty Beach. Charcoal fires blazed in the iron *chulas* of food vendors, and the scent of skewered kebabs and spiced lentils and potatoes drifted on the dusk. A breeze lifted off the dark sea, which lay beneath a few lurid swirls of cloud, and from a speaker on a pole above the crush of people, sitar music blared into the swelling murmur of voices. In the surging throng he caught sight of a man juggling knives—a troupe of performing monkeys on leashes—a tightrope artist sliding his bare feet along a wire, arms outstretched as he tipped from side to side on the blue evening.

Later, drawn by the flicker of torches, Kordt stopped to gaze down at a *sadhu*, buried alive. Apart from the hands and forearms of the holy man, nothing else projected from the sand. As Kordt watched in fascination, the fingers of one hand closed slowly into a fist, then opened again.

How was it possible?

In the moving, half-lit shadows, an Indian in a dhoti and soiled turban pressed forward, smiling. His face had an oily gleam in the firelight, and one eye was only a slit of atrophied tissue.

"Does it astonish you so much?" he asked in singsong English.

"Why doesn't he suffocate?" Kordt said.

"Because he concentrates on the Supreme Spirit until he is able to establish identity of consciousness with the deity."

"Are you sure it's not a trick?"

The young Hindu stopped smiling, hurt by the accusation. "In the mystic state, his mind becomes one with the Spirit so that he is beyond pain and can exist outside himself."

The longer Kordt watched, the more his excitement mounted, as if some microcosm of wisdom were waiting to be revealed in the disembodied hands. Beyond the dancing gout of flame, the curled fingers moved once more, as if beckoning to him to pass through the fire.

Six years later, the ship bringing Kordt back from India docked in Bremerhaven. From the port, he took a train to Berlin to visit his sister. Rutger Kordt was now twenty-eight, and his face, though yet unlined, was more ascetic in its contours than in his days at the university—the face of a man disciplined to physical hardship beyond the normal limits of endurance. The deep tan emblazoned over it made the gray eyes all the more startling in their paleness, like winter light.

At the Bahnhof, passengers were swarming over the platform as he stepped from the train. Above the sound of a pea whistle, a girl's familiar voice called out his name. He looked through the crowd and saw Anna and her husband, Karl, standing near the gates. Karl lifted a hand. Anna ran toward Kordt. Her long legs flashed above the high heels, and excitement left a dark flush on her cheeks.

Kordt put down his bags, not a moment too soon. Anna flung herself into his arms. The laughter of her warm mouth on his smothered his greeting. Still in his arms, she threw back her head and cried, "Are you really home? For good?"

"Who knows?" Kordt smiled.

Karl came through the crowd. Thinning hair and wire-rimmed glasses made him seem older than his thirty-four years, and he wore the armband of a Party official on the sleeve of his coat.

"Welcome home, Rutger. Let me help you with your things."

Karl picked up one of the bags. Kordt carried the other. Anna walked beside him, clinging to his arm.

"We've planned a wonderful homecoming for you tonight," she said. "All sorts of important people will be there."

"Yes, it's true." Karl nodded. "Some very important people. One of them is quite close to the Führer. I told him all about you. His name is Canaris."

Later in the week Kordt joined Admiral Wilhelm Canaris for an aperitif in the gardens of the Hotel Esplanade. The chief of German intelligence had issued the invitation the night of the party. Now, as Kordt arrived, he saw Canaris alone at a table under the trees near the dance platform. The musicians were in shirtsleeves and it was pleasant, after the hot day, to feel the breeze stirring the leaves overhead and listen to the Viennese tunes played by the men who sat on wooden chairs in front of their music stands.

"I've brought along your book," Canaris said. "I thought you might be kind enough to inscribe it for me."

Kordt looked down at the book on the white tablecloth and saw that it was his translation into German from the original Sanskrit of the epic poem *The Ramayana*. It was not the sort of reading matter he had imagined would interest the chief of the Abwehr. But Canaris was full of surprises. From Karl's description, before the party, Kordt had expected an imposing figure in gold-braided uniform. The slight man in the dark, rumpled suit had turned out to be physically unimpressive, hardly the model of a senior naval officer in an important position. He had given Kordt a limp hand to shake while the restive eyes in their hooded pouches had avoided contact. After no more than a dozen words, smiling thinly, he had drifted off into the crowd, as if he wished to blend out of view like a chameleon with its deceits of color.

"I'm surprised you found a copy," Kordt said. "Poetry is out of fashion, these days."

"Not for everyone."

Already, Kordt's opinion of the other man had changed. Canaris no longer struck him as stiff and cold. His gaze, tonight, was open and direct, and his manner had an old-world charm.

"Tell me about India," he said. "What kept you there for six years?"

"Curiosity." Kordt smiled.

"Have you satisfied it?"

"Temporarily."

"Like a mistress one grows tired of?"

"No, Herr Admiral." Kordt smiled again. "More, I should say, like a beautiful woman you can never possess, so you fall in love forever with her mystery."

Canaris ignored his aperitif and said, "What do you propose to do with yourself, now that you're home?"

"I haven't given it much thought," Kordt said. "The Kaiser Friedrich Museum has offered me a post. My sister would like me to take it and stay in Berlin."

For the first time, Canaris stared off at the last light dissolving in the leaves above the long shadows of the trees on the cropped turf. Finally, he gazed across the table at Kordt. "I will tell you something frankly, and rely on your discretion not to repeat it. In my opinion, Germany will be at war within a year."

"Herr Admiral . . ." Kordt frowned through his surprise. "I find that hard to believe."

"Assume that it's true. What will you do?"

Kordt struggled with the question. At last he replied, "One has a duty . . ."

"Exactly so." The admiral nodded. "It has already been made clear to me by Karl that yours could best be carried out in the intelligence service."

"But you know nothing about me," Kordt protested.

The musicians finished their Strauss and laid their instruments down. The chatter at the other tables went on, a pleasant sound among the windblown shades of evening in this elegant corner of Berlin.

"There was a fellow at Heidelberg," Canaris said, "a bullying pig, to be sure. It seems you turned him out, one night. Just the two of you beneath the walls of the old castle. He got what he deserved."

"I'd nearly forgotten." Kordt shook his head.

"At Cambridge, you admired the works of T. E. Lawrence. I should think the walking trip Lawrence took alone through Syria to gather material for a thesis was not so different from your own experience in India. Lawrence was also a brilliant scholar. When war broke out, he served British intelligence. In view of his background, it was the logical place for him. The same reasoning could apply to you."

"Except," Kordt said, "that war hasn't broken out."

A waiter came up and lit the candle in the saucer on their table. Canaris was staring off once more. The admiral had a way of retreating into himself at odd moments.

"Tell me," he said after the waiter had moved off. "Is it true that the holy fakirs of India can perform feats that would seem to be impossible by ordinary physical laws?"

"Yes," Kordt said without hesitation.

"How do you explain it?"

"The mystic, Patanjali, was the first holy man to seek liberation of the spirit from matter. He believed it was possible through the practice of certain exercises having to do with posture and the control of breathing, and through mental concentration so intense as to separate the mind from all consciousness of the senses. In that state, it was said by his followers that he could be in more than one place at the same time, and could see the past and the future."

"Do you believe such things are possible?"

For what seemed a long time, Kordt did not answer. Finally, the gray eyes shifted to Canaris and held steady, as if they had absorbed the cold force of some spiritual vision into the very centers of the pupils. They might have been looking through the admiral at the flicker of candles in the twilight at the other tables. Slowly, Kordt moved his right hand over the flame until his open palm rested less than an inch from the fire.

Ten seconds went by—fifteen. A frown worked its way into Canaris's brow. After thirty seconds, he abruptly reached out and snatched the candle away. Then he grasped Kordt's wrist, turning the palm upward. Where the flesh should have been blackened, it was unmarked, and he could see no blisters forming under the skin.

The admiral released Kordt's wrist, but the hooded eyes remained fixed in amazement on the younger man, as if the chief of intelligence, an expert in splendid deceptions, could not quite accept what he had seen.

8

Darkness had settled over Bombay in skirmishes of twilight when Mrs. Vora's limousine dropped Carr in front of the Malabar Arms. The power was out, the lift not working. A candle flickered at the desk. The clerk stood up in its glow and said, "The hotel is without power. Some bloody fellow has run off with the fuses. I have sent the *chowkidar* out for replacements."

Carr went into the garden and mounted the outer stairs to the upper gallery. In the dark, he had trouble fitting his key into the lock, but at last the door gave way and he stepped into the room.

The cord sang down, biting into his throat, choking off his breath. The pressure dragged him backward, off balance. Going down, he twisted to get the floor under his hands. A knee slammed into his back, pinning him against the leverage of the cord. In the silent struggle the oxygen went quickly from his lungs while his heart hammered for more.

Something blunt cracked into his skull and the sound of shattering glass seemed miles away. Stunned, he rolled on the floor. The knee was gone from his back. The garrote, still coiled about his neck, no longer bit into the flesh. He lurched onto the gallery, dragging the cord loose with his fingers. The attacker was already somewhere below him on the stairs, and Carr bolted after him.

By the time he reached the lower landing, there was no sign of the other man. Then, moving along the balustrade, he caught sight of a darting shape beyond the stone fountain in the garden. The figure melted from view where the foliage swelled into a larger blackness.

Carr vaulted the rail and ran to the fountain. He peered hard into the shadows, but saw nothing. Above the dry stone dish, a statue of Victoria reigned—a useless witness—decapitated by anti-British vandals.

He moved past the headless monarch into the leafy blackness of the neglected garden. Farther back stood the shell of a gazebo, caught fast in the grip of vegetation. In earlier times, British officers would have sat in its shade, sipping whiskey and wiping their moustaches. Now, under the crush of vines and creepers, the roof had caved in. Carr ducked beneath the overhang, ransacking the dark for movement.

A rattle fell across the stillness, jerking him in its direction. The shadows pulled at him once more as he slipped through the tangled growth, and a garden wall came up suddenly. A pile of rubble lay banked in the corner where the stones joined the side of the building. From a corroded pipe, higher up, sewage seeped down onto the debris. It left a slimy coating on the mortar, and the stench had attracted a pair of rats. He caught the swirl of a tail, a glistening movement of fur, and another loose rattle of metal.

The rats would not retreat. They might have been staking ownership of the litter, which included Victoria's severed head, blighted by dark patches of lichen, yet imperious, still, in its decay. Probably the man had gone over the wall.

Carr climbed the stairs to his room. Glass crunched underfoot in the dark. He struck a match and saw that the shards came from a smashed bulb. Before the match went out, he touched it to a candle in a saucer, and shut the door.

The arrangement of his personal effects made it clear the room had been searched, though nothing had been left in disarray. In the bathroom he set the candle on the shelf below the mirror and turned on the tap. Blood and bits of glass shone in his scalp. He dipped a hand towel in cold water, made a compress, and held it to his scalp. The garrote had left a rope burn around his neck. The hands twisting it had been unnaturally large, powerful, and skilled in the practice of homicide. Another few seconds of tension on the cord . . . but the constricting pressure had been deliberately eased. *Why?*

"It could have been a prowler," Paine said, "trying to steal from you. They're a problem for the police."

The two were alone in the morning shade of trees clumped on a fringe of the Azad Maidan. Farther out, on the cropped green, a cricket match had drawn a ragged throng. The players were garbed in white, and the batsman and wicket keeper wore shin guards. The crack of the bat and shouts from the field drifted in and out of hearing.

Carr said, "He used a lamp cord."

"The thuggees were fond of silken ones. They treated murder as a religious duty and dedicated their victims to Kali."

"Remind me to make an obeisance to Kali in gratitude for my deliverence."

On the chalked turf, the bowler ran forward, delivering his high overhand pitch. The crack of the paddle drove the ball over the head of the nearest fielder.

Carr said, "Mrs. Vora wants me to meet someone."

"She didn't say who?"

"Only that the party was interested in guns."

"Couldn't be Kordt." Paine shook his head. "He wouldn't be that cheeky. Not until he'd done some checking on you."

"Tell that to the men who were at the bridge."

"Mark you," Paine said, "I'm not saying it wouldn't be a spot of luck if it were him."

Carr lit a cigarette and said, "How close was Mrs. Vora to Bose?"

"Peas in a bloody pod, sir."

"What do your files say about her father?"

"Sir Colin? He made a packet in textiles. Liked to muck about with women and racing boats. I suppose one or the other was bound to do the bugger in. He was killed going for a speed record on a Scottish loch in thirty-eight. The experimental craft went air-borne on the water and blew to bits."

On the green, the bat cracked again, looping the ball high. A fielder caught it on the run, ending the match, and the spectators broke ranks.

"Did Mrs. Vora say when this meeting might take place?" Paine asked.

"Only that there wasn't much time left."

"Was she talking about China Blue, do you think?"

Carr shrugged, and said, "I don't read minds."

"Right," Paine said. "I'll pass your report along to Bloody Albert."

"Bloody Albert?"

"Sorry. It's what the lads call the colonel when he's not about. Term of affection."

"Is that what he inspires?"

"You'll get used to him, sir. Bloody Albert's not a bad sort. The problem is, he has a nineteenth-century idea of India—house full of wog servants, string of polo ponies, sipping whiskey in the afternoon—all that colonial rot. Me—I say give it back to the wogs."

Carr said, "You won't get an argument from Bose, or Mrs. Vora."

"I expect they'll put a watch on you. It won't do for us to meet in the open again. We don't want to take any risks now."

9

Carr sent a note around to Mrs. Vora, making himself available for the meeting she had proposed. He expected a call from her, but none came. Nor were any messages left for him at the desk. Several evenings later, coming back to the hotel, he found her limousine parked in the street. The window was rolled down and he saw the black gleam of her hair against the whiteness of her upturned face as she leaned forward into the twilight.

"Get in," she said calmly. "We've only a little time."

"What is it?"

"Don't ask questions that I can't answer."

Carr climbed in beside her, slammed the door, and the hotel swung away on the glass.

"Can't you tell me where we're going?" He leaned back on the cushioned leather and caught the fragrance of some expensive scent.

"Not far," she replied.

The chrome angel on the hood of the Rolls plunged smoothly along the boulevard in the sparse traffic. In a little while, its outstretched wings banked toward the dark shape of Malabar Hill and Carr thought they must be bound for Mrs. Vora's house, but the driver took a different turning.

The city fell away as they climbed above it into the woods. The road snaked back on itself and Carr had a glimpse, over the tops of the trees, of the barrage balloons anchored on long cables to the turf of the Oval Maidan and floating high against the dusk. Beyond their soaring dark bloom, a few lights streaked out to the harbor, where the toy ships and loading cranes were illuminated like a film set.

Near the crown of the hill, the limousine rolled to a stop beside a high stone wall, and the driver cut the motor. He scrambled out and opened the door on Ashley's side. Carr ducked out behind her.

"This way," she said.

In the shadow of the wall, an iron gate lay ajar. They slipped through it and mounted several tiers of steps, chipped and crumbling in the leafy darkness, to a footpath. Ashley paused, and he felt the pressure of her fingers on his arm.

"This place is called Doongarwadi," she murmured. "It is where the Parsis leave their dead." She pointed through the trees, leeched by vines and vegetation, to a high dark shape. "One of the *dakhmas*," she went on, "the receptacles for the dead. There are seven altogether, but now only a few are used."

Each of the circular, walled enclaves, Carr knew, was open on top and slanted down to a central pit lined with charcoal. Parsi dead were borne in on litters and left exposed for the vultures to pick clean. Then the bones were thrown into the pits. If the rite lacked a certain utility, the corpses were beyond caring, and the vultures would not complain.

The footpath took them uphill through the falling thicket. Overhead, the moon poured its light into the creepers, and Carr could feel the pull of the leaf shadows on his face as he climbed higher.

The *dakhma* drifted into view, its stone weathered and streaked black like basalt, and Carr could make out the dull shine of an iron door in the dark under the portal arch. Once more, Ashley turned to him.

"Before we go in," she said, "it will be necessary for you to be searched. A security measure . . ."

A rail-thin Indian stepped out from the shadow of a tree. In the white jacket and trousers, and white shoes, he might have been a figure chalked on the darkness—probably one of the hereditary litter bearers of the Parsi dead. The hands traveling over Carr's frame in a simple frisk had a wiry strength. Afterward, the man stepped back and nodded to Ashley.

"He'll keep watch," Ashley said. "But don't worry, no one ever disturbs this place. There's a smell of death about it. People call these *dakhmas* the towers of silence."

The soft clang of iron rang hollowly upward into the tunnel passage as the door swung open. They mounted the worn, uneven steps to the main enclave. The crater shell gaped across the sky, the floor and center pit drenched in the shadow of the trees soaring above the rim.

Carr peered hard into the darkness, but nothing moved. Overhead, a black shape flapped out of the trees and alit atop the wall. More birds followed, a soft, black beating of wings across the silence. In moments, they formed a ragged circle of scavengers on the crumbling rim where the moon burned like a stage light.

Carr lowered his gaze, and his nerves absorbed a shock. The other man was suddenly just there, as if by an act of teleportation. In the pool of shadow around the pit, he had the look of some grainy half-formed image in an old-fashioned daguerreotype. Then he moved slowly toward them along the circular slant of the stones. In the khaki shooting jacket, he might have stepped intact from the veldt, and even his hair had the sun-yellow gleam of savanna.

"I *am* sorry," he said in a clipped, British way, "about the gloomy surroundings."

"As long as the vultures don't object," Carr said.

"They prefer to attend corpses," Kordt said, "not meetings."

"I don't mind contributing to their disappointment," Carr said.

"Nor I," the German replied with a short laugh.

"Are you British?" Carr asked.

"Don't I look to be?" Behind some residual gleam of humor Kordt's stare had the open distances of the veldt in it, too.

"I suppose this could even be a pub off Piccadilly," Carr said. "It probably is."

"No skittles or warm beer, I'm afraid."

"What does that leave?"

"Certain opportunities," Kordt replied.

"Of what sort?"

"I should think that would depend where you stand on the issue of British rule in India."

"It doesn't matter where I stand. You can only change colonial policy by an act of Parliament."

"Or guns," Ashley said.

"Armed revolt?" Carr said, and glanced up at the rim of the *dakhma*, its outline broken by the hunched curve of feathered backs and gleam of hooked beaks. The birds would gather whenever they sensed that death was about to be practiced. Perhaps they could not distinguish between a dead Parsi and a dead empire.

Kordt said, "Aristotle concluded that revolutions are carried out in two ways—by force or by fraud."

"That's the problem with revolutions," Carr said. "They're easier to make theories about than to bring off."

In the dark, the smile on the German's mouth seemed to be shaped by an interior melancholy. He looked to be solidly built, engineered for hard use, like a machine connected to a power source. Even if the cable link were cut, the mechanical parts would continue to operate on the ether of some ascetic force and sheer will.

"All situations are hypothetical," he said, "to some degree. For instance, a cargo of weapons is captured. Enfield rifles and Bren guns. It turns out that the Brens are missing their body locking pins and spring rods, and none of the Enfields has its striker nose. It seems the parts were shipped separately—a security measure against theft in transit."

"I'm no expert," Carr said, "but I believe the striker pin is an essential feature of the firing cycle."

"As a nonexpert," Kordt said, "do you think the missing parts could be gotten hold of?"

"Anything can be gotten hold of for a price."

"That has not proven to be the case, so far. Where would you imagine they'd come from?"

Carr's gaze went from Kordt to Ashley and back to the German again. They might have been negotiating the sale of a fake Matisse.

"Out of Berbera, most likely," he replied.

"British Somaliland?" Kordt frowned reflectively.

"I know a chap there," Carr said.

"If arrangements were undertaken now," the German said, "how soon could delivery be made?"

"That's hard to say. Apart from the merchandise, there's the problem of shipment. It has to be gotten past customs at both ports."

Ashley said, "The bill of lading will list the cargo as machinery for my husband's plantation. Customs in Bombay won't be a problem."

"How long?" Kordt pressed him.

"Three to four weeks," Carr said.

"Delivery must be no later than the end of March. Can you guarantee it?"

"There are U-boats off the horn of Africa," Carr said. "They don't always respect guarantees."

"Understood," Kordt said. "Can we proceed?"

"I'll need your requirements. Specific nomenclature and quantity. Certain inquiries have to be made before I can quote you a price."

"Make them," Ashley said quietly.

Carr shook his head and warned, "It won't be cheap."

"Nothing is cheap, these days," Kordt said, and once more his smile had a touch of fatalistic melancholy, "except life, perhaps."

10

As the limousine pulled away from Doongarwadi, Carr glanced through the rear glass at the woods sliding off against the night, and said, "Who is he?"

"Names aren't important," Ashley said. "You can call him Alex."

"Alex," Carr said. "The cloak looks to be Saville Row, but I'm not sure about the dagger."

"Does it make any difference?"

"Only if it's sticking in your back."

"You've no reason to be concerned."

"When you're handed cards," he said, "it's easier if you know the game."

In the moving darkness she turned her head, and the violent eyes stared straight into his. "Do you really want to know what it's about?" she said. "All right, I'll show you."

She leaned forward on the seat, opened the glass panel, and spoke in Marathi to the driver.

Below Malabar Hill they turned east onto a road lit only by the moon and cruised out to a square that looked across to the swelling dome of the Raudat Mosque.

Several *ghoda-ghadis* were parked at the curb, the drivers asleep in the carriages. Ashley woke one, who sat up, yawning and rubbing a hand over his prickly stubble as he listened to her directions. Even the horse seemed disinterested, its head drooping low in the traces and festooned about the ears with a loop of wilted flowers.

"We can't take the limousine," Ashley said to Carr. "The streets are too narrow where we're going."

The springs creaked under his weight as he swung up beside her in the dark under the canopy. The ragged upholstery smelled strongly of sweat and fodder. The driver climbed up on the high seat beside the unlit brass lamp, gave the reins a flick, and the cab started forward with a jerk. He laid his whip across the bony flanks of the horse, and the flat paving stones of the road under the smoothly rocking carriage picked up speed until they were streaming past.

"You've seen the part of Bombay that is British," Ashley said. "It's time you had a look at the Indian half."

The clop of hooves echoed hollowly into the darkness beyond the grinding wheels of the carriage, taking them toward the rising mill-stacks of Cotton Green and Parel. The quarter pressed in on them, a crush of darkened shops and stalls, some late traffic, and the dark shapes of people curled up in alcoves.

Later, they turned down an unpaved alley where the high broken outline of roofs on either side left only a narrow streak of sky above the canopy. The lane emptied into a dirt square flanked by *chawls*, the multistory tenement houses built for mill workers. A few women and children queued with pails in front of a standpipe where the flashing trickle of water muddied the ground.

Ashley told the driver to wait. He gave them a sidelong look that fell just short of a worldly smirk, climbed down, and hooked the burlap feeding bag over the muzzle of the horse.

"This way," she said to Carr.

The stairs of the tenement rose narrowly, past sleeping figures on the landings, and the thin walls gave up the murmur of voices. On the top floor, tenants waited in the dim hallway outside a communal toilet.

Ashley groped in her purse for a key and unlocked one of the cubicles. She did not light the kerosene lamp, but instead opened the tall shutters. The bloom of moonlight came up on the walls, darkly leeched by water stains from a leaking roof. The room was bare except for a narrow plank bed and tick mattress, and a crate that served as a stand for the lamp. A brass chamber pot shone in the corner, and there was a small burner for cooking, fueled by cow dung.

"Who lives here?" Carr said.

"What does that matter?" she replied. "It's only a room with a view—different from the one you get at the Malabar Arms. I wanted you to see it, that's all."

The shutters gaped open on the slum, a labyrinth of dank passageways, sagging galleries, and windows barred against intrusion, lit now by the moon as if deliberately to expose the dark lesions left by mortar crumbling away, the dry rot of timbers, and tiles missing from slate roofs. Off to the right, hovels of scrap wood and tin crowded down on each other. The stench of refuse piles drifted up on the night along with the sounds of the district—squalling children, voices in argument.

"A while ago you asked me what it was about," Ashley said. "This is the best answer I can give you. These *chawls*, for example. People sleep five to a room in them, and sometimes more."

"It's not your fault," Carr said, "that Bombay is overcrowded."

"My father built some of these tenements to house his mill workers. He made a fortune on cheap Indian labor." She stared out across the crush of the slum, her black hair drawn back from the oval gleam of the earring against her neck. She was leaning against the shutter post, her hands behind her, and in the glaze of moonlight Carr saw that something lifted her breasts into the tight cotton blouse, an undergarment so sheer it left the tips faintly indented into the fabric. Tonight her manner had a cool sexuality, and she wore it like another expensive accessory.

"My mother," she went on, "was high caste. She came from a wealthy, educated family. They opposed her marriage to an Englishman. She was young and stupidly infatuated, and she did the unthinkable—ran off with him. Apart from being handsome and dashing, he was shallow and utterly selfish. There were always other women. Eventually he went off to Europe with a brigadier's wife. They were living together when he was killed in a powerboat crash. I was just out of medical school. Nine months later my mother died from complications of untreated syphilis. Mercury might have arrested the disease early on, but she'd felt too much shame and disgrace to seek medical help. The truth was, she hadn't the will to live. I suppose my father typified the British presence in India. He took what he wanted, and left only misery behind."

Her tone had a flat calm, as if all the emotions had been suppressed. It made Carr wonder to what extent the perception of her father extended to other men. Clearly it did not include her husband. He was too old to be unfaithful. In the nuptial contract of fidelity, age was the best collateral of all.

"Why did you give up medicine?" Carr said.

"When you've watched enough children die in these slums, you start to perceive life differently. At first, you ask yourself what kind of a deity would permit such cruelty, and you can only conclude that God is imperfect, or doesn't exist at all, and suddenly the old values lose all relevance. You begin to look for new solutions. I abandoned medicine for politics. Revolutionary politics. You can't eradicate disease and mass poverty until you overturn the social conditions that breed them."

"That sounds like Gandhi," Carr said. "Or is it Subhas Bose?"

"Shall I tell you the difference between the two? Gandhi's view of freedom is wholly utopian. Bose understands that revolutions don't occur peacefully on their own, and he acts on that historical principle. Political tyrannies are brought down by guns and explosives, not moral superiority."

The nearby squalling had turned into a muffled whimpering, like the children of Hamelin lost in their mountain. Bose was the piper who would rid Bombay of its British rats.

"Guns don't change anything," Carr said, "unless you have people trained to use them."

She glanced at him sharply and said, "That's not a problem for you to be concerned about."

It seemed to Carr that he had pushed the conversation as far in that direction as it was likely to go without arousing suspicion. He shrugged and glanced out over the district where the faint glimmer of rush lamps escaped into the night. In this part of the city, blackout restrictions were only haphazardly enforced. Perhaps the British had decided that if enemy planes came over, the slum might as well attract their bombs.

On a gallery below, a blanket was carelessly draped across a missing shutter, and a family wept for a deceased. The figure of the dead man, stretched out on a mat with his thumbs bound together, showed partially in the flicker of a candle.

"Tomorrow they will take him on a litter in procession to a burning ghat," Ashley murmured. "The two most common things you will find in Bombay are beauty and death."

The first respirations of sultry air slid over the quarter and she closed her eyes. Carr saw her breast lift in the half darkness, and thought that it must be chaste, notwithstanding its erotic swell in the thin garment. A valve opened inside him, and the easy desire flowing out of it surprised him. The bed on the edge of his vision seemed connected to some alluring promise. He raised his head and saw the same glimmer of concupiscent surprise on her own dark stare. In the passing moment it was as if they were caught fast in some force field of awareness, sharply physical, and then suddenly it was shut down. Now they might have been nothing more than actors improvising an unscripted love scene on a film set. Even the empty bed struck him as a stage prop. None of it was real. Whatever sexual conflicts she possessed were locked away in a psychological portfolio behind a cold purpose that had less to do with her husband than the man in the *dakhma*, and China Blue.

He could remember Gage, in Estoril, saying, "We want answers, not people. What the devil is China Blue?"

What the devil . . . Carr smiled to himself.

11

On a January day, more than a year earlier, a light snow had fallen along the stone quay above the black waters of the Landwehrkanal in Berlin. The wet, sleety crusts were freezing on the Tirpitz Ufer where the headquarters of the Abwehr thrust its dank, gray stone high against the mother-of-pearl sky.

In his office on the top floor, Admiral Wilhelm Canaris was curled asleep on a black leather couch. The chief of German intelligence had worked well into the night at his big lamplit desk, and on this raw Sunday morning he was dreaming about a summer day long ago when he had joined friends on an estate outside Berlin for a fox hunt. The sun was just up, warming the fields and forests on the other side of the white road and low stone wall, and the hunting party was already mounted on the cobbled circle in front of the manor house. The hollow clop of impatient hooves against the paving stones mingled in the crisp air with the distant barking of foxhounds eager to take up the chase, for they already had the scent of the fox in his wire pen. The admiral put a hand on the smooth neck of his bay to calm him and stared through the woods, still steeped in cool shadows, at the glint of sunburnt grain running off on the other side. Suddenly the barking of the dogs grew shrill, and someone said, *They've put the fox into the field*.

The steady rap of knuckles on the tall double doors pulled him out of the dream. A balding staff officer poked his head into the high-ceilinged room and said, "Sir, Colonel von Lahousen and his visitor are here."

Von Lahousen, a tall Austrian, was chief of the Sabotage and Insurrection Division.

"Very well," Canaris replied. "Send them in, and bring coffee, please."

Standing, the admiral ran a hand across his thinning hair. The desk lamp, which had burned through the night, heightened the unhealthy pallor of his face with its pouched eyes and slack creases. Only the shrewdness in it remained untouched by the years.

Colonel von Lahousen entered the room first.

"Herr Admiral," he said, stepping aside, "may I present the famous Indian Nationalist, Subhas Bose?"

The Indian was short and plump in his khaki uniform, trousers flared above black jackboots, tunic buttoned all the way up to the high collar where his brown neck bulged. His dark hair was trimmed short and receding on a high forehead, and the heavy-rimmed glasses gave his flat Bengali features a studious look. He raised his arm in a brief Roman salute by way of a military courtesy, which Canaris acknowledged.

"Sit down, please," the admiral said, speaking in passable English. "Be comfortable."

"Thank you," Bose replied, taking a chair opposite. "I am most gratified that we could meet before my departure. As you know, I shall be working closely with your staff in the coming struggle."

A second German in a gray double-breasted suit had stepped into the room after Bose. This was *Hauptmann* Kordt, whom the admiral had recently placed on von Lahousen's staff. Now Kordt closed the double doors and went over to stand behind von Lahousen's seated figure where he could bend down and translate in a soft tone the key points of the conversation.

Canaris said to Bose, "When do you leave for Singapore?"

"Within the next two weeks. We go out of Kiel by U-boat and sail around Africa to a rendezvous south of Madagascar. A Japanese submarine will carry us across the Indian Ocean to Sumatra. From there, we go on to Tokyo by air. I shall meet with Premier Tojo for discussions, then return to Singapore to begin the task."

"I hope you like submarines," Canaris said, and noted the dark nicotine stains on two of the Indian's fingers. "It is a long voyage."

"It is a small inconvenience. In any case, one doesn't suffer *mal de mer* beneath the sea, I'm told."

Already, the admiral had discerned two things about Bose—that he was a chain-smoker and a blind optimist. Both habits were destructive.

"Tell me," he said. "How do you propose to raise an army of sixty thousand?"

"There are two million Indian nationals in Burma and Malaya from which to draw manpower. Apart from this source, sixty thousand Indian troops were surrendered to the Japanese by the British garrison on Singapore Island. What are they now except slaves rotting in prison camps on behalf of their British masters? Give them the key to their freedom, and they will soon be persuaded to fit it into the lock."

"I assume," Canaris said, "you have given some thought to logistics and training. Realistically, how long will it take you to put an army into the field?"

"I should think nine months at most, once we have established a provisional government. Then we march with our Japanese comrades into Assam. The battle for Imphal will be critical. After we have taken it and moved into Bengal, British resistance will crumble, and the Indian people will rally to our cause."

The admiral tapped his desk reflectively, his gaze focused on a ceramic piece of three monkeys posturing to see, hear, and speak no evil. These days, one could only *think* evil in safety, and it was the admiral's thought that Bose possessed a grand streak of megalomania. So did Hitler, of course. Perhaps it was the season, after all, for mad visions that would come true.

A knock at the door brought coffee. Only Kordt declined a cup. The balding major who had served it departed on a sharp click of heels.

Canaris said, "And what about China Blue?"

Over the top of his cup and saucer, Bose stared hard at the admiral. "We cannot succeed without the German effort," he replied.

Canaris nodded. At least the Indian leader had some appreciation, however basic, for tactics. Some of his contempt for the other man receded. He glanced from Bose to Kordt. "Well, Hauptmann," he said. "China Blue is your piece of mischief. You had better bring me up to date on developments."

"Yes, Herr Admiral." Kordt stepped over to the world map spread across one wall and picked up a pointer. The gray suit fitted him nicely, and he moved with the loose assurance of an athlete, as if the compact frame could draw indefinitely on some inner latent power. "At present, our force consists of twenty-five *Kampfgruppen.* Each combat team is made up of three men. All were volunteers, chosen from the best of the Indian Legion recruited at Annaburg Camp. They are undergoing specialized training at our agents' school outside Meseritz."

"Seventy-five men," Canaris said, "can hardly be expected to stop a British counteroffensive."

"Once in place," Kordt said, "each cell will begin to recruit and train sympathizers. We anticipate a dramatic expansion of the force after the cadre is on Indian soil."

"How do you propose to supply them?"

"Two sources," Kordt said. "Submarine drops by the Japanese navy off both coasts of India will provide the bulk of arms and ammunition. On the premise that some shipments won't get through, it will be necessary to make up deficits through hit-and-run attacks on British weapons depots and arms in transit. Sufficient ordnance will be needed to support guerilla operations for six months." He glanced at Bose, who sat holding his cup and saucer on his crossed legs. "At that point, the war in India will have been won or lost, and China Blue will no longer be a factor."

"I assume these stockpiles will be dispersed," Canaris said.

"To thirteen sites."

"How do you know the sites are secure?"

Under Kordt's pale, unflinching gaze, his smile had a touch of fatalistic humor. He replied, "Because I selected them myself, Herr Admiral."

"Targets, too?"

Kordt turned once more to the map and used his pointer. "We anticipate that the main thrust of Japanese and Indian divisions into Assam will take place no later than the end of March of next year. As Herr Bose has pointed out, the struggle for Imphal will be crucial. The British will be compelled to commit the bulk of their forces to the defense. Once the battle is joined—by early April— China Blue irregulars will launch simultaneous assaults on the allied airfield at Chabua, and rail lines running north from Dacca and south from Nowgong. These strikes will cut the major enemy supply routes to the Imphal plain." The tip of the pointer jumped across the vast stretches of central India to the printed green whorls of the Western Ghats. "There are three rail arteries out of Bombay normally used for the shipment of war materiel across the subcontinent from the port. Severing these will have a major effect on the flow of goods critical to the British defense of Imphal."

"How long can you keep them cut? In the east, for example?"

"The overland supply route to the Imphal front runs for nine hundred kilometers. Along the way, it alternates between broad- and narrow-gauge track and river crossings by barge. At each point, materiel must be unloaded by hand and put aboard the new conveyance. The system cannot be defended against guerilla-type attacks. The British will be forced to supply their troops in the field by air, and pack animal, until the May monsoon—which will curtail air operations."

Canaris nodded slowly, his closed fist against his mouth. Finally he said, "Tell me frankly. What are the chances of success?"

Kordt said without hesitation, "I should think about the same as for the Greeks at the walls of Troy."

"Are you drawing a historical parallel on the order of battle, or the outcome?"

"The British in India believe they are safely out of the war. It's a Trojan mentality. They are not inclined to beware of Greeks bearing gifts."

The admiral smiled at the subtle reference to his own Greek ancestry, and took a sip of coffee.

Bose said to Canaris, "The operation will succeed precisely because it *is* bold, and not simply a half measure."

"It is also expensive," Canaris replied. "I have no wish to explain to the Führer another expensive failure."

"When the campaign is over," Bose said, "and you have India as an ally, it will have been a cheap success."

For a full minute, the admiral reflected in silence. At last, he raised his head. "I will approve the plan," he said to Bose, "with one reservation. We will infiltrate no cadre onto the subcontinent until you are established in Singapore and have the necessary assurances of support from Tokyo. If you should be lost at sea, God forbid, it seems to me the whole business falls apart."

"I have faith in the German U-boat service." Bose smiled for the first time. "Haven't you?"

"Of course," Canaris said. "But, then, we're only taking you halfway."

"Very well," Bose said. "I'll send a cipher from Singapore. I expect it will have to come to you through the Japanese attaché here in Berlin. How shall I word it?"

For no reason at all the admiral thought once more of the fox hunt. The broken dream fragments passed for a moment across his stare, the sunlit flashes of meadow in the racing trees as he threw his weight forward in the saddle astride the galloping horse.

"Just say in your message," he replied, "to put the fox into the field."

12

The place Paine had chosen for their meeting was a brothel in Kamatipura, and on his way there Carr was followed by a Sikh on a motorbike. It was not that the bike was so small—but the rider so huge—that gave the machine the look of a two-wheeled toy. There was no way to lose him in the traffic, except on foot, and Carr told the taxi driver to stop at the Chor Bazaar.

The narrow streets around the bazaar could hardly contain the glut of people among the open-fronted shops and stalls. Hawkers shouted over the noisy swell of dialects, and from one murky shop, the voice of Caruso crackled through the brass horn on an antique gramophone. In the Thieves' Market you could get anything, Carr thought, even opera.

He stopped in the shade under the awning of another shop and stared at the reflections moving on the glass. The big Sikh suddenly loomed in the crowd ghosting the pane—like one of Ali's bearded thieves. Carr, who topped six-feet-three, was sure the other man must have eight or nine inches on him and another hundred pounds. The cavernous brow below the turban could have been cut from stone, and all his features looked out of size, from the gigantic neck to the massive hands.

Carr drifted away in the throng, the Sikh trailing well behind. The sun beat down into the narrow lanes that trapped the late afternoon heat. Carr stepped around several old women squatting beside their baskets of lemons and tomatoes on the pavement, then ducked through the shop of a *farsan walla* and out the other side into the press of bodies and was gone.

13

For several minutes the big Sikh drifted with the crowd away from the *farsan walla's* shop. Canvas shelters on tall poles kept the sun out of vendors' stalls, where the shade, strewn like a patchwork of camouflage, deceived the eye. Everywhere, the seething movement of people took on a repetitive sameness, and the babel of Marathi, Tamil, Gujarati, and English seemed to conspire with some higher power to confuse the pursuit. Here and there, shop windows trapped the streaming reflections, but Carr had already passed beyond them. He might have been lost in a glimmer of brass from a darkened interior, or absorbed into the murky shine of a mirror, unyielding and still, which gave nothing back to the Sikh except his own image, like a portrait.

Ram Singh was the oldest son of a railway laborer, and he had grown up near Simla in the hill country of the Punjab. When the boy was ten, his father took him to worship in the Golden Temple in Amritsar. They traveled on a railway pass, signed by an assistant traffic superintendent, and left at dawn for Kalka, the junction for the main rail line between Delhi and Amritsar.

A cool breeze blew in the open window of the compartment onto the passengers crammed together on the straight wooden seats of the third-class carriage. The train snaked downward over a grade of looping track where the valleys plunged away into morning mists and rose steeply in far-off ridges that seemed to hang in the sky. The sun, coming up, burned the mists from the valleys and warmed the stone arches of bridges in lemon light that did not yet slant all the way down into the shade of the dry culverts where goats grazed on grass.

His father had an arm around him and smiled quietly as he pointed out sights to the boy with a flick of one brown finger. His father was deeply religious, and it pleased him to be taking his son on pilgrimage.

In Amritsar that night they slept on their bedrolls on the floor of the station, and the next day went to the temple. Surrounded by a wide, clear pool, the soaring domes lay in shimmering reflections of white marble on the water. His father bought rice for the doves, and two flowers to be blessed, before they crossed the causeway over the pool and entered the holy shrine.

Inside, the boy gazed in awe at the opulent brilliance, his head thrown back on his shoulders. The walls rose in a glimmer of gilt copper and burnished metalwork, and upon an altar draped in silks and brocades rested the sacred scripture. Incense left a smoldering fragrance on the air, and high overhead a pair of doves fluttered among the sunlit pillars.

For much of the day, Ram Singh sat beside his father and listened to the priest read from the holy *Granth*. Though not yet eleven, the boy already loomed a full head taller than others his age and was conscious of a latent power in his physical being that could be dangerous if ever it went unchecked. In the smooth, brown face the eyes had a bituminous shine, as if the suppressed violence were already lit like a pilot flame in some deep recess. He admired his father's patience and self-control, for the boy himself was quick to anger, and unforgiving of a slight.

Later, he watched his father in the tight trousers and threadbare frock coat, patched at both elbows, approach the altar and hold out two flowers to the priest. The priest placed them on the gilded cover of the *Granth*, then handed them back. His father pressed the petals of one against his eyes, afterward fitting the flower into a fold of his turban. The other he gave to Ram Singh to do the same. Outside, the two threw rice to the doves.

That evening, they joined the torchlit procession moving across the footbridge from the temple to the marble sanctuary where the swords of the ancient Sikh kings were kept. Priests carried the sacred book, wrapped in veils of gold thread, and the torches of the chanting faithful swam on the black water like fiery snakes. As the priests entered the holy vault to rest the *Granth* in a gem-laden hollow, Ram Singh stood on the footbridge above the drowning gleams of firelight and prayed that the spirit of the warrior prophet, Govind, would descend on him with gifts of strength and courage.

On the train, south of Amritsar, his father discovered that the railway pass had been lost. He knew no one on the Delhi main line, nor was he himself a familiar figure. The conductor-guard glared at him out of a sallow, perspiring face. The heat in the sweltering carriages had left him short-tempered and intolerant of passengers trying to ride without tickets.

"You will have to get off at Jullundur," he said.

"But I am also a railroad person," his father insisted, "and I tell you that I had a letter of authority for travel to Simla."

The other passengers who were crammed into the third-class compartment watched solemnly.

"Where is this letter of authority?"

His father smiled desperately and lifted his hands. "Well, I have misplaced it, surely."

The conductor-guard's air of supreme authority grew more openly contemptuous. "*I don't believe you.*"

Ram Singh saw his father's face darken. It was the only time he could remember him in a temper. Or perhaps the dark flush had to do with his loss of dignity and embarrassment in front of others.

"I speak the truth," he murmured.

"I suppose you think you are entitled to some special privilege, eh? Just because the boy is with you? Well, you can pay for your fare like everyone else."

"I haven't enough rupees for a ticket."

"Then you bloody well can walk," the conductor-guard roared back.

"Oh, but it is too far."

"You should have thought of that before you tried to cheat the railway."

Once more, humiliation burned into his father's cheeks below the turban. He was a soft-spoken man, unused to confrontations. Now, all eyes in the compartment were on him.

"Someone at Kalka will know me," he pleaded. "At least let us ride that far and see."

"And have you slip off before we get there? Don't you think I know all the dirty tricks by now?"

"I am a railway person," his father stammered hoarsely. "I am entitled . . ."

"If it weren't for the boy, I would stop the train and put you off here. Be grateful that I'm letting you ride to Jullundur. There is a railway policeman on this train. If you give me any more nonsense, I will have you arrested.

The two men were staring at each other, and Ram Singh saw his father break. Under the overbearing force of the words, his father's gaze dropped to the floor while his face darkened even more in the hot shame of surrender.

The conductor-guard was gone. In the compartment, the passengers were silent. No one glanced at his father now. The train ran on, flinging the country away from the window, and the only sound was the click of the rails under the wheels.

They were five days on foot, and by horse-drawn tonga, getting to the cool green country at Kalka where the hills vaulted down from the Himalayas. There they boarded a train for the five-hour climb to Simla. In the dusty frock coat and soiled turban his father seemed still sadly withdrawn, as if chafing under some permanent defeat, and the boy sat with the wilted flower from the temple clenched in his fist, along with his hate for the conductor-guard.

By his eighteenth year, Ram Singh had reached his full height of six feet, eleven inches. His shoulders sloped down from an unnaturally thick neck in two columns of packed muscle, and he could lift loads that two men of ordinary size could not budge. That was the year his father lost a hand in a coupling accident at Barog and could no longer work. The British were recruiting men for service in the North-West Frontier Province, and Ram Singh went into the army.

Two years later he was in Tobruk—a city under siege by Rommel's Afrika Korps—where the course of his life would turn on a tiny, improbable event.

The sector headquarters was a cave bunker inside the mine field and barbed wire of the subperimeter, and at 0430 hours on an April morning Ram Singh and his havildar were there being debriefed by a sandy-haired British captain. They had come back from a patrol into enemy lines beyond Ras el Medauer, where they had made contact with a rifle regiment of Italian Bersaglieri.

"I say," the captain protested, shaking his head, "these estimates of enemy dead can't be right."

"With the Captain-Sahib's pardon, they are truly counted," the havildar replied.

"Twenty Bersaglieri killed?"

"And one prisoner," the havildar added.

"And only five of you?" Under the sandy moustache, the captain's thin smile was twisted by skepticism. He ran a freckled hand across his thinning pompadour and a few scales of dead skin drifted across the light of the hurricane lamp on the table. "See here, Suresh. I can't send these figures in. The Old Man just gave the staff a rocket for overestimating enemy dead."

"Bersaglieri do not fight well in the dark," the havildar said.

"You're missing the bloody point," the captain said tartly. "You'll have to change these figures."

From the shadows behind the sergeant, Ram Singh spoke to the officer. "My havildar speaks the truth."

The captain gazed up at the big Sikh whose turban touched the low ceiling of the cave. From collar to leggings his uniform was caked with desert dust. The captain frowned at what he perceived to be a glint of surly arrogance.

"I don't believe you," he said.

A vein swelled at the Sikh's temple, and the image of a train compartment slowly burned itself out on the black heat of his pupils, but he did not reply.

Dawn was spilling across the desert like flame overturned from a crucible when the Sikh and the havildar reached their dugout on the outer defense line. Ram Singh used a camel's-thorn switch to dust their tracks from the sand so their position would not be spotted in daylight by German Stukas. He could endure the oppressive heat, the swarming flies, the lice and sand fleas, but not the screaming nuisance of a diving Stuka, for he had asked to go on patrol again that night, and he wanted sleep.

The patrol slipped away after dark, squirming on their backs through a gap cut in the wire, then setting out across no-man's-land. Each soldier carried five ten-round magazines, two grenades, a day's rations, water bottle, backpack and entrenching tool, and four drawstring bags that could be filled with sand for a hasty fortification. In addition, Ram Singh carried his *khanda*, whetted razor sharp, on his web belt next to his compass and bayonet.

The star-burnt night was clear, the desert dim under a sickle moon. The patrol covered the first thousand meters in good time, pausing only to take a compass reading and set a new azimuth. Not until they halted a second time did the leader realize one of his men was missing.

An hour later Ram Singh was crouched in the shadows near the rock-strewn mouth of a dry wadi. He did not go into the ravine but worked his way instead around the flank of the low escarpment, climbing through sand and scrub to the top. Beyond it, the dunes slumped to a desert plain and he saw what looked to be a staging area. A dozen Panzer III tanks were spread out in line, camouflage nets draped across them to break the outline of the tracks and turret guns. Deployed along the flanks were 150-mm artillery pieces, their crews asleep under shelter quarters beside the batteries. Troop trucks were parked near a stockpile of fifty-gallon fuel drums. Fighting emplacements ringed the area, most of them manned by one rifleman except for mortar and machine-gun pits.

A wind was blowing from the south, sweeping streamers of sand across the bivouac. The heavy gusts had the feel of a *khamsin*, a hot wind off the Sahara, and if that were so it would only be a matter of minutes before the tidal wave of sand, hundreds of feet high, engulfed them in its blinding surge. He was sure more Germans must be dug in somewhere along the high ground and he crawled forward in the dark near the crown of the escarpment. He had covered no more than thirty meters when he spotted the machine-gun nest. The two-man crew had capped the muzzle of the MG34 above its tripod to keep the barrel free of blowing sand. Now they sat, adjusting their goggles and face masks, their backs to the wind.

For a full moment the Sikh did not move, absorbed in the two figures. Then he crept forward. The wail of the wind rose and died as the gale drew nearer. In one swift lunge he was on them, and the crack of their heads together in his huge hands sounded like the stroke of a cleaver into a coconut. One of the gunners, knocked senseless, fell against the sandbags. The other thrashed until Ram Singh snapped his neck.

The wind was raging now, driving sand off the desert floor with stinging force, and the stars were only a few racing points of light. Gazing down at the dead Germans, the Sikh drew his khanda. After he had opened their throats, he cut the left ear from each head.

In the cave bunker, Ram Singh stood once more before the sandy-haired captain. Overturned on its crown, the officer's cap lay on the table, flakes of dead skin from his scalp trapped on the greasy sweatband.

"Why did you stay out two days?" he asked.

"I was caught in the khamsin, Captain-Sahib."

Under the sandy moustache, the captain's mouth twisted down in sneering disbelief. "You are telling me," he said, "that you lost contact with your patrol in the dark, stayed out two days, infiltrated an enemy supply base, and single-handedly killed thirty men. Is this your report?"

"*This* is my report," he said, using his khanda to slit open one of the drawstring bags so that the contents spilled out like the guts of a fish slit from gill to vent. The hurricane lamp shone on thirty severed ears, rank in the heat, and still coated with blood-slime.

The color drained from the captain's face, and he gripped the table, trying not to be sick.

At a temporary field headquarters near a desert well, General Erwin Rommel was meeting with staff officers under a tarpaulin stretched for shade beside his command car. In flared breeches and boots, the general sat on a canvas folding chair with his legs crossed, his Zeiss binoculars dangling from a leather strap against his gray tunic, and a pair of Perspex sand-and-sun goggles raised above the brim of his peaked cap. The morning was clear, and he intended to be aloft in his Storch aircraft by 1000 hours for a reconnaissance of the front. Now, he was listening with interest to a report from his intelligence officer about an incident at a staging area south of Ras el Medauer.

"And why do you assume it was the work of one man?" the general asked.

"From the method of killing, Herr General, and the fact that no attack was made against other targets."

"He infiltrated on two successive nights?"

"During the sandstorm, Herr General. Visibility was sharply reduced."

"No more for us than for him," the general snapped.

"One soldier survived the attack. He is paralyzed with a broken neck, and bled heavily after an ear was slashed off, but he gave a description. The attacker may have been an Indian. His face was concealed behind goggles and a sand mask, but he wore a turban. He was quite enormous—eight feet tall. . . ."

"Indeed," Rommel scoffed.

"The men are calling him 'The Ghost.' I think they are somewhat unnerved by the exploit."

"The British have one lion among their donkeys, eh?" Rommel said scathingly, but the story appealed to his sense of theater. It was the material of myth. A legend could grow swiftly, like a dust devil into a sandstorm that swallowed armies, unless it were stopped. "The lion always comes back to his kill," the general went on. "Catch him, next time."

"*Catch* him, Herr General?"

"Alive, if possible."

"Yes, Herr General, though I am wondering how?"

In the tanned face, the gray-blue eyes sparkled with a hard force. "How do you catch a lion? You bait a trap for him and when he comes you spring it. Then you put the lion in a cage where he is no longer feared."

But it was another six weeks before Rommel, in battle at Hafid Ridge, got word that the infiltrator who was fond of slashing the ears from German dead had been taken alive. In hand-to-hand combat with a dozen troops he had gone berserk, and even after being twice bayonetted—in the side and leg—had managed to crush the skull of one sergeant and nearly decapitate another with an entrenching tool. Now he was on his way to Annaburg Camp near Dresden where Indian prisoners were being interned at the request of the exiled leader, Subhas Bose. The report ended on a wry note. Once a prisoner, it said, the Sikh had become quite docile.

Like a lion, Rommel thought, *in captivity*. . . .

14

Carr reached the brothel district by horse cab as dusk was falling. Mill workers and clerks thronged the streets, and the gutters gleamed in the flares of the foodstalls. From an upper window, a Nepalese girl screamed obscenities at a man in the crowd below—probably an unfaithful lover who had spent his six rupees on a rival prostitute.

The house Carr was looking for squatted at the end of a dirt lane. Two prostitutes in long silk dresses stood barefooted under a plane tree in the walled court. One of the girls was smoking. The brown, braceleted arm came up lazily, the tip of the cigarette glowed in the leafy darkness, and she blew smoke toward him.

The madam, a frail Frenchwoman in her seventies, led him upstairs past a dozen cubicles, some occupied, and stopped before a door at the end of a dim hall.

"He waits for you in there," she said in a croaking whisper.

Carr rapped once with his knuckles and heard the scrape of a chair. Paine opened the door and said, "Come in, sir. It's late. I was starting to worry about you."

"A man followed me from the hotel."

"Did you lose him?"

"In the Chor Bazaar."

"I don't suppose you got a good look at him?"

"He was a Sikh," Carr said. "Close to seven feet. You can't miss him in a crowd."

"Well, one thing's clear," Paine said. "They're not taking any chances with you."

"Why should they?" Carr said.

They sat at a flimsy table where a lamp threw the imprint of its tasseled shade across the pocked mortar of the wall and struck a gleam from the brass rail of the rumpled bed.

"Your spare parts for the Brens and Enfields will be shipped out of Berbera next week," Paine said. "The vessel should make Bombay by the twenty-eighth."

"What registry?"

"Turkish," Paine said. "The *Yildiz*."

"Mrs. Vora will be glad to hear it."

"I dare say," Paine agreed. "We can't fill our own indents on time, and we're filling theirs double quick. It's a risk Bloody Albert wasn't keen on taking. He's gambling a packet on keeping track of the shipment to its final destination."

"Tell him gambling is a destructive habit."

"Right," Paine said. "You bet I'll tell him that."

The room had a rank smell of burnt incense mixed with carnal sweat and seminal waste. Carr lit a cigarette and said, "By the way, what made you ship weapons with missing parts in the first place?"

"The order went down from Battalion to the port after two similar raids in Bengal."

"China Blue?" Carr said.

"That would be pure speculation since we don't know what China Blue is about."

"Always assume the worst, Paine, if you want the percentages to operate in your favor."

They were silent for a moment, and then Paine said, "Tell me about Kordt, sir. What sort of beggar is he?"

"As British as you," Carr said, "and then some."

"No accent at all?"

"He talks like a Cambridge don."

"Anything else? Any unusual trait?"

"I suppose—an air of disillusionment."

"About what, sir?"

"What do people get disillusioned about these days? Civilization? God? Cricket scores?"

"Cynical, you mean?"

"Cynics aren't troubled by the woes of mankind. They know civilization is a loose league of fools. They accept that on faith. Disillusionment is something else."

"I wouldn't know about that, sir," Paine said. "When will you see him again?"

Carr shrugged and said, "When he's ready."

"What do you make of Mrs. Vora?"

"The basic difference between Kordt and Mrs. Vora," Carr said, "is that she hates the British."

"Why, I wonder?"

"Maybe she doesn't want to be caught in the middle. When it comes down to it, she's an Anglo-Indian, isn't she?"

Later, as they were about to leave, Paine said, "I damn well almost forgot the most important part. We had an odd bit of intelligence in from Delhi. A Gurkha patrol near Mualbem spotted a large Jap force. Estimated strength of two thousand, and they were moving west."

"Toward Assam?"

"That's not all. A detachment of Indian troops was sighted with the column. The Gurkha patrol leader thought they might have been acting as scouts for the Japanese."

"What do they make of it in Delhi?"

"They can't put an enemy force that size together with anything. They're still trying to confirm the report."

"Maybe the Gurkhas got into the rum ration," Carr said.

"A tot too many?" Paine said. "Yes, let's hope so. I shouldn't like to think anything that size could be connected to China Blue."

15

Over the telephone, Ashley had told him, "Be at the Flora Fountain at six, and someone will fetch you."

But at six, no one was there except the beggars squatting below the monument, and a *sadhu*, his face and body coated in the white ash of renunciation. Across the traffic loop, a taxi driver leaned against the door of his Renault while a *kan-saf walla* poured warm mustard oil into his ear and removed wax with a small pointed spoon. People came and went, dropping a few annas into the alms dish of the *sadhu*.

At half past six, the taxi driver wandered over to the fountain. "You please are coming," he said to Carr. "I taking you now."

They drove down past the green sprawl of the *maidans* to the long curve of Marine Drive lit against the sea in the dusk. The cab turned off the boulevard and climbed the hill to the garden park above the beach, and Carr saw the black gleam of Mrs. Vora's limousine under the trees. After the taxi had rattled off, he walked back to the Rolls and opened the door. Ashley sat alone in the passenger compartment, the curtains drawn on the windows. A cigarette smoldered in her long fingers where the silk of her sari melted over her crossed legs.

"Please get in."

She leaned forward to crush the cigarette, and Carr saw the smudge of lipstick on two other broken cylinders in the ashtray as he ducked in beside her and shut the door. Evidently she was a bit nervous, too. The limousine was already moving. Ashley drew a colored scarf from her purse.

"I'm sorry," she said. "You'll have to wear a blindfold."

"Are you taking me to be shot?"

"We can't afford to compromise this particular location."

Carr smiled and said, "What you mean is that your friend Alex doesn't trust me."

"Is it such a sacrifice?" She smiled back at him. "Come, I'll tie it for you."

She lifted her arms and Carr had a glimpse of the dampness at the armpits of her tight cotton blouse and the heavy crease of flesh where the opulently rounded breasts spilled together, and the image opened a blood valve of male hardness before he could stop it.

"There," she said. "It's tied."

"I suppose you've heard the reports," he said, "that a Japanese force has crossed the frontier into Assam."

"I heard it on the wireless," she replied.

"There's a rumor around the city that Bose's troops are in the fight."

"I shouldn't imagine the colonial administration would confirm that," she said, "even if it were true."

"Indians fighting Indians," Carr said. "Do you believe it?"

This time she hesitated before she replied. "As long as British censors control the release of news from the front, why should you imagine that any of it is true? Even a Japanese invasion?"

It seemed to Carr that they drove aimlessly about the district for awhile solely to confuse him. When he tried to bring up the subject of Bose again, she put him off. He gave up on talk and asked for a cigarette.

"Here," she murmured, just before her warm fingers grazed his mouth. A lighter clicked, threw its moving brightness across the silk band, and went out.

Later, the limousine rolled to a stop, and he heard the driver get out.

"We're here," Ashley said. "Give me your hand, and mind your head, getting out. It's only a short way. There's a footpath to the hut. Don't worry, I'll lead you."

One hand gripped him above the elbow, the other clasped his wrist, and, once, when she pressed close, her breast was briefly steeped against his arm. It felt hard and heavy as some large over-ripe fruit, and quite warm, and then was gone. Tall grass brushed against his trouser legs. Ahead, in the dark, the sea made a languorous sound washing up against a beach. A shift of wind brought the reek of decaying fish. Amid the whisper of its own fronds, a coconut palm creaked. The hand on his arm tightened, signaling a halt.

"A door," she said. "You are too tall. Bend down."

They were inside. Carr heard the door shut behind them. Fingers loosened the scarf, which fell away from his eyes, and he blinked at the tallow candle that threw its glimmer across the walls and low ceiling of the cane-and-mud hut. Near the boarded window stood Rutger Kordt, clad in a dark one-piece jump suit, belted at the waist, his face smeared with burnt cork under a seaman's wool cap pulled down over his ears.

"Sorry." The German's teeth flashed whitely in the blackened face. "I can't offer you tea."

"That could spell the end of civilization," Carr said.

"Would it be such a loss, I wonder?" Kordt gazed at him.

"You're asking the wrong man," Carr said. "Try Aristotle."

"Let's hope it will survive long enough for us to finish our business."

"That may be a high expectation," Carr said. "In any case, the parts for your Brens and Enfields are sitting at the port."

"The second payment was deposited to your Zurich account yesterday," Kordt said, "as we agreed. You should have received confirmation by now."

"As soon as I have it, I'll cable Berbera."

"The ship is the *Yildiz*, I believe?"

"Old, but seaworthy," Carr said, "assuming no one puts a torpedo into her."

"No one will," Kordt said.

"Shall I gamble on that?"

Kordt smiled again and said, "Why not? Gambling's your business, isn't it? Don't you usually win your bets?"

Carr's nerves were suddenly alive to some new direction in the conversation. He shrugged, and replied, "What's the point of losing?"

"I expect the grand casinos would like to know how you avoid it."

"That would take all the fun out of it for them."

"And the profit for you?"

"Did the police tell you that?" Carr asked, and could remember Paine saying, *They'll do some checking on you.*

"The police are more interested in your appreciation of fine art," Kordt said. "It seems you've had a run of luck in acquiring obscure early works by modern artists, and moving them into private collections."

The information, Carr thought, might have been dropped by Gage to the police in Estoril, in which case the account of his activities was likely to be thorough. Or it could have been supplied to the German ambassador in Lisbon by the dark-haired girl whom he had last seen in the casino. He remembered that she had posed for Valadon. The artist in Emile had been intrigued by the two white breasts that did not quite match, as if one were an imperfect forgery of the other.

"The paintings were authenticated by experts," Carr replied.

"I dare say they were. But who authenticated the signatures of the experts?"

"Don't worry." Carr smiled. "You'll get your merchandise. A Picasso is easier to counterfeit than a firing pin."

It struck Carr that his own credentials were being examined, and it was the German who would either authenticate them as genuine, or declare them a fake. The irony was that they were real.

"Art, gambling, and guns." Kordt shook his head. "It's a bit hard to find any logic in that combination of enterprises."

"Most behavior is illogical," Carr said. "Why should you take such a particular interest in mine?"

"Consider it part of a process," Kordt said, "to identify your loyalties."

"Maybe I don't have any," Carr said.

"You don't take sides in the war, for example."

"Why should I?"

"On the other hand," Kordt said, "why shouldn't you?"

"It's a hazardous occupation."

"So is cheating at cards."

"But one pays better."

Kordt laughed softly and said, "Does that mean you'd be willing to absorb some risk for the proper reward?"

"That would depend on the risk and the reward."

Ashley said, "Suppose the risk had to do with the cause of a free India?"

Carr glanced at her.

"Or the release of an Indian patriot," she added, "from a British gaol?"

"British gaols are bulging with Indian patriots," he said. "It's the only thing that keeps them in business."

"This one is special," she murmured.

"They're all special," Carr said. "Aren't they?"

Kordt said, "The operation needs someone who can pass for British. It shouldn't involve much risk—no more than the sale of a fake painting."

There were voices outside, and a rap of knuckles. Kordt pinched out the candle and slipped across in the dark to the plank door. He opened it part way, and Carr caught sight of the towering figure blocking the slot. There was no mistaking the big Sikh who had followed him into the Chor Bazaar. Sheer size made him impossible to confuse with anyone else. Now he spoke to Kordt in a guttural mixture of Panjabi and Marathi. Carr understood none of it, but, twice, he picked up the German word for submarine.

Kordt left the Sikh standing in the open doorway and came back. "British patrols," he said, "making a sweep. They'll have roadblocks up. We should get out now. It won't be safe to move if we wait."

16

They drove no more than five or six kilometers, then swung onto a side road, rutted and sandy, and crept along it in low gear, and finally stopped. The driver got out and went off in the dark. In a few minutes he was back, chattering in Marathi to Ashley through the window that she had rolled down.

She turned to Carr and said, "There are roadblocks into the city. This is Juhu. I have a place here. Better to wait than risk a lot of questions."

They got out and Carr stood in the road while Ashley told the driver what to do. The limousine backed into the leafy scrub to turn around, then drove off down the lane, and the sound of the motor died out.

"He'll come back for us when it's safe," she said.

Carr followed her along the sandy footpath in the scrub, where the slow roll of her hips in the sari caught the gleam of speckled moonlight. Ahead, the bungalow squatted above the beach in a line of coconut palms soaring on the blue darkness. A salt breeze blew off the water, stirring the fronds, and the surf was barely a whisper.

Ashley unlocked the door under the portico arch, and they went in. The bungalow had been closed too long, turning it musty. The moon flooded the room with its radiant blaze as she drew back the curtains and opened several windows.

Carr said, "Alex is German, isn't he?"

"Does it make any difference?" she replied.

"Not to me," he said, "but maybe to the British. They have some silly rules about spies. They hang them."

"First they have to catch them," she said.

"Suppose they do," Carr said. "Where does that leave *you*?"

"It's a risk I'm prepared to take."

"I'm not sure that I am."

"You've taken risks before," she said.

"That's not a strong argument for continuing the practice."

She had been standing at the window, her head and one shoulder tipped against the frame, her black hair curving down across her cheek and shining against the glitter of the sea. Now she turned away and sat down in a wicker armchair, leaning back and crossing her legs in the sari.

"What can I do to make you change your mind?" she said, and it struck Carr that her behavior was suddenly more English than Indian.

He lit a cigarette and replied, "I'm probably vulnerable to a wide range of inducements. But that's not the point."

"What *is* the point, then?"

"I've never been fond of surprises."

"I don't intend to provide any," she said, and asked for a cigarette.

The flame wavered across her face as she leaned toward it with the cigarette. For once, her dark eyes were calm, the violence suppressed on the pupils. Her hand came up to his on the lighter, but did not quite touch it, as if her fingers were deliberately resisting contact. A damp glaze of perspiration showed between her breasts, which gave up a faint scent of musk, and then the image flickered out.

Carr said, "If Subhas Bose is leading an Indian National army into Assam alongside the Japanese, you can bet the British will tighten security in Bombay."

"Because they are more afraid of Indian liberation," Ashley said, "than Japanese domination."

"The British call it treason," Carr said, "not liberation. Treason has an inflationary value in wartime. It's a high-stakes game, and the odds are with the house."

"I thought you preferred games with high stakes."

"Only when I'm winning."

"You've managed not to lose, most of the time."

"I've always taken care to see who else was in the game."

She blew a thin, impatient stream of smoke into the darkness and said, "I already know that about you."

"What else do you know?"

"Enough," she said.

"For what?" Carr smiled.

"My own satisfaction."

"Who provided the details?"

"Various sources."

"Confidential?"

"Some," Ashley said. "Did you know that Scotland Yard has a special file on you? And there's Suleiman Hadim, the man who supplied the arms you took into Ethiopia. He lives in a grand villa on a hill overlooking the Bosphorus in Istanbul. He had quite a lot to say about you, and—by the way—he's enormously proud of the Matisse on his wall. In fact, he's convinced that he got a wonderful bargain."

"Quite true." Carr nodded. "It's probably better than Matisse could have done."

"I don't doubt it," Ashley said, "if you say so."

"I've been thinking," Carr said, "there might be a market here in Bombay, before long, for some modern art. No Constable or Turner, of course. Postimpressionists, mostly. The value's always soaring."

"I suppose that idea *just* struck you?"

Carr's shadow advanced over the moonlit tiles. He might have been an actor taking center stage. "For instance, that wall. It needs something. A touch of color . . ." He glanced at her and said, "Your husband's bungalow, is it?"

She hesitated, and replied, "It belonged to my father."

He could not see her face clearly in the diagonal of shadow, only the full shape of her crossed legs in the sari, and the smoke prowling up from the neglected cigarette in her long fingers. But he could sense the interior change, the psychological barriers going up.

"When I was a child," she went on, "we came here occasionally on a weekend. It was a lonely stretch of coast, and still is. But in those days, there was nothing. Only the waves breaking and sliding up on the beach, and at night the stars looked as if they'd been poured off the horizon—like a pirate's treasure—because the sky was so dark and clear."

The memory, once out, seemed to stir some restless dissatisfaction in her. She got up from the wicker chair, went over to a table by the far wall, and ground out the cigarette with an angry violence. Books and papers cluttered the teakwood surface, along with a humidor of Irish porcelain, a rack of briar pipes, and a riding crop. Carr half expected her to sweep the objects away with one temperamental blow from her open hand, but instead her fingers only closed on the riding crop.

"He liked to ride by the sea. I remember him taking me along once against my mother's protests. He put the horse into a gallop. We flew down the beach. The palm trees kept racing by in the wind. I was holding on to the stallion's mane with both hands, and my father was holding me, and I was laughing because I was afraid."

"He's been dead a while," Carr said, "but you've never sorted through his effects."

"Not because of sentiment," Ashley said. "Only lack of interest. Probably he brought other women here. They weren't so different from his horses and racing boats. He could break a horse, or a woman, or a speed record with roughly the same sense of accomplishment after the fact."

On the wall above the table was a news photo under glass of a smiling, helmeted figure waving into the camera from the cockpit of a powerboat. The long, silver shape had the look of a floating rocket.

"An early model," Ashley said, "of the experimental craft that he was finally killed in. It was a quick, exhilarating, flamboyant way to die—not at all like the death he gave my mother."

"Everyone has an exclusive contract." Carr shrugged. "Immortality isn't one of the options."

"Did your friend Valadon teach you that, too?"

"He taught me how to recognize a fake. But, then, Emile was always his own best forgery." Carr crushed out his cigarette and looked at her. "Like you."

"I doubt we have any characteristics in common," she replied coldly. "Least of all that one."

They were close enough for Carr to pick up some odd tension in her nerves behind the improvised calm of her stare.

"You can put on a sari and cast yourself in the role of Lakshmi," he said, "and I suppose you can even sanctify the impersonation with an Indian marriage. But you're still half English. When are you going to stop running away from it?"

"That's a bit arrogant, isn't it," she said, "from a man who makes his living cheating at casinos and swindling the art world?"

Once more he caught the damp scent of a musky perfume, only now it mingled with some natural female scent that was excited and overripe and which the glands could not hold back.

"Why not be honest for a change?" Carr said. "You came here to find out something about yourself. It has nothing to do with British roadblocks—only with being a woman."

He saw the flash of antagonistic heat on her stare, and then he was holding the side of his neck. His hand came away with a smear of blood from the welt left by the riding crop.

He smiled, and said, "Was that from Ashley Farrar, or Mrs. Vora?"

She tried to slash again with the crop, but Carr snatched her wrist and twisted it behind her. She gave a cry of pain, and the leather quirt dropped from her grasp. He wasn't sure how long their mouths ground together in the quick Fahrenheit of sexual heat that swept all the barriers down. She murmured "Damn you" through the kiss, but the words had no anger. They seemed almost an expression of complicity, lacking altogether any resistance. Even as their mouths still clung together, Carr swung her off her feet, across the ensemble of shadows, to the couch. His hand went at once to the silk undergarment, already moist where the pubic thatch lay matted against the fabric, and his two curled fingers tore away the elastic band and sought her clitoris with an exquisitely pleasurable caress that drew more of love's honey thickness from some unfamiliar cove of feeling.

Later, she lifted her arms above her head while he pulled the cotton blouse free, and then she clung to him, her lips buried on his neck, while he unfastened the hooks of her brassiere. They came loose and Ashley leaned back on the cushion, without the garment, and Carr saw that her bare breasts were unbelievably rounded and heavy, like overripe fruit, and that the tips, even unstimulated, stood erect. A shiver went through her and she slid her fingers into the heavy matting of black hair on his chest.

He was not sure how many long minutes passed before the same fingers that had been tentative and halting on his chest became insistent and carnal in the fruit of some new knowledge, guiding the hard thickness of him into herself, and the vaginal walls gave up their first startled pain to enclose him, like an anemone closing in a sea pool, so there would be no escape from that intrusion of pleasure. His thrust deepened almost at once to the very source of her mounting contractions, which hurled their wet secrets back upon the armor shape in a taunting struggle that would win from it, at all costs, that final seminal rush. Her eyes were tightly shut and her body moved heatedly under his, her pelvis straining upward to gain maximum penetration from him, forcing at last the surrender of that warm heavy flood of himself.

The night breathed its warm respirations through the open windows into the room, and for a long time he remained in her, their mouths no longer grinding one against the other but now only grazing softly. Finally, they drew apart and lay eye to eye and listened to the surf running. Carr stroked her flank, the bare swell of her breast erotically steeped against him, and said nothing.

Later, they slipped outside to the beach under the stars. On the horizon clouds were banked low, like a distant ghost surf breaking into the moon's immaculate blaze. The sea was deliciously cool, and the dark surface had the shimmer of quicksilver around them as they swam. In deep water, Carr snatched her ankle, and she let herself be swept against him among the drowning stars. Her arms slid around his neck, and her laughing mouth on his gave back a kiss as her legs drifted about him in the weightless density among the refractions of shattered light. They broke apart, then stroked slowly back to shore.

Hand in hand they waded in through the flashing swells and shallows to the wet slant of beach and lay, half-submerged, in a tidal pool left by the retreating surf. Ashley leaned back on her elbows, one knee uplifted, her head thrown back on her shoulders. Her breasts were heavily tilted and wide apart, the tips pointed and gleaming, and drops of water glistened on her skin. For a long time she stared at the immense dome of night, as if the silver dust of the galaxies held the answer to some secret about herself.

"A little while ago I was certain of everything," she murmured, "and suddenly I'm not sure of anything."

"It's too late," Carr said, "to change it back."

"I know," Ashley said. "I don't want to."

"Then I suppose we have to decide what we're going to do about it."

"It's not that simple."

"Or that complicated," Carr said.

"I love my husband," she said. "I could never openly hurt him."

An odd tremor of jealousy cut through Carr. Passion could survive an attack of guilt, but not of pity. The dangerous emotions always lay close to the heart.

A shooting star flashed down the sky and went out.

"You can't put that star back into the sky, either," he said.

"The early civilization on the Indus Plain thought every falling star was an omen. It meant the gods were about to reveal a secret."

"Some secrets are meant to be kept," he said.

She closed her eyes under the weight of the night, and Carr became absorbed in the long line of her neck, and the wet thatch of black hair streaming down.

"Can't we pretend," she said, "there are only the two of us and it's the beginning of the world?"

He thought of the bombs dropping across Europe, more plentiful than falling stars, and said, "More likely the end of it."

"Beginnings are better than endings."

"There was a serpent in the Garden," Carr said. "Remember?"

"A cynical one?"

"He couldn't distinguish between beginnings and endings."

"That's expediency," she said, "not wisdom."

"So is pretending," Carr said.

Above them, on the beach, the coconut palms swayed and creaked in the night wind.

Ashley turned her head to gaze at him and said, "I don't want to love you."

Carr stretched across the stars and kissed her breast, then took her mouth, which was impassively cool in some last thin denial—or gesture of posthumous fidelity. But almost at once her lips stirred, and the kiss quickly overheated, and her tongue passed a burning response back to him.

He drew her legs apart underwater and felt the shiver of dark excitement pass through her body at love's first groping touch, then heard the gasp of surprise at the intrusion of thickness into her vaginal canal for the second time, and knew the sound was only a different kind of forgery, not surprise at all, but some exquisite shock of feeling beyond the threshold of entry. Another long gasp was torn from her throat—and another—as he touched over and over again the erotic secret of her being at the wet freshets of its source. Already her eyes were glazed with the promise of first orgasm, and long before his hardness broke he felt the quickening, seismic response within her own straining body. Finally, the blinding parcels of moonlight no longer rippled in bands across the sea pool, and there was only the spent glimmer of stars on the clear surface like bits of ejaculated light.

When he started to withdraw, her arms locked about his neck. She whispered, "Don't leave me yet," and the sudden tightening of vaginal muscles wrenched another pleasurable spasm from him.

The lashes were black against the white of her cheeks, but after a moment the lids opened slowly upon some dark center of truth in the pupils that locked fast on his until he could feel their flat penetration.

"I want nothing from you," she murmured, "unless you love me, too, and then I only want your promise to help us."

"Free a political prisoner?" Carr almost smiled at the act of sexual extortion. Even the grip of her arms, and her bare breasts pressing against his chest, struck him as elements of a conspiracy to force his cooperation. Yet, the devastating calm of her unflinching stare made him think otherwise. Some cold purity of emotion in it lacked altogether the properties of a lie, or premeditation. He said, "What makes one prisoner in a British gaol so important?"

"He's my brother," Ashley said.

17

While Carr and Ashley lay under the starry darkness of Juhu, the man about whom they spoke—Jai Devar—was stretched out on a plank bed in a cell in Yeravda Prison near Poona. His features were predominantly Indian, as if the English genes had sought anonymity in his dusky complexion and passionate eyes, which were full of brown color and luminous, like a stag's. He lay on his side, both hands flattened together under his cheek, and stared across the cell at the aperture higher up in the stone wall. In his poet's mind, it became a corner cut from the universe and set like a gemstone to show off a million tiny points of brilliance.

His mother, whose name was Radha, had come from a village on the sunburnt plain below Thana. At fifteen, she had been sold by her parents to a tout for money to buy seed for the planting season. She would go to Madras, the tout told her family, to work as a maidservant in the household of a government official. Instead, he took her to a Bombay brothel that specialized in the procurement of virgins for a wealthy clientele.

The brothel had once been a house for child prostitutes, and the windows were barred to prevent escape. The madam, an aging courtesan from Simla, took to herself the task of instructing Radha in the pleasures and perversions of sex. The girl accepted all of this with an air of passive complicity, as if the overripe curves of her body had been purposely engineered into it for carnal use. Even the translucent eyes seemed to brim with some dark concupiscent secret melting outward on each unblinking stare.

"I have something special this time," the courtesan said to Colin Farrar. "If you wish, I will send her to you. I promise you won't be disappointed."

Sir Colin was not one to pass up a sexual audition. The girl had managed to convey, in the ardent twisting of her body and half-stifled cries, a fierce pleasure, notwithstanding the faint sheen of blood on her inner thighs afterward. Dazed knowledge lay lovingly in her eyes. At the sink, she wet a towel in warm water, wringing out the excess moisture, then came back to the bed to wipe the traces of pink blood from his own swollen maleness.

The oil lamp cast its flicker on her brown nakedness. Some air of corrupted innocence, placidly detached from evil, attracted the Englishman. Instead of sending her back to the brothel, he had installed her in Colaba in a small house half-concealed in dark tropical foliage and an abundance of flowering bougainvillaea and hibiscus whose wind-stirred leaves now and then gave up a glimpse of the sea.

This arrangement lasted for three years, until she found that she was carrying a child. By the fifth month, she could no longer conceal her bodily changes and confessed her pregnancy. The next day, an Indian doctor gripping a medical bag turned up at the house. He had come, he said, to abort her fetus. Terrified, she had run past him down the overfoliaged path, dankly mottled in shade, to the road and screamed at the driver of a *ghoda-ghadi* to take her away.

While cutting wheat in the fields behind her village, she had gone into labor and delivered the child on the spot. An older woman came over to help, using the sickle blade to sever the umbilical cord from the extruded placenta. During the final contractions of pain, Radha's eyes had been squeezed shut in the sun, and now she opened them to see the woman, like an afterimage on the blinding disc, taking the baby away to a pond to wash the mucous from it. She turned her head slightly and saw the grain glinting on the sky above her. The golden sparkle was like a promise for her son, but on the ground the flattened stalks were matted with the shine of blood. She worried that no priest was present, no one to offer a *puja* to the gods, no one to chant from a holy text to make the time of birth fortunate. She named the boy Jai, and resolved to go as soon as possible to an astrologer to chart her son's horoscope.

The boy's English paternity might be concealed in his dusky skin, but a marriage arrangement for Radha was out of the question. There seemed to be no future for her, except, perhaps, outside the village as a domestic servant. But a working prostitute would earn more in a month than a maid might make in a year. So she had left the boy in the care of her married sister in Thana and found work in a Sonargachi brothel in Calcutta, sending back what money she could.

Jai was raised as part of his aunt's family in a two-room hut near the tidal marsh. The shack had no electricity or running water, and meals were cooked on an iron burner fueled by cow dung. The children slept on mats on the floor, and after dark the only light came from a kerosene lamp slung from a peg on the wall next to the oil drum of water. When he was old enough to understand, Jai was told that his parents had drowned in a ferryboat accident in Gujarat. In Thana, he attended a missionary school for Indian youth and early on showed an aptitude for books and poetry.

At sixteen, he left his aunt's household and went to work in a cotton mill in Bombay. He was by nature solitary, devout in his Hindu faith, and with the small amount of money that had been put away for him he was able to find a cheap attic room in a slum of Kalbadevi. Plank stairs, rotting and stained red from expectorations of *paan*, rose narrowly in the cramped darkness where he had to climb, half-bent, to avoid striking his head on the low crossbeams. In the morning he was up before daybreak to dress, heat water for tea, then walk to work while the smudges of smoke from the distant factory stacks boiled blackly upward into the pink dawn.

He worked a twelve-hour shift, close to the throbbing roar of a press and huge pistons, and in the last weeks before the monsoon the humid temperatures in the mill often soared to 120 degrees. After the steam whistle shrilled, he would walk the thronged road back to the slum in the first pale of evening, place a fresh blossom before the colored picture of Vishnu, and meditate in prayer while a joss stick lifted its plume above a bowl of warm scented oil. Later, he would bathe in water drawn from a standpipe and cook a meal of rice and lentils, which he ate with his fingers from a tin dish, sitting cross-legged on the floor; and sometimes he would go out to see a film.

Then, one Sunday, his uncle turned up in Kalbadevi in a monsoon torrent that had driven the crowds to cover. The older man stood, dripping, in the dank attic room under the tin roof where the rain hammered.

"It is time you knew the truth," he said. "Unfortunately, I have myself only just learned it."

Jai's mother, he informed the youth, had not died in a ferry accident years ago, but on a Calcutta street, in recent months, from consumption. Sadly, that was not the worst of the lie. The uncle stared for a long moment at the flash of rain beyond the open shutters. Jai himself was not of the true Sudra caste, but a half-caste, fathered outside marriage by an Englishman.

"I do not wish to speak the abomination of his name, but I have written it." He laid a sheet of folded notepaper beside the floating blossom and joss stick, as if to expose their hypocrisy, and left. Jai had a last glimpse of him, below, in the flooded street, his umbrella spread like a bat wing against the splinters of rain, his cotton trousers rolled above his knees as he waded in the black water backed up from storm drains.

The irony of being a laborer in one of his father's own mills worked on Jai in subtle ways. He could not separate shame from curiosity, and for several weeks he brooded over what to do. Finally, huddled beside the flaming wick of the oil lamp in his room above the evening din of the slum, he composed a letter of introduction. In formal English, he wrote the facts of his background as he knew them, and asked for a meeting.

Next morning, clad in spotless white trousers and shirt, he presented the letter personally to a secretary outside Sir Colin's offices high above the green of Cross Maidan and told her he would wait for a reply.

He waited through the afternoon while businessmen came and went, and finally he was alone on the long bench beneath the lemon patch of sunlight high up on the wall. On the other side of the railing, the clerks were clearing off their desks.

Once more, Jai stood before the secretary. "Excuse me," he said, "but are you sure my letter was delivered?"

"Of course it was delivered. I handed it to Sir Colin myself."

On her desk, the telephones no longer rang impatiently. Soon, the civil servants and clerks would be streaming into the streets from office buildings and rushing to catch trains out of Victoria Terminus or Churchgate Station.

The secretary rose, clutching pad and pencil, and disappeared behind two massive doors paneled in teak. After a minute she came back, sleek and aloof in her gold-trimmed sari.

"Sir Colin has gone," she said. "He is a very busy man, you know. Perhaps if you came back tomorrow . . ."

Early the next day, he was back, waiting once more on the bench beyond the sari-clad figure of the secretary, who sat like a Sphinx guarding a tomb, and no one would solve her riddle. At midmorning, she vanished once more behind the crypt-heavy doors. Her manner when she came out was neither friendly nor unfriendly, but only austere in its reserve.

"Sir Colin is gone for the day," she said. "I am afraid his appointment calendar is filled for quite some time. . . ." Her brown fingers strayed to a spiral book, and he saw, blocked out under the date: *Willingdon Sports Club*.

He could not get past the gate onto the grounds of the sporting club. Sir Colin Farrar, they told him, was on the golf course.

Jai trailed along the fence in the sun and squinted under cupped hands at the toy figures on the fairways spotted with sand traps and clumps of trees. The golfers, with their caddies, were too far off to distinguish one from the other. Perhaps Sir Colin had already finished on the links and retired to the dining terrace by the swimming pool. The tables would sport a mixed crowd of prosperous Indians and British sipping pink gin and beer, and dining on stuffed fowl, or pomfret and fresh oysters.

At five o'clock Jai was still waiting in the shade by the wall outside the gate when the cream-yellow Continental Touring Saloon rolled down the drive from the clubhouse. Sir Colin had an Englishwoman beside him in the back seat. The sideburns of his dark, thinning hair left a flash of silver against features that looked more Florentine than British. Only the eyes remained Celtic in their cold blue. They caught sight of Jai and held fast for a passing moment. The heavy mouth lost the shape of its smile to some vague memory—disturbing, perhaps—for the face behind the glass turned back, all at once, to the woman.

Jai's own stare followed the limousine as it shrank from view. In that suspended instant, as their glances had met, he had almost started to smile. It was an unconscious reflex, arising from a sense of biological identity, a stillborn affection, and it was followed immediately by keen disappointment as the sleek Rolls ground past without stopping. Suddenly he was angry with himself, and the anger was directed at his own false expectations.

The gaunt, bespeckled Indian, waiting outside the factory a few days later, stepped forward to introduce himself. He was a solicitor, he explained, acting at the behest of Sir Colin Farrar.

"My firm has offices near High Court." His English had some exaggerated cadence of Oxford in its lofty flow. "If you are free, I have a taxi waiting."

The offices were deserted and dim at this late hour of the day, like a rendezvous for secret agents. But that was as it should be. A bastard, Jai thought, was not much more than a product of sexual espionage.

"Sir Colin," the solicitor said, "acknowledges no responsibility in the matter of your claim to a filial relationship. However, he wishes to see to your education. He has agreed to undertake the expense of sending you through the engineering college at Poona. It is his firm belief that India needs engineers . . ." The solicitor paused to make his point, and added, "Not poets."

Jai said nothing, but the odd stab of pain came and went. He could not even identify it with an emotion.

"In return for your education, and a reasonable allowance to see you through the process, you will be required to sign papers disavowing any claim to paternity such as you have expressed in *this* . . ." He lifted a paper, and Jai recognized his letter to his father in which he had mentioned his interest in poetry. "You are to make no further representations of this sort in the future, regardless of circumstances in which you may find yourself. On the assumption that you would most certainly agree to these conditions, I have drawn up the necessary papers. You need only to sign them, and we can conclude these proceedings."

By the end of his third year at the college he was an active disciple of Gandhi and committed to the concept of nonviolent civil disobedience. In Whitehall, Parliament had passed the Government of India Act, but it was a hollow concession that retained for the viceroy and his British governors the power to veto legislation. Jai had joined other students in a march of protest that began at dusk outside the guardhouse of Peshwa Palace, its gates still fortified with spikes against elephant charges, and they had crossed the bridge over the river to the Government House and lit candles in a silent vigil through the night. Perhaps because of its intrinsic melodrama, the incident had been reported in the Bombay press. A few days later, the gaunt solicitor who had arranged for his education paid him a visit in Poona.

"It is your sponsor's wish," he said, "that you refrain from all political activity, forthwith, or risk the loss of financial support."

It was a long time before Jai could bring himself to answer. "I prefer to risk the loss of financial support," he said, "than the loss of my conscience."

"Very well, but I think it is a decision you will come to regret dearly," the solicitor said. He added with a small sneer of wry wisdom, "A conscience is a poor collateral for success in British India."

Jai did not stand for his final examinations. Six weeks later he was arrested with a dozen others for obstructing railway traffic in the hills to the south. In the early dawn they had taken up a segment of track where a goods train would pass within the hour, and when the engine finally came into view, pounding slowly up the grade out of a river valley, they had run, shouting and waving red flags alongside the cab to prevent a derailment. Below, where the train had climbed out of the valley, a second group was already taking up more track and flinging it off the trestle over the river, isolating the string of boxcars on the hill.

In the same manner, they had marooned two more locomotives chugging to the scene with repair crews and spare rails. Finally, arms linked, they had huddled together on the track to form a human barrier. They were all young, their mood festive, as if they had succeeded at a college prank.

At the stockade in Kolhapur, the deputy superintendent of police arrived in a Rover to question him. Jai would not answer and watched the anger bloom on the Englishman's cheeks until they were pink like the shell of a crab drawn out of a steam vat. At last the superintendent stood up under the grinding paddle fan and told Jai that he and the others would be taken to the military garrison at Poona for further questioning.

The Army havildar in charge of the transport was a Madrassi with blue-black skin slackly drawn over tough features, broken rather than arranged across his face. Sepoy guards herded the prisoners into two stakebed trucks, and they headed north on the winding mountain roads, the sun hot on the canvas overhead. Long before they reached Poona, the lorries turned onto a branch road, rutted and dusty, that ran out to a shack on the rail line. Scrub and spear grass grew alongside the elevated cinder bed of the track, and the long tin roof of the shed flashed in the sun.

The dust plumed earthward after the vehicles had rolled to a stop. A sepoy lifted the pins from the tailgate, which clanged hollowly as it fell. The havildar gazed at each prisoner sitting cross-legged in the bed of the lorry. Finally the rum-red eyes settled on Jai, and he told him to get down. A tremor of apprehension shot through Jai, but he did as he was told.

The spear grass rustled against his legs as he was led to the shack. The havildar opened the padlock and motioned Jai to go in. Now his alarm mounted, like an ether of fear loose in the nerves. Perhaps they meant to put a bullet into the back of his head and leave him. The heat under the tin roof was suffocating, and the ties stacked in the dirt against the wall smelled of creosote. Only a little light seeped through the cracks in the sideboards, and he could hear the buzz of flies in the darkness.

The havildar said, "Look, I haven't time to waste with you in this heat. The police say you were uncooperative. You have information they want. I'll give you a chance to start talking." He wagged a finger. "One chance. That's all."

Two sepoys stood in the doorway, their uniforms dusty and sweat-streaked. Both were dark-skinned, and one had a slack smile on his mouth beneath a stare of round absorption. The fear had condensed to moisture in Jai's palms, and his mouth felt too dry even to swallow.

"They told me in Kolhapur you were a caste Hindu," the havildar said.

Jai wanted to reply, "No, I'm Anglo-Indian," but could not bring himself to say it. Instead, he said nothing.

"The others out there, too," the havildar went on. "They all have caste. These sepoys are *ajanya*. Untouchable. They could do with a woman, but they can't afford one. Anyhow, it's dark enough in here. I suppose they can pretend they're having a woman."

In the bed of the moving lorry Jai huddled by himself in one corner, his face buried in his crossed arms. The memory was all part of a fragmented darkness, the touch of a rifle barrel behind his ear, the dirt floor of the shed against his cheek, screams turning to sobs, the buzz of flies on the silence . . . Before they had even dragged him outside into the blinding sun, the others were telling the havildar what he wanted to know.

Jai spent nine months in Yeravda Prison, and was let out. The defilement by his captors in the railway line shack still festered inside him, a psychological sore that would not heal. The humiliation had attached itself to his soul like some prurient rot. Nothing would burn it out. Only his hatred of the British served as a therapeutic agent.

Soon after his release from prison Jai carried a letter of introduction, written by a local Congress leader, to Subhas Bose in Calcutta. The train rolled into Howrah depot at sundown, and he spent the first night in the station on the floor under one of the steel girders that soared high up toward the glass-domed ceiling. The next morning, with his bedroll under his arm, he shouldered his way through the teeming crowd, past the water vendors, newsboys, and peddlers hawking rice and sweetmeats, and crossed Howrah Bridge on foot into the city. The cantilevered span above the mud-brown river was jammed solidly with motorcars, bicycles, bullock carts, rickshaws, and human traffic.

He had read in the paper that Subhas Bose would address an outdoor political rally that day, and he made his way up the strand on the bank of the river to the Maidan. By midmorning a huge crowd had massed on the green in the sweltering heat, and a deafening shout went up as Bose mounted the speaker's platform, its timbers swathed in green and yellow bunting. For a full hour, the fiery new president of the Indian National Congress assailed the British.

"The struggle for freedom," he had shouted, "cannot be won by passive mysticism. Freedom is never given. It is taken. . . ."

Even as the words blared from loudspeakers and proliferated into echoes, they struck some center of blocked-up feeling in Jai. It was as though a psychological axis shifted in his mind, dislodging a flood of accumulated anger and insight. From that moment, he was committed to a course of radical politics.

A few days later, in response to the letter of introduction, the Indian leader received him in his home. Clad in a loose, white cotton khaddar, which had been spun and woven on a hand loom, Bose looked to be in his early forties—perhaps even younger. They drank tea in the garden, and the politician said, "Why have you come to Calcutta?"

"To be of help," Jai answered without hesitation.

There was no humor in the flat Bengali face, only dark vitality and uncompromising purpose. Even the stare seemed to hover on his glasses in refractions of force that would cut through any subterfuge.

"In what way?" he said.

"In whatever way I can be useful."

"Even if it means prison?"

"There are worse things," Jai said, "than prison."

For the next three years, he served as a political organizer and secretary to the Congress leader, and twice went with him by train into the Bengali countryside. In the damp heat of summer they traveled in ordinary second class, and sometimes villagers who could not afford the fare scrambled onto the top of the coach. They were taking sheaves of hay to market, and from the window of the compartment Jai could see the outline of their shadows streaming on the landscape below the glass and into his own consciousness.

"Bengal," Bose said, "will be the heart of a free India. It is already beating in those shadows that you are watching. Now I will tell you something. One day, the struggle will be won or lost here."

"Yes," Jai said, though he had no idea what the militant Indian leader meant.

In Calcutta, Jai lived alone above a cheap restaurant. It was built in an L-shape, the grill and scullery set apart from the dining room by beaded curtains. Only one of two paddle fans worked, and the sluggish blades would not disperse the smoke and cooking smells from the kitchen. Tables and chairs that did not match ran across the bare floor, often slick underfoot where the waiters tracked in oily deposits from grease traps that had overflowed. There were two waiters, unshaven and sweaty as the proprietor, and at night Jai could hear them shouting at the cook, and sometimes at each other, for the walls were thin as matchwood.

One afternoon when he came back to his room there was a note stuck to the door telling him to see the proprietor. He found him at a table downstairs, wolfing a meal of sliced potatoes that had been smothered in onions and spices and baked in a deep dish.

"A woman was here looking for you," the proprietor said. "I thought she must be English. She looks and dresses English, but speaks Hindi. I am not sure what she is."

"What did she want?"

The proprietor used his tongue to dislodge a morsel from his teeth while pouring mustard oil over his *canhki*. "She would like you to meet her tomorrow at two o'clock beneath the queen's statue in the Victoria Memorial. That's all I know."

Next afternoon, Jai walked up Chowringhee to the memorial. The young woman waiting alone under the statue of Victoria wore white gloves and carried a purse to match, and the creamy silk of her dress had a white gleam, too, where the fabric melted into the contours of her body. Only her eyes and hair were stunningly black against the English-pale skin. After a moment, she caught sight of him in the crowd, and the dark pupils seemed almost to widen in the dilations of some instinctive recognition. She approached him and said, "My name is Ashley Farrar. It seems we had the same father."

He invited her back to his room for tea. In the horse cab, clopping across Dalhousie Square, Ashley told him Colin Farrar was dead. She had learned of Jai's existence, she said, a year ago through the solicitor handling the estate. The police had traced him, finally, to Calcutta.

"He was no father to me," Jai said. "Now, he is my shame, just as I was his."

At the restaurant, they climbed the stairs to his room from the cobbled alley strewn with fish heads and garbage. Inside, she looked around sadly at the drab surroundings, but said nothing. Jai heated water on the electric ring, and afterward they sat facing each other on mats on the floor, sipping tea and retracing their lives.

Later, she said, "I want you to come back to Bombay with me. There's no reason for you to live like this, now. He was very rich. I intend to settle an allowance on you—the one you should have had from him."

He was silent, his head bowed so that she could not see his expression. At last he stood up and drifted to the window where the shutters gaped open on the quarter. Dirt lanes twisted back through the slum, still jammed with moving figures, and here and there the shadows gave up a black gleam of sewage. Ashley rose to join him.

"Did you know," he said, "that jackals used to prowl this district at night, looking for the dead? You hear stories about a pack ripping away gangrenous flesh from a dying man. I have always thought it was a fitting metaphor for British rule in India, because that is their true legacy to us, not memorials in white marble to dead queens. No, I cannot leave Calcutta. There's exciting work here."

The first shades of twilight were bathing the quarter when Jai and Ashley descended the outer stairs to the alley. The cobbles shone with a grimy film under the litter of scum and garbage. A block from the restaurant, they found a horse cab. The canopy was folded down, and Jai helped her into the open carriage and insisted on paying the driver. From the pavement, he gazed up at her and said, "I should very much like you to meet Subhas Bose before you leave Calcutta. He is the future of India. You will see."

But he had come back to Bombay, after all, following Bose's flight out of the country, and within ten months found himself once more confined to Yeravda Prison, this time for terrorism and sedition.

Now he lay on the plank bed, his hands flattened together under his cheek, staring up at the stars crammed into the open slot in the thick wall of the cell. He rarely let his mind drift too far into the past. There were too many dark, psychological undertows—and especially one—waiting to take him down. But he often thought about his sister and the day she had come unexpectedly into his life. He saw her now in the horse-drawn carriage, moving off in the warm twilight, looking back with a smile and lifting one white-gloved hand. For a long time the clop of hooves carried her away into the past, until the white gleam of her dress was only another point of brilliance on the night. At last, on his stare, it became a shooting star that flashed down the sky and went out.

18

At Juhu, they both saw the second star streak down the horizon and burn out.

"Another secret?" Carr smiled.

"I shouldn't have thought we had any of those left," Ashley said.

She still lay with her elbows in the sand, one knee uplifted against the glimmer of the night. She had referred several times to Subhas Bose as *Netaji*—Revered Leader. If Hitler could call himself *Führer*, and Mussolini make himself the *Duce*, at least Bose would not be outdone in the choice of sobriquets.

"How did Bose get out of the country?" Carr said.

"He escaped from house arrest in the middle of the night and was taken by motorcar to Gomoh. Jai was waiting for him with tickets at the railway station and they boarded a train for Peshawar. From there, they took another car over back roads into the Khyber Pass to a tribal village. Netaji was posing as a deaf mute. They set out on foot with a Pathan escort. Jai left them near the frontier. Netaji was bound for the Soviet embassy in Kabul."

"And now he's with the Japanese, knocking on the back door," Carr said. "Better than house arrest, I suppose."

"The British were about to try him for sedition. He would have been rotting in prison, instead of leading a liberation army."

"This business of getting your brother out of gaol—does it have anything to do with Bose's military operation in Assam?"

She turned her head to gaze at him, the shadows touching out her features, and the night wind took the black of her hair across light years of scattered stars. "Perhaps," she replied.

111

"It won't be easy," Carr said.

"No one expects it to be. If you agree to help, then tomorrow, when the car comes for us, we'll drive directly to the tea plantation. You can't go back to your hotel."

"Why?"

"For security reasons. You can be sure the British CID is watching your hotel. In any case, Alex is the one who makes the rules."

Kordt, again. Carr did his best to hold back a smile, and said, "But Alex gets his orders from Berlin."

"You should believe me," Ashley said, "when I tell you he's a man, above everything else, of personal honor. He spent many years here in India before the war."

"Doing what?" It seemed to Carr that she was inching toward trust like a beautiful sleek doe investigating a scent and ready to spring away from danger.

"A scholar of Indian religious history," she replied. "He was very much fascinated by some of the *sadhu* mystics and spent quite a lot of time with them. Some of his work is still represented in the Prince of Wales Museum in Bombay. I told you once that India belongs to those who love her. In this case, a German."

"Your brother, too?"

She leaned closer in the shadows, her breast swelling as a glimmer of flesh, and he felt the light, insistent pressure of her fingers on his chest. "Will you help him," she murmured, "for my sake?"

Was there a male on the planet, Carr wondered, who could have refused? Her mouth grazed his, not as a plea, but a caress, and the mixture of trust and love in her stare was disarmingly real. For the first time ever, quite apart from being a cheat, he felt like one. In the sale of fake canvases, one could at least put a value on irony. Now, there was a moment when he came close to saying no, but in the end he took her kiss, like a deposit on another forgery, and stared past the warm curve of her shoulder at the distant flash of surf down the coast.

19

"What made you decide to join us?" Kordt said.

Carr looked at Ashley, whose dark pupils smuggled back the answer like contraband.

"I was persuaded," he replied, "by sentiment."

The plantation lay a few kilometers off the mountain road between Mahad and Mahabaleshwar. They had driven down the coast before noon, then up through the pass away from the sea, turning off into a long valley where the terraced hillsides were planted in tea. Kordt had not appeared until dusk. Now the three of them were alone in the walled garden as the early darkness settled like a sediment over the distant ridges.

"I suppose it's as good a reason as any." Kordt shrugged. "Everything of value is in short ration, these days. Even sentiment."

"When does this miracle of deliverance begin?" Carr said.

"Tonight," Kordt said.

Carr let a smile drift over his surprise. "You don't believe in wasting time."

"Change of plans, I'm afraid. The British are transferring their prisoner to a garrison in Madras. The move wasn't to take place for another fortnight, but they've set the date forward."

"Why?"

"I expect it has to do with the Japanese advance into Assam. Devar has quite a lot of political sympathy in the Bombay region, and he's a key figure in Bose's Forward Bloc Party. I should think the British are worried about civil demonstrations—perhaps even an attempt to break him out of Yeravda."

"Tell me something." Carr lit a cigarette. "How do you know Bose has an army fighting alongside the Japanese on Indian soil? The newspapers haven't reported it."

Kordt smiled impassively, and said, "I know."

A servant holding a lamp came from the house into the garden. He whispered something to Ashley, and Carr saw a flicker of concern.

"It may be that my husband has suffered another small stroke," she said. "I must go to him. If it's true, we will have to fetch a doctor."

Her dark gaze settled on Carr, and the look in it seemed to pass beyond distress into some dimension of anger and self-guilt, as if their adultery were responsible. Moral contrition could not distinguish between infidelity and a blocked artery. But then the expression softened, and she said, "Be careful, won't you?"

He watched her moving off beside the servant who held the lamp above his turbaned head, pooling light over the ground.

Carr said to Kordt, "Don't you think it's time I knew who you were?"

"As you've probably guessed," the other replied, "I'm a German officer, acting under orders."

"You'll be shot as a spy if you're caught out of uniform."

"A bullet is always a soldier's risk, whether it comes from a firing squad or somewhere else. It can only kill you once." Kordt laughed softly. "In any case, we'll both be in uniform soon enough. British, of course."

"How soon can I celebrate my commission?"

"In about seventy-two hours, actually. That's not much time, is it? If you've finished your cigarette, perhaps we should get cracking."

Half an hour later, the lights of the tea plantation were falling away behind them as they climbed on horseback out of the valley. In addition to Kordt and Carr there were two others—the Sikh, whose massive frame seemed to dwarf that of the horse, and a mountain tribesman who wore a hooded garment draped as far as his loincloth and who trailed a string of two pack mules. Kordt would say only that they were bound for a jungle base camp.

They went over the first low ridge, dropped down into a shallow basin, and skirted a lake spiked with reeds. The moon burned on the water, and there was no sound except the soft slow thud of hooves and the creak of the leather pack saddles that bulged with supplies on either side of the mules.

The floor of the basin rose, and the trail climbed over switchbacks through a pass. Scrub gave way to jungle spilling down from ridges, dark against the stars. There was no sign of a village, and twice, over the next hour, Carr heard a panther scream.

Later, they followed a stream into the mouth of a gorge, and Kordt halted beside a deep pool. From a ledge thirty feet up, a waterfall thundered down, its mists blowing. The riders dismounted, and the Sikh went back in the dark to unstrap the packs from the mules. Afterward, the second Indian led the animals away.

"There's a hamlet not far from here," Kordt said, "where the animals can be looked after. We used to picket them in here, until a tiger killed one of the mules."

"That means we're walking, doesn't it?" Carr said.

"The climb up this gorge is too steep for the horses, I'm afraid."

"What about the packs?"

"Ram Singh will carry one tonight and come back for the other in the morning."

Carr thought the base camp could not be too far. He watched Ram Singh move off the trail and slip one of the saddle packs into a cavernous hollow where the talon-shaped roots of a tree bulked above the ground. Then the Sikh swung the other pack, as if it had no weight at all, across his shoulder.

They set out in single file. Higher up in the gorge, a falling sheet of granite gleamed in the moonlight. By the time they reached the top of the falls, Carr was sweating. The trail angled steeply upward in the jungle beside the streambed of tumbled boulders where the water dropped down in a series of pools. Now and then the roaring torrent was close enough in the tangled foliage for Carr to feel the spray on his face, but at other times it was only a silver flash beyond the black leaves of the rain forest.

For another hour they worked their way up the flank. Twice Carr glanced back and caught sight of the Sikh coming up from below, the pack still balanced over one massive shoulder, his big hands stretching out to grip the cable-heavy vines.

They had come level with the sheer granite face that had been visible from below the falls. Now the vertical slab was sinking into shadow on the other side of the chasm. The crest of rimrock they were on gave itself up grudgingly, and with each few meters of new ground Carr could feel his heartbeat accelerate against the empty reserve of oxygen in his lungs.

Finally the top of the ridge rested under their feet. Below, the gorge was no more than a toy landscape, the waterfall a bit of twisting light where it fell into the clear pit of the rocky pool.

"How much farther?" Carr said.

"Not far," the German replied.

Ahead, the temple squatted above them in the grip of the jungle. The top was gone from a colonnade and the broken pillars rose on the night. Friezes and figures ornamented the exterior blocks, beasts and gods sculpted into coexistence. Time had eroded many of the faces, leaving a leprous look—a nose lopped off, an ear or fingers missing, an eye gouged from a socket.

"Welcome to Nagaraja," Kordt said.

They mounted the broad stone steps, crumbling and chinked with vegetation, to the ruined colonnade. Chalky debris crunched underfoot as the German led them into a high-domed chamber. A dozen vents at the top cut the moonlight into falling beams which converged on colossal images projected in relief on the walls— Shiva in the fondling embrace of his consorts, Parvati, goddess of battle, and Kali, goddess of death.

In another panel, Shiva performed the dance of creation, wearing a serpent armband and grasping a great cobra entwined around one muscular leg and passing between his thighs like a phallus.

Kordt said, "The faithful believe that the serpent brings life as well as death. Childless women used to come here with offerings of bananas and milk for Nagaraja and beg for the gift of fertility."

"I suppose the one thing India needs," Carr said, "is more people."

"It's late," Kordt said. "Better get some sleep. You'll find a bedroll in the supply pack." The German looked fresh, as if the fatigue and strain of the climb had not touched him at all. In the moonlight, he smiled at the figures cut from stone. "Tonight you'll rest in the lap of the gods."

The sun was up when Carr woke. A few rays fell through the slitted dome in a tangle of light, and he saw that Ram Singh still slept under the blanket that was too small for his huge frame. Kordt's bedroll lay untouched nearby, as if it had not been used.

Carr rose quietly and went out to the colonnade, its stone still cold in the first sunlight. He caught sight of Kordt, stripped to the waist, bathing at a spring in the jungle below the steps.

He heard the scrape of a sandal and turned his head sharply. In the felled shadows of the columns stood an old Brahmin priest, his dhoti gathered between his bare legs, which were thin and brittle as sticks.

Kordt had seen the two of them and was striding up from the spring, a towel draped over his neck across the hard, flat muscles of his chest. He took the steps two at a time to the top, and joined his outstretched palms in a prayerlike fashion, raising them briefly to the height of his mouth. Then he spoke to the priest in Marathi. The old man, whose face was wrinkled and black like the skin of a prune, replied in a lisping, toothless whisper, and went off.

"Sleep well?" Kordt asked.

"Like a sinner absolved," Carr said.

"If you are so pure of heart," the German said, smiling, "you must be hungry. Come along. The old Brahmin has set a breakfast for us."

Behind a pillar in the domed enclave, steps spiraled down into a cavernous chamber lit by flares on pikes. Kordt paused on a U-shaped ledge above a pit that looked to be about twelve feet deep and at least thirty feet across. At the center, a massive sculpture of the serpent god rose above a round, low slab of rock.

"The god, Vasuki," the German said, "he of the many feet. He guards the ark in which Manu, the father of all men, was saved from the flood."

There was movement in the shadows below the idol, and a priestess stepped into view. She placed a bronze vessel of milk on the granite slab. Then she went forward to one of several lattice covers flush with the wall and lifted a stakepin.

After several moments, there was a gleam in the dark aperture. A narrow snout appeared, patterned across the top with scaly fissures, and Carr watched a great hamadryad—a king cobra—glide out. It seemed to come forever, like something extruded from the rock. In motion, the snake's head remained aloft, hood slightly extended, while its long shape melted over the ground in a bending curve. The shiny seeds of eyes had the glint of a fierce homicide on their lidless stare and the split tongue flicked from the scaly mouth.

Carr was suddenly aware of a cold frost of moisture above his upper lip. He drew the back of his hand across it.

"Vasuki is also the Serpent King, Nagaraja," Kordt explained. "This cobra is thought to be the incarnation of the god. The priestess cares for him."

"Is she the old priest's wife?"

"Once she was his wife, but then she was consecrated and became the wife of the deity. After that, she ceased to be married to her husband."

The cobra, Carr thought, would measure at least sixteen feet. There was a sinister grace in the way the curved head and hooded neck hovered, above the slab, in a full moment of arrested motion, then spilled across the granite in a final gliding thrust to the milk.

The priestess had closed the thatched cover and moved back to the bronze saucer. The hamadryad could have reared to strike the robed figure, but it displayed no aggression toward her. Instead, it drank from the vessel near her bare feet.

"The hamadryad is our security watch," Kordt said. "He has certain advantages over a conventional sentry. For instance, he stands duty round the clock and requires no relief. His enemies fear him, but he has no fear of them. He's a highly intelligent creature, and one strike from his fangs can inject enough venom to kill an elephant."

"What does he protect?"

"Come and see for yourself," Kordt said, and lit a rush candle from one of the flares.

The cobra's lair was a damp cavern of ledges and crevices flaring away from the rushlight. Behind a cleft, a plank door opened on another passage where half a dozen rooms, hewn out of the rock, slid into the glare of a hanging lantern. Kordt pinched out the candle and said, "These cells were once the living quarters of priests. Now they serve as an operations center and mess."

In one of the rooms, they sat cross-legged on mats and ate roti—flat, unleavened bread—and drank tea that the old priest had brewed.

"Don't you worry about uninvited visitors?" Carr asked.

"You saw the plaited covers in Vasuki's pit. The cobras are enough to stop anyone coming down to this level."

"Even the faithful?"

"The Cult of the Serpent died out here centuries ago. Today it only exists in the south."

"*You* found it, didn't you?"

"It's what I did before the war, here in India. This region has quite a lot of cave temples and old forts. Some of the ruins don't even appear on British maps."

"That's convenient."

"If you value privacy." Kordt smiled. "Finish your tea, and I'll take you along to our clothing stores. We still have to turn you out smartly in uniform. I expect it may require a bit of stitching, and a brush and press. Then I want to get you briefed on the operation. It all begins on a train. . . ."

20

From the barred window of his first-class compartment, Carr looked out across the railway platform in Poona. The lights of the station burned across the darkness and left a gleam on the tracks in the yards, but at this hour there was not much activity. A few barefooted porters dozed beside iron-wheeled carts. Others bore on their turbaned heads the baggage of passengers changing from the broad-gauge line out of Bombay to the meter-gauge system for the trip south through the mountains.

Later, he saw a detachment of troops escort the prisoner across the platform from the main concourse. The party consisted of three riflemen, a havildar, and a company grade British officer in charge. Two of the men broke off and passed by Carr below his window on their way to the rear. Probably one of them would take a position on the roof of the last coach to keep the top of the train clear of riders who had no tickets. The third rifleman went forward to ride with the engineer and fireman in the cab. The officer and havildar boarded the other first-class coach with Devar, whose wrists were handcuffed in front of him.

Twice, from the front of the train, a pea whistle blew. In the cab of the locomotive the engineer opened the regulator. A puff of steam billowed out from the underside of the boiler as the engine gave three quick chugs. The coaches lurched into motion, and Carr watched the platform sliding away. The train rolled slowly out of the yards under the signal gantries, the wheels clicking over the switchplates, the steel joints of the undercarriage creaking as the coach swayed.

The lights of Poona faded behind them, and Carr could see bits of broken landscape on the streaming darkness outside the window. The chunks of terrain flew fast as the train pounded across the valley toward the dark ridges cutting across the stars.

There was a rap of knuckles at the door, and the conductor-guard stepped into the compartment to look at Carr's ticket.

"What was the delay about at Poona?" Carr said.

"Military business, sir," the conductor replied. "The army is transporting a prisoner to Bangalore."

"He must be important. I saw four guards and an officer getting on the train."

"It's Devar, the terrorist. They are taking no chances with him."

"Never heard of the chap."

"Then the colonel must not be from this region," the conductor replied, "or he would know the bloody fellow."

"I'm only here on a spot of leave," Carr said, "thanks to a Jap bullet in Burma." He smiled to give the impression he was taking the conductor into his confidence.

"Of course, sir." The conductor was staring at the row of battle ribbons above the breast pocket of Carr's tunic. "I understand. You are going to Madras? You will change trains again at Bangalore. From there, the track is broad gauge. I should like to be informed if there is anything we can do to make the colonel more comfortable. Have a pleasant trip, and I wish the colonel a speedy recovery from his wounds."

The conductor was gone. The far-off glimmer of villages sank into the valley, and the beat of the engine slowed to a tramp-tramp-tramp as it labored up a winding grade through a pass. The stars took a long time drawing near, only to be cut adrift again and driven off by more lunging ridges. On each sharp curve the engine swung into view, sparks streaming from the funnel like fireflies blown into the night.

Carr switched off the lamp, lit a cigarette, and stared at the steep country through the soldier's image ghosting the pane. Valadon would have been pleased with the forgery of the battle-hardened lieutenant colonel. But the authentication of the portrait, and its sale to the British, were still an hour away in the plunging darkness outside the window.

Around midnight, Carr saw the first lanterns swinging out of the dark beside the track, and a red flag waving in the glow, and felt the brakes lock, wrenching forward motion from the wheels with enough force and friction to send sparks flying from the steel. No sooner had the train slid to a stop than the whistle shrilled, a hoot of angry protest, and a geyser of steam erupted from the safety valve. The Indian who had flagged the train hurried down the line toward the cab.

The train had ground to a halt on a curve, not far from a bridge, and Carr could see the engine and tender on the track, and the shine of arched girders in the moonlight where the trestle crossed the river. A dirt road came in from the woods on the right and there were cut logs across it to mark the dead end. A Bedford lorry was backed up in the clearing, and he saw Kordt standing on the running board and leaning on the top frame of the open door. Four sepoys wearing turbans and Sikh beards were dispersed around the truck, their rifles already off their shoulders and at the ready.

In full battle dress, Kordt looked every bit the professional soldier. Short puttees held his jungle green trousers fast to the tops of his nailed boots. Hooked to the web belt round his waist, below the battle vest, were an ammunition pouch, compass, and water bottle, and a *kukri* sheathed in its leather case. His carbine was slung, muzzle down, from one shoulder, and his wide-brimmed Gurkha hat sported the numbered badge of his regiment.

"On the lower quadrant of the window, the conductor came into view, gripping a lantern in its brass cradle. Already, Kordt was striding toward him into the light. The two men spoke briefly, and the conductor pointed back at the train. Now the escort officer joined them in the cut between the woods and the track. His appearance could have come on cue. It was very nearly like a play that they had already done in rehearsal, and Carr's presence on stage would be next.

21

Kordt watched the stocky escort officer step from the coach and stride with a stiff, short-legged gait away from the track bed and into the lamplight pooled on the ground. At the same time, the Indian who had flagged down the engine trotted back from the cab.

The officer, who looked a bit old to be a captain and who had the truculent features and curling underlip of a toy bulldog, saluted Kordt, and said to the conductor, "Why have we stopped?"

"The second bridge down the line is out," the conductor said. "This fellow with the flag is a local stationmaster. I know him by sight."

"An explosive charge is being wired to the bridge and set off," the stationmaster said breathlessly. He was a rail-thin Moslem, and a film of nervous sweat gleamed on his dark face. "It is jolly well being sabotage by dastardly persons."

"Why weren't we alerted at the last stop?" the captain said. "We went right on through."

"Maybe signal problem." The stationmaster shrugged. "Who can be knowing the cause in this bloody awful confusion?"

"Be grateful we caught you," Kordt said. "These coaches sink fast, and it's a dark night for swimming. Is your name Parker, by the way?"

"Sir," the captain replied smartly in a tone that meant yes.

"I have orders from General Welply in Poona to assume custody of your prisoner. We'll be transporting him under tight security, by lorry, to Bangalore."

Kordt saw the involuntary jerk of wariness in the gray-green pupils and knew the captain would not be easily fooled. He had the look of an accountant or civil inspector who had donned his uniform and rank for the war. Even the Webley revolver looked unused and out of place on his plump hip.

"I see," he replied. "May I have a look at those orders, sir?"

"Hardly," Kordt said. "They're verbal."

The captain swallowed uncomfortably and said, "Might I request that the colonel identify himself?"

"My name is Ross," Kordt said. "On loan, at present, to the Jungle and Mountain Warfare Center at Wilson Point. I supervise instruction in land navigation and long-range patrols. As best I know, we're the only military unit operating in this area at the moment. I expect that's the reason we were pressed into service."

"It is being truly spoken," the stationmaster said. "I myself am receiving a most urgent call from the district traffic superintendent who is mentioning the colonel-sahib by name."

"How do you know for sure it was the district traffic superintendent you talked to?" the captain said.

"Because he is my cousin," the stationmaster said.

"And the railway police?" The captain glanced about. "Why aren't they here with you?"

"The railway police are being now dispatched to the scene of bloody mischief," the stationmaster replied. "They will work this way up the line. All culverts and bridges must be for thorough checking."

Kordt said, "There's a breakdown train with a crane and repair crew coming up from Kolhapur. The bridge should be patched up by noon tomorrow. The orders out of Division are for you and your men to stay with the train and provide security. Once repairs to the bridge are complete, you're to proceed as far south as Sangli."

While the four men stood conferring in the bright gleam of the lantern, the lance corporal who had ridden on the footplate between the engine and tender had dropped down onto the ballast and doubled back to the coach where the prisoner was held. Apart from the conductor and Captain Parker, no one else had left the train, though faces were pressed to the lighted panes. The sight of armed soldiers was enough to keep the passengers shut in their compartments. But now the havildar swung down from his stand-

ing coach, his rifle slung over his shoulder, and Kordt watched him
drift toward the lorry.

The captain said, "Very good, sir. But I shall have to verify that,
I'm afraid, since it's in conflict with the written orders I'm carrying. There's no provision in them for releasing the prisoner to anyone except the authorities in Bangalore."

"I dare say there's no provision in them for a sabotaged bridge,
either. It may have escaped your attention, but there's a rutting
war on. Orders sometimes have to be changed in the field. The
textbooks call it military necessity."

The heat burned quickly into the captain's cheeks, and a touch
of pugnacity showed in the thrust of his underlip. "Very sorry,
indeed, sir, but I shall *have* to verify the order."

"You can use the wireless pack in the lorry," Kordt said. "It'll
put you through to our field headquarters."

The captain fell silent, but the curled underlip held its militant
air. Finally he said, "I shall need a land line to put through a call to
my own headquarters."

Kordt said to the stationmaster, "How far is the nearest telephone?"

"Dear goodness me." The stationmaster pointed to the fin
shape of jungled terrain rising to the west. "Five kilometers in that
direction."

"How do you propose to get there?" Kordt asked the other officer.

The captain flushed again and glanced at the lorry. His frustra-
tion was giving way to impatience under the pressure of decision.
"You mean to say there's no damned trouble box on the bridge?"
he snapped at the stationmaster.

"Indeed, yes, there is existing one such instrument at the location you mention."

"Well, then . . ." The captain relaxed.

"But it is unworkable. Two years ago villainous persons were
cutting lines as soon as they were connected up. Finally, to be solv-
ing the problem, repairs were stopped to said instrument. Now, I
am reporting this discrepancy every month to the district traffic
superintendent. Jolly bad show, I say. But perhaps after this we are
seeing some action."

Beyond the sweaty glint of the stationmaster's face, Kordt
could see the havildar staring at the lorry. He had stayed clear of

the four sepoys dispersed out from the vehicle at opposite points. An inquisitive sergeant was not a factor choreographed into the situation during the planning stage. Time, Kordt thought, to play his wild card. He tugged at his ear, and his manner changed from one of sardonic tolerance to crisp command.

"I understand your problem, Captain. I can't solve it for you. A section of bridge was blown, down the line. It may well have been part of an attempt to take your prisoner by force. If that's so, something obviously got botched, but whoever is behind it is probably heading this way right now. The solution is to get the target out of here as quickly as possible. I don't propose to stand about negotiating through the night. Apart from the prisoner, I can make room in the lorry for one more man. Your orders from your division commander are to stay with the train. If you want to disobey them, you can send along one man with us, or come yourself. We'll drop you at the first telephone to make your call, but I bloody well can't bring you back. Now, let's get on with it."

22

From his darkened compartment, Carr saw Kordt tug casually at his ear and knew it was time to join the ensemble. As he swung down from the coach, gripping the handrail, he could hear the distant clank of a steam valve, and the drip of moisture onto the ballasted ties from the sweating undercarriage. The small rocks crunched and slid underfoot as he went down the embankment away from the amber light beaded along the ground below the windows.

"Trouble?" he called out to the group standing in the lantern's glow.

Kordt shielded his eyes and said, "Roger? Is that you, or am I bloody crazy?"

"Jack!" Carr gave a short laugh and advanced with his hand out. "Jack Ross. Well, I'm damned. What the devil are you doing out here? Playing soldier?"

"Semidetached for duty," Kordt said. "And you?"

"Convalescent leave," Carr said. "A Jap sniper arranged it."

The captain, who had been listening to the exchange, said to Carr, "Then you know this officer, sir?"

"Never laid eyes on him before in my life. Can't you spot a damned impostor?" Carr winked, and another grin broke from his mouth. "Of course I know him. We came down from Sandhurst together in thirty-one. One of us should probably have been at Borstal instead of the Royal Military College. I won't say which."

"We've run into a sticky wicket here, I'm afraid," the captain explained, and Carr noticed that he rubbed his thumb and forefinger together in a reflex of nervous tension. "It involves the custody of a wog terrorist on board the train. Conflict of orders. There isn't time to properly set the mess straight. If you can show me some proper identification, and in turn vouch for the colonel before these witnesses, I'm willing to sign over custody of the prisoner. I shall require a written receipt, of course."

"I've a set of leave orders in my kit," Carr said. "You can match them up with other I.D., if you like."

"Right," Kordt said, taking charge. "Suppose you go along to your compartment with the captain, Roger, and satisfy him as to your true identity. I'll write out a receipt for the prisoner while you're fetching him back here."

The havildar, who was a Kshatriya and had a pitted, brown, uneven face in which even the slyness seemed broken down into small partitions of guile, had slipped across from the train to speak with one of the sepoys. He had first inquired about his unit and the soldier had replied that he was undergoing special training in jungle warfare at Wilson Point.

"We are quite some distance from Wilson Point," the havildar said.

"There is a temporary field headquarters and bivouac not far from here," the sepoy replied. "They are training us for the long-range penetration of enemy terrain and the destruction of railway supply lines. That's why it's necessary to work close to the railroad."

The sepoy carried a portable radio in a canvas harness on his back, the periscope antenna poking above his shoulder, and his carbine rested in the crook of his arm.

"And your officer?" the havildar said. "What does he do?"

"The colonel-sahib is an advisor who comes from the Fourth Gurkha Rifles and has knowledge of jungle combat. Tonight we were ordered out on a special mission to escort a prisoner to Bangalore. It was all very sudden. Less than forty-five minutes ago. Whatever is happening is not part of the usual drill."

The havildar nodded, then drifted closer to the lorry. Except for a petrol drum lashed down, and an ammunition tin, the bed of the truck looked empty in the shadow under the canvas stretched over the bows. The sepoys carried no field packs. But perhaps the packs had been left behind to make more room in the vehicle. Still, something struck him as being wrong. The silence, for example. No transmissions were crackling over the radio. Wouldn't a field headquarters be trying to get information on the situation?

Slowly, the havildar circled the lorry. The body had been repainted not too long ago. He used his thumbnail to scrape a bit of black pigment from the I.D. number. A flake of old paint under the primer peeled loose. It proved nothing, except that the vehicle had probably needed repainting. He glanced up and caught sight of a hairline crack in the windshield. It left a small diagonal of cloudy glass, like a cataract forming high up in the panel on the passenger side. The havildar frowned, then moved at once around the headlights to a convex dent in the fender. It bubbled upward into the steel skin, and he pressed his palm over it, as if he needed to confirm its existence, *and then he knew*.

From the aisle outside the compartment, Carr had his first glimpse of Devar seated on a lower berth, his shackled wrists resting on his knees. He raised his head, and in the gleam of the panel lamp his features were smoothly burnished, the large eyes darkly lit.

"On your feet," the captain said briskly. "There's a bridge out, down the line. You're going on to Bangalore by lorry. Come along."

The captain was first into the aisle, followed by Devar, with the armed lance corporal close behind. Carr brought up the rear. In front of him, the three men dropped down onto the crushed ballast beside the track. The captain said to the lance corporal, "Stand fast with the prisoner until I have a receipt."

Carr remained on the last step of the coach, his fingers curled around both handrails. He watched the captain moving with his stiff, springing gait toward Kordt. It was at that point the havildar cried out.

"Don't release the prisoner! This is a stolen lorry! It was taken during the attack on the weapons convoy coming up from Prince's Dock!" The havildar was already snatching the rifle off his shoulder as he broke into a run.

"Shoot him," Kordt called out in a clear voice, never taking his eyes from the captain.

The sepoy with the radio backpack leveled his carbine and fired twice. The havildar pitched forward with a sharp outcry and did not move. The sepoy advanced on the crumpled figure and took the rifle.

The captain dithered for a full second, immobilized by panic and foolishly silhouetted in the lights from the train. In the coach behind him a woman screamed. He clawed open the flap of his holster and fumbled for his sidearm.

"Don't," Kordt said.

Perhaps the captain's mind was too confused to judge the danger. The muzzle of the revolver had barely cleared the holster when Kordt fired. The Webley flew from the captain's grasp as if it had been jerked loose by a wire. The officer spun half around and was down, both hands pressed to his side. One palm came away bloody, and he gazed at it and at the wet dark stain spreading over the khaki jacket above the pistol belt.

Kordt snatched the lantern from the conductor and hurled it off to the left. It sailed high, and even before it smashed on some rocks, bursting into a ring of flame, Kordt was diving for cover away from the first burst of fire from the lance corporal at the train. Puffs of dirt hung in the air where the German had been standing. The conductor and stationmaster lay on the ground in the open, their hands clamped over their heads.

The lance corporal fired again. Behind him, Carr gripped the handrails tightly and kicked out with both feet. He could feel the wind go out of the soldier who tumbled down the embankment.

"The lorry!" Kordt yelled. "Get to the lorry!"

"Over there," Carr said to Devar and pointed. "Make a run for it."

But they had no chance to break away. More rifle fire erupted from the rear of the train. A ricochet sang off the rail near Carr's head, and bits of flying rock stung his arm and cheek. The rifle that the lance corporal had lost when Carr's feet had slammed into him lay midway down the bank of cinders. Carr started to lunge for it, but another burst stopped him.

The lance corporal recovered his weapon, and the muzzle swung up, pointing at Carr's sternum. The whole scenario, for Carr, seemed to click into stop-action, and the moment became enormous, and he knew he was already dead. His death lacked only some millisecond of tension on a trigger before the bits of bone exploded out of his chest. But it was Kordt's shot, passing through the throat of the lance corporal, that disconnected the moment from its own cold eternity. The lance corporal was facedown on the cinders, and Kordt had drawn the fire from the rear of the train.

Carr shouted to Devar, "Try to make it down the back side!"

They ducked under the coach close to the rods and standing wheels of the undercarriage, slipped down the embankment on the other side, and ran, crouching, along the defile between the track and jungle. After the first shots, there had been much screaming from the train. Now the passengers were quiet, cringing on the floor away from the windows and the crack of rifles.

The havildar had been hit from behind as he tried to bolt. A rib had deflected the bullet upward and it had exited below the right pectoral muscle near the armpit. Though it bled profusely, the wound was not critical. He had feigned unconsciousness on the ground a dozen feet from the dangling tailgate of the lorry, one arm flung out above his head. He heard the quick pounding of boots as the sepoy who had shot him ran up, and he remained limp and did not resist as the other man wrenched the rifle from his grasp.

He did not see the captain go down, but heard the crack of rifles from the rear of the train and the impacting thud of bullets near the lorry as his men engaged the enemy. He turned his head a fraction of an inch and saw the darting shapes of the sepoys as they fanned out into a skirmish line on the edge of the jungle. Gasoline fumes drifted toward him over the ground. His gaze swiveled back to the lorry and he caught sight of a wet shine on the tailgate and knew at once that a stray shot had ruptured the jerry can of petrol.

The blood had soaked through his tunic into the dirt, leaving the khaki fabric congealed to flesh around the wound. He felt dizzy and light-headed, but his mind was clear. The ground slipped past his cheek a few inches at a time as he crept toward the transparent ribbon of fuel twisting down in the dark.

By the time he reached the shadow of the lorry, the spill had slowed to a drip, pooling under the chassis. A clammy sweat beaded through the oily grime on his face, and his racing heart seemed unable to move the blood blocked up in the aortic chambers. He was afraid he would pass out, but some last, thin reserve of adrenalin kept him out of shock. He rolled onto his left side and groped for the matches in his breast pocket. His fingers shook badly and had no strength at all.

He dragged the match twice across the striking zone on the box before the sulphur head flared, and he heard the nearest sepoy shout from the edge of the trees. Then the hammering of the carbine, its muzzle flash, and the chewed-up dirt racing toward him, were all part of the same instant of white-hot pain that exploded behind his eyes like a solar flare and took him away in its expanding brightness.

As he dashed with Devar along the ditch beside the track Carr had a clear view, through the open gaps under the train, of the action on the other side. He saw the fire erupt under the lorry in an orange flash, and the flames surge upward on the combustible fumes in great, engulfing petals. The canvas top caught and burned like damp paper, the blackness spreading across the fabric, which disintegrated in seconds.

"The lorry!" Devar shouted.

Below the engine and tender, Carr hesitated. He glanced up and saw the two firemen, stripped to the waist, on the footplate in the cab. The heavier one held the shovel like a weapon.

"Forget the lorry," Carr said. "Go for the bridge."

The funnel of light blazing out from the front of the boiler above the cowcatcher bathed the rails in its brightness and spread down the ballast into the culvert. It picked the girders out of the darkness ahead and left them hanging like steel vertebrae across the night. The two men bolted forward into the glow, their running shadows projected across the wall of jungle leaves.

"Halt!" a voice behind them yelled. "Hands up!"

Carr darted a look over his shoulder and saw one of the soldiers, his rifle half-raised, silhouetted in the blinding disc of the headlamp.

"Keep your head down," he said to Devar, and shoved the Indian ahead of him onto the walkway that ran low along the side of the trestle above the river.

Their soles pounded hollowly on the planks that were warped and old, and through the gaps Carr saw the black gleam of the water, thirty feet below, sliding past the stone piles. Before they were halfway across the span, the rifle cracked. The bullet, whining off a girder, made a tone like a tuning fork.

Devar stopped running and cried, "It's no use! We can't make it across!"

"Right," Carr said. "Over the side, then. Into the water."

"I cannot swim with these!" Devar waved the handcuffs.

Another shot rang out, clipping wood from the timbers above their heads.

"I'm afraid you'll have to." Carr snatched Devar's wrist and threw a shoulder into his midsection, lifting him off his feet. He tossed the smaller man over the handrail and vaulted it himself. Both men hit the water with a splash, plunging deep in a quicksilver chain of erupting air. Carr was the first to come up, the night air breaking against his face. He gazed around on the streaming blackness. Twenty feet away, Devar bobbed to the surface. The current muscled them past the stone piling and out from under the shadow of the trestle.

Devar had swallowed water down his windpipe. It left him choking as he struggled to stay afloat, his head arched back, feet kicking, the manacled wrists flailing in panic. Carr swam to him and said, "Hang on to my shoulder."

The trestle, high above them on the sky, was gliding away. A figure had run out onto the footramp beneath the crossed timbers, but there were no more shots. Suddenly, a bright ball of flame swelled into view above the cutting where the engine stood, and seconds later the blast shook the night. Bits of flaming debris from the lorry went spinning upward on the darkness, then fell back to earth. No sound of firing came from the train. Probably Kordt had broken off the fight and slipped back into the jungle.

The bridge still drifted away, the girders shrinking to a glimmer of steel. On either side of the river, the banks flowed blackly. The current in midchannel was smooth and fast, and Carr thought they could not be far from rapids.

The river swung into a curve, not as wide as he would have liked, but he decided it would have to do. They could not risk running into white water around a blind bend.

"Hang on and kick," Carr shouted, and felt the current tighten its grip, as if it had no intention of letting them go.

23

The bank was high and dark, and it swung fast in a semicircle, rushing before them like a clip of movie film where the camera has panned too swiftly. It came no closer as they kicked and struggled, and Carr felt the drain on his strength against the more powerful resistance of the water. But suddenly the stream slowed into an eddy, and the current weakened at the calm center of its own centrifugal motion.

His nerves shut off their alarm and he put his head down in the water and kicked hard against the hydrostatic force, throwing his shoulders into each stroke, and imagined that the bank was drawing toward him in the magnetic pull of his own Zen vision of it. All at once, it was there in his grip—the tangle of roots which had been exposed by the cutting edge of the current—and even after his mind had unlocked from the image, his heart went on hammering. Beside him, Devar was choking, his fingers still clamped around the shoulder strap of Carr's Sam Browne belt.

They heaved themselves, dripping, into the spear grass on the bank. The bridge was out of sight, a kilometer upstream, but the fire still left a yellowish tint on the sky.

"Who are you?" Devar said. Water ran down his face, and his hair was soddenly plastered against his skull.

"A bloody wet fool." Carr gave a low chuckle. "In the company of a second bloody wet fool."

"I wouldn't have gone off the bridge." Devar shook his head.

"The odds were better than even," Carr replied, "barring a broken neck in the fall."

Devar smiled and said, "You are British?"

"Sometimes."

"And the other fellow in uniform?"

"A German officer. Calls himself Alex, but I doubt that's his name. Ask Mrs. Vora. Maybe she'll tell you."

"Then my sister was responsible for my escape?" Devar said.

"Partly."

"I was alerted a fortnight ago that an attempt would be made, but I had no idea of the details, or who was behind it. Tell me, what is the news of Netaji?"

"Bose? The best rumor is that he's crossed the frontier into Assam with an army, fighting alongside the Japanese."

"If it's true," Devar said, "then India will soon be free."

Carr could see the glow of fanatical conviction on the wet, shining face. He said, "I expect Alex can tell you."

"I pray he was not killed at the train."

"He's a clever chap, not the sort to get killed."

"Cleverness won't stop a bullet."

"Luck will," Carr said. "He has that, too. But we're pressing ours the longer we stay here. Better move, if you're up to it."

"Where?"

"There was a rendezvous point set up near Wai in case we had to scatter. We'll try for it tomorrow."

In the flattened spear grass they took the time to wring the water from their clothing. Then they set out into the hills. As they climbed higher around the side of the bluff, the stretch of river beyond the bend drifted into view, and Carr saw the rapids streaming down over snags of tumbled rock in a long silver flash lit to cold brilliance by the moon.

Devar shook his head. "We would have drowned, surely."

The slump of dark hills on the starry sky ahead pulled them away from the river. A tired soreness worked itself into Carr's muscles under the wet clothing, but he kept moving for another hour toward the higher ground. He wanted to be nowhere near the river when daylight came.

The morning chill woke Carr as the first pink of dawn touched the sky over the hills in the east. The horizon ignited quickly, burning the darkness off the ridges lunging toward the sea.

Nearby, Devar was asleep on the ground below an outcrop of seamed granite that crowned the high point of terrain. Carr's clothing was still damp, and he was ravenously hungry. He got to his feet, shivering, and climbed up along the spine of rock to have a look at the country.

Below, the basin sank into its own shadow, and he saw the river uncoiling and stretching into a far-off valley between low hills. A ribbon of smoke trailed up out of the purple haze on the other side of the basin and he thought it must be a village. He heard rock chips falling and glanced back to see Devar climbing toward him.

"Do you see any British patrols?" the Indian called out.

"No," Carr said. "But they're out, all right. They can't afford to let you slip away."

"Where are we, do you think?"

"The river's over there." Carr pointed. "The main road to Kolhapur can't be more than a dozen kilometers to the west. If we follow the sun, we can't go wrong. We'll try to pick up some food along the way and get rid of those handcuffs."

"Do you think it is safe to go into a village while you are still in a British uniform?"

"Hardly."

"Then how will you get food?"

"Steal it," Carr said, "from a farmer. It can be his contribution to *Hind Swaraj*."

"I do not like to steal from the people."

Carr smiled and said, "Give your belly another six hours without food, and you'll be astonished at how easy it becomes."

The rendezvous was a crumbling pavilion in the scrub a few kilometers out of Wai, and they did not reach it until dusk of the second day. Thirty meters from the ruin, they halted off the trail beneath a banyon tree that soared on the evening. Hundreds of aerial shoots had dropped and taken root, spreading out more branches, and monkeys scrambled about in the solid thatch on top.

"Stay here," Carr said, "while I have a look."

He slipped past the murmur of a spring. It ran down into a rocky defile in the jungle, where the flashing trickle disappeared among some crimson flowers in the leafy darkness. The pavilion drifted near in the vegetation. Under a dome supported by stone columns, a three-headed deity glared down.

Carr mounted the steps and stared up at the sculpted faces, disfigured by spores of mold and caught fast in creepers that had worked up under the dome. He heard the scrape of a sandal, and Ram Singh loomed suddenly in the dark next to one of the pillars. The shadows touched out his sockets, and one oversized hand gripped the column as if it were a pasteboard prop that could be torn out easily.

"Where's Alex?" Carr said.

"He was here," the Sikh replied, "but now he is gone."

"I've brought Devar."

"My eyes have seen it."

"So have the eyes of a foot-constable," Carr said, "about an hour ago. We had to make a run for it. They'll be combing this part of the country."

"There is a bullock cart nearby. Two men can lie in the bottom and be covered by bundles of firewood. It will get you through the last of the villages without being seen. After that, it will be safe to go on foot."

"Where?"

The Sikh only shrugged and said, "You will see."

Later, they left the bullock cart outside a hamlet near a stream and climbed a footpath into the hills. The country was rocky, the valleys gutted with grass and patches of jungle and the glint of bamboo and sometimes a far-off steel flash of water. Stars burned above stampeding ridges in the camouflage of the night, and Carr had no idea where they were.

Around midnight, they picked their way up a dry ravine, steeped in shadow, that lifted out of the scrub toward a high slab of rock set like a conning tower in the glaze of the moon. Midway to the top, the Sikh halted.

"I will go alone," he said, "to speak to the sentry."

He moved off in the dark, leaving Carr and Devar in the dense gloom of the rising rock.

"I have never thanked you properly," Jai said, "for saving my life."

"I'm the one who got you into a tight spot in the first place."

"You could have gone off the bridge without me."

"I nearly did."

Devar gazed at the flint-struck light of stars above the rimrock.

"You cannot know how it feels to breathe the air outside a British cell. Without you, it would not have happened. The only thing I can offer in payment is my friendship, always."

The words hit a nerve. At least Valadon's forgeries had an intrinsic value. Carr's own was worthless, and in terms of the payment offered it was overpriced.

"Always is a long time," he said. After two days on the run from police and British patrols, it was impossible not to develop a bond of comradeship. But it was not something Carr had set out to arrange.

In a few minutes Ram Singh came back and they followed him uphill in the dark. Carr saw the crescent shadow of the cavern set well back under its mantel of rock. Tarpaulins were stretched across the mouth, and the Sikh drew aside the canvas.

The interior widened before them in a scallop shape, and a distant oil lamp threw its light across a plunging wall. Carr's stare took in everything at once—the lorries parked in two tight ranks, petrol cans stacked along a gallery, shipping crates with Japanese markings piled to the ceiling. Whatever China Blue was, Carr thought, it had to involve a sustained operation. Why else would Kordt stockpile supplies?

The Sikh led them off to another chamber where the ceiling sloped low. At least a dozen figures were curled asleep in bedrolls. Ram Singh pointed to three supply packs and said, "We will carry these tomorrow to Nagaraja. There are blankets and rations in them. Now you should sleep. I will wake you in three hours."

"What pressing business do we have at Nagaraja?" Carr said. The prospect of only three hours sleep irritated him.

The Sikh stared at him and for the second time replied, "You will see."

24

They climbed, sweating, up through the final two hundred meters of rain forest to Nagaraja, and Carr saw Kordt coming from the pavilion. His hair caught the sun, and the faded khaki shirt exaggerated the tan emblazoned over his face and forearms.

"So you made it after all." His smile flashed warm approval. "Bloody marvelous!"

"I suppose that sums it up." Carr nodded wryly.

The German joined his palms in the traditional greeting of *anjali*, and Devar responded in kind, and said, "It would be impossible to express my gratitude for what you did at the train."

"I expect you could use a spot of tea," Kordt said. "Come along. There's someone else waiting to see you."

As they mounted the steps, Ashley appeared in the colonnade. She wore tan jodhpurs and riding boots, and the thin cotton pullover above the belted waist showed the opulent swell of her breasts. Her black hair, drawn back on the nape of her neck, shone against the pearl-smooth skin. Out of sari, she looked strikingly English, as if she had come fresh from a ride on the moors. She stopped short of embracing Devar, perhaps because of the others present, but Carr saw tears form in the dark, violent eyes.

"I am so pleased," she murmured. Then her gaze shifted to Carr. Something went out of it, and something altogether different came into it, but the depth of feeling remained untouched, and she repeated for him, "I am so pleased."

In the lower region of the temple, lit by oil lamps, they drank tea served with *mitahis*, and Kordt said, "We'd almost given you up. How did you manage it?"

"Vishnu the Preserver," Carr said. "It had to be."

"Things have got cracking in Assam. The Japanese have crossed the mountains onto the Imphal Plain with a full division of the Indian National Army. The fight for the Capital is underway."

"And China Blue?" Devar said.

Kordt started to reply, then glanced at Carr, who tried to smother some odd excitement pouring into his nerves.

"Perhaps I'd better leave," he said.

"No." Kordt shook his head. "I dare say you've earned the right to stay. In any case, China Blue will be a *fait accompli* by the time you leave here. The operation goes in seventy-two hours."

"What's it about?"

"I can tell you it involves guerilla operations by irregular forces under the command of Subhas Bose and Provisional Government of Azad Hind. The immediate objective is to cut supply lines to General Slim's army on the Imphal front. Once the Capital falls, there is nothing to stop a quick thrust into Bengal where Netaji has a wide base of support. His presence there should be more than enough to foment a popular uprising against British rule that will spread across the subcontinent. The final phase of China Blue will unfold here in the west, and Bombay will be the key. The port is quite vulnerable, actually."

"Irregular forces have to be supplied," Carr said. "How can you do it without airdrops?"

"Supplies have been moving into place for nine months," Kordt said. "The depots are well dispersed and hidden. By the way, the replacement parts for the Brens and Enfields have come in from Berbera. I'm off, tomorrow, to have a look."

"Shipping them east?" Carr said.

"No. They'll stay in Bombay."

They were sitting in a circle on the floor, their legs crossed. In the lamp's flicker, Carr turned to Ashley, who was next to him, and said, "Your husband—how is he?"

"His condition is stabilized," she replied. "But he is confined to bed under round-the-clock nursing care. The paralysis is more extensive than before. Mercifully, it was a small stroke and he survived it."

"Are you going back to him?"

"Yes." She gazed at Carr across the clay cup of tea in her hands. "But not tonight."

The night burned its alchemy into the sky above the colonnade where Carr had spread his sleeping bag. He was sure she would come, and he lay with his fingers laced behind his head on the flannel lining of the down-filled bag, and watched the drift of the stars in the tops of the pillars. A sharp memory of Juhu and Ashley's straining body floated up behind his gaze, and the image unlocked some deep seminal wish that went slowly from a desire to a need in his nerves, and after an hour of waiting, it was backed up in some male center of his being that lay, inaccessible, across the light years of distance that still poured into his stare.

Around midnight, he heard a sound from the pavilion and leaned up on one elbow in the dark. There was a quick, darting movement among the shadows of the pillars, and a moment later he caught sight of her in a slash of moonlight. She had a thin blanket clutched round her shoulders, and she was barefooted on the stone.

Carr called out softly, and she came to the cove of shadow and dropped the blanket from her shoulders and slipped, naked, into the sleeping robe beside him, and for a long time their mouths clung together. Then her lips opened and she sucked languorously on his tongue in a direct, explicit way that needed no words, and the ducts of his own seminal urge came open in the first sticky dampening of seed under the pressure of desire. The tip of her breast was already swollen hard when he touched it, and his hand moved to the damp nest between her legs, which stirred and parted at his touch, and almost at once his fingers found the estuary of sexual heat where the clitoris swelled erect.

Suddenly her own fingers moved in a surprising conquest to force penetration, and he smiled and guided her hips with his hands until she was astride him in a posture of mock dominance that gave her control of the pleasure within her. Above the dark tilt of the heavy breasts, her head was arched back in the moon's pale radiance, and he was aware of some blind gratification in the parted lips and tightly shut eyes as she impaled herself again and again on his captive hardness, and her hair tossed like a black flame against the stars. He let her bring herself to climax, and heard the sobbing gasps of breath from her before she drew down and took his mouth, and the black flame that had tossed against the stars now spilled down and grazed his face as if to shut out the world above them during the final moments when love became a quivering flow in her loins.

Still in her, he forced her to come over on her back, and this time pushed to the deeper zone of orgasm, and could see the points of light on her eyes where the stars gleamed like their own silver on a sea at night, and her lids closed on yet another breathless outcry, and opened once, then closed again on some tidal surge of feeling, and Carr could feel it break on its own interior shore in wet salt waves and flood the tidal pools, and much later, when her eyes opened, he saw once more the star glimmer on the pupils, dark and deep in their love for him, and some new, impossible tenderness in them claimed from him the same unspoken admission of love.

Ashley was gone, and all around Carr the colonnade lay deserted and still, like a surreal landscape of stone and shadow. She had asked if he would stay in Bombay, and he had replied evasively, "Is it important?"

In the dark, her fingers had grazed his cheek in a loving caress as she murmured, "I could not bear it if you left now."

The whole scenario, Carr thought, had gone bad. One could pass a fake Matisse in good conscience on the inflated currencies of the art world, where the risk might even be construed as a form of shady valor. Love lacked the simple element of deceit, and so it could not coexist with deception. Mixing the two produced an impossible conflict, and the psychological liability for damages would be exacted in payments of pain on which the interest was compounded. The worst part was that he could not tell her. It would be like telling someone you had sold them a bad painting and spent the money.

I've got to finish it now, he thought, *or else walk away from it.*

But how could he walk away? The British had taken care to blackmail his livelihood, not his conscience, and the chain of extortion, which had begun in Estoril, could only end in Bombay. It did not matter to Carr that he had given his word—that was the easiest forgery of all. Worthless copies of it existed in all the grand casinos of Europe. A cheat's honor could hardly be warranted in a contract. What counted, now, was that he found himself in a game where the bets were made in lives, not the blood-red checks on a *chemin de fer* table.

Seventy-two hours, Kordt had said, and China Blue would be a *fait accompli*. How many lives, Carr wondered, equaled a *coup du deshonneur*?

He pulled on his trousers and shirt, buttoning them slowly. He was in no hurry, though time was running down. He stretched forward to lace his shoes, then lit a cigarette and palmed the burning tip in his curled fingers. For a long time he sat dead still, the pillar against his back, and stared across the sterile landscape to the mouth of the pavilion. All the while he ransacked his mind for an excuse not to go down, but each proposition had a taint of cowardice, and in the end it was his vanity, and a belief in his own luck, that made the risk acceptable. He crushed out the cigarette and slipped across to the pavilion.

Inside, parcels of moonlight fell through the vented dome, touching the massive relief of Shiva entwined with the serpent in their phallic dance of creation.

Carr moved beneath the towering divinity to the far end of the hall where a stone archway formed a crumbling impression on the darkness. Worn steps spiraled down, and in the dark he could only feel his way.

The altar pit bloomed before him in the glint of a flare on the far side. The great sculpture of Vasuki, guarding the ark of Manu, floated up out of the half-lit shadows.

Carr looked for the hamadryad. The plaited cover to its den was in place. The cobra had to be somewhere below in the pit, but Carr preferred to make sure. Finally he caught sight of it, a shining loop in the half darkness.

Carr moved along the rim past the idol and down into the cobra's empty lair. The damp ledges trailing past his head reflected the faint glimmer of a distant lamp turned low for the night. At the juncture of the complex he heard a cough from one of the cells. The sound went into his nerves with the impact of a bullet, and he flattened himself against the wall away from the light. Nothing stirred, and after a few moments the silence was again drum tight. He slipped down the passage that angled off to the operations room, found the door in the dark, and was quickly inside.

He struck a match, and the ceiling ran away from the flame in shadowy ribbons. On a long bamboo table, strewn with papers, was a kerosene lamp, and he lifted the glass chimney and touched the match to the wick.

Two large flags draped the wall behind the table—the swastika of Germany, and the banner of Bose's provisional government, a springing tiger imprinted on the green, white, and yellow tricolor of the Congress. The Japanese, Carr thought, would surely feel slighted.

Wires from a field switchboard ran up through a conduit in the ceiling, and atop a wireless set lay a cipher book. Carr stuffed the cipher into his waistband and squatted beside a cardboard box containing several folders. He thumbed through these but could find nothing that looked important.

The materials cluttering the table were chiefly British—army manuals, railway schedules, a blueprint of Bombay Port from Timber Bunder to Sassoon Dock—but no reference to China Blue.

He glanced round the room once more, taking in more detail—a pail filled with sand for the disposal of cigarettes, a tin of kerosene for the lamps, a large wire basket with three railway signal flares in the bottom. Probably the flares were there for the emergency burning of documents should Kordt have to get out fast.

Once more his gaze rested on the flags. He put down the lamp and drew the bunting apart. The military maps, riddled with pins of different colors, seemed almost indecently exposed, and this time his nerves absorbed a small, quick thrill of discovery. But that soon paled, for there was no legend to explain the configuration of the pins, or their colors.

Then he caught sight of a solitary pin in the lower right quadrant of the panel—the only blue one on the board—and scrawled beside it were thirteen grid coordinates.

It was as close, Carr thought, as he would get to China Blue, and he copied the grids down on the back cover of the cipher. But he had no chance to plot the locations on the map, for the plank door swung open behind him, and Kordt's voice cut short the exercise.

"Don't turn around just yet, unless you fancy a bullet in the liver."

25

The lamp threw its moving glint across Kordt's bare chest and the blued steel of the carbine cradled in his arm. He glanced at the cipher book that Ram Singh had taken from Carr, and said, "You would have found it dull reading."

"I was borrowing it for a sick friend," Carr said.

"I dare say." Kordt nodded. "It's a silly business, after all. But then, war is nothing more than absurdity in a more deadly form."

"Tell that to all the sods in eastern Europe. They seem to have missed the joke. No sense of humor, I suppose. They actually think your Führer is mean-spirited. The blockheads."

"They're no worse off than India under the British."

A few feet from Carr, the Sikh was bareheaded, his hair tied in a knot and held by a comb on the crown of his head. Ashley stepped into the open doorway. She was barefooted still, and had slipped into the riding trousers and cotton shirt. Carr wasn't sure how long she had been standing there, or how much she had heard, though it hardly mattered at this point. Her dark gaze held fast to his and the undertow of violent feeling in the pupils pulled the truth from him without a word being spoken.

She approached him slowly, as if the unhurried motion of her body could more forcefully communicate the extent of her scorn, and stopped in front of him. He saw her mouth tremble and the combustible heat in her stare dissolve across the sad edge of betrayal that formed into the wet brilliance of a solitary tear that did not fall but drew back instead onto a tiny sheen of watery hate. Then she was gone from the room, and the flash of pain from the slap that left a red welt on the side of his face was already fading.

Only the stinging contempt remained like a psychological toxin that would never be altogether absorbed.

Kordt said, "You're rather a clever fellow."

"Not clever enough," Carr said, "or I'd be holding the gun."

The muzzle of the carbine was lazily trained on Carr's midsection. Kordt smiled and said, "I always worried that your background was a bit too pat. How long have you been working for the British?"

"Is *that* what you think?" Carr tipped back his head and laughed. "What bloody nonsense. I work under a self-employment scheme. There's a brisk market for military information these days. As long as your politics are neutral, you can sell to either side."

"And yours are neutral?"

"Only a fool would limit his sources of revenue."

"You copied some grids onto the back of the cipher book. What would you have done with the information?"

"Sold it to the high bidder," Carr said. "I would have given you the final shot at it, of course."

"Out of professional courtesy?"

"And fiduciary sentiment."

"Or perhaps taken our reichsmarks, and then sold it to British intelligence."

"Sell it twice?" Carr affected a look of hurt surprise. "But that would be dishonest. Neither side would ever want to deal with me again. Just because espionage is a commerce of lies doesn't mean you can get by on a sullied reputation."

"You've gone to considerable risk for some numbers on a map." Kordt smiled and shook his head. "The irony is, they've been right under Bloody Albert's nose all along."

A nerve flinched in Carr's cheek at the reference to *Bloody Albert*. It could only mean Kordt had someone close to Sterns—or Paine—operating in Bombay.

"You should have stayed with cards and the sale of art," Kordt said. "It's a less hazardous occupation."

"Perhaps we can discuss my early return to it," Carr said.

"I dare say we'll have some long chats," Kordt said, "as quickly as I can get back from Bombay."

The cell door slammed shut on Carr and he heard the locking timber drop down into the iron U-joints bolted into the outer frame. From the peephole slot he watched the Sikh's moving shadow disappear from the passage wall. Only the glimmer from a distant lamp clung to the stone.

The cell was unlit and Carr waited for his eyes to adjust. His arms were lashed to a horizontal rod that ran across his back, leaving them outstretched, like a scarecrow in a field. A full minute passed before the walls took shape on his pupils, and he saw that the cell was cramped and bare, lacking even a plank bed and latrine bucket. He circled the room slowly, then explored the seam of the door with his fingers. The door was solid core and he could find no latch or hinges. He slid to a sitting position, his back against the wall. Voices drifted in and out, too faint and far-off for him to pick up the dialogue.

The voices had been still for some time. Carr thought it must be well into the morning. Kordt would be off to Bombay. Probably Ashley had taken Devar to the plantation. Unless you counted the old Brahmin and his priestess, that left only Ram Singh, and possibly a guard or two topside.

Carr waited another half hour by the slot. No sound came down the dank passage where the distant lamp left only a faint smear of light on the stone.

In the pat-down search, the Sikh had neglected the matches in Carr's shirt pocket. Bent at the waist, Carr tried to shake them loose. Finally, with the tip of his shirt collar between his teeth, he worked the matchbook free and it dropped to the floor near his head.

Only three matches were left. He went down on his back, head and shoulders against the wall. The ropes were tight at his wrists, shutting off circulation to his fingers, which felt numb and clumsy. Still, they managed to manipulate a match sideways out of the book, taking care not to tear the stem loose, but bending it twice into a U-shape so that the sulphur tip rested over the striking zone. With the book pinned against the floor, he used his forefinger to scrape the head into flame.

The petal of fire bloomed upward and he moved his wrist over it and watched the loop of rope begin to blacken as the fibers smoldered. The intensity of the heat on his skin surprised him and he winced. The match went out, and the fibers, which had burned about halfway through the thickness of the rope, were the last to lose their red glow.

Carr lit a second match in the same fashion, and this time beads of sweat popped out on his face as the flame scorched his wrist. All the while, he could see the internal strands of the rope igniting and disintegrating into singed ends of burnt hemp. The match flickered out on its own blackened stub. Carr pushed to his feet. Only a few charred braids held the rope intact, and he sawed them against the sharp edge of stone where the door was recessed into the wall. They separated easily and he twisted the rope from one arm, then the other, and flexed his fingers. The flesh on the underside of his right wrist was already swollen red and blistering.

The peephole slot ran eight inches across and two inches high, and with his eye pressed to it he could see only the top of the locking timber. He stuffed a loop of rope through the opening and tried to snare the end of the timber to lift it. Time and again, the rope missed its target. He twisted the ends to bring more tension into play, but still the bar resisted capture. After twenty minutes he grew impatient and shoved the rope carelessly through the slot. This time the loop fell half across the blunt end of the timber. He twisted one segment slowly until the coil gave a wiggle and dropped like a noose into place.

In the passage, Carr gripped the rod that had been used to secure his arms. He slipped past the cubicles toward the glow of the hanging lamp. No sound drifted from any of them, and he was sure the enclave must be deserted. The lamp burned behind him now as shallow steps, cut from the stone, took him down to the last barrier door. There was shadowy movement even as he opened it, and he saw a sinuous gleam of patterned muscle lifting on the darkness no more than ten feet away in the cavern, and he spun back, bracing his shoulder into the door after it had swung shut.

He ducked back into the enclave, took the lamp from its peg, and went down to the operations room. Nothing was changed. He overturned the sand bucket, unscrewed the cap from the jerry can, and poured kerosene into the pail until it was full. He snatched the flags from the wall, tore the bunting into strips, and tied them on the end of the rod to make a ball. Not the ideal flare, but it would have to do. He thrust the wad into the kerosene to soak, then stepped back to the mesh-wire bin. The three pyrotechnic devices lay in the bottom, and he slipped them into his waistband. They were tube-shaped and red and looked to be standard railway flares.

Carr left the lamp in the passage at the top of the steps and slipped down to the barrier door. He struck the flare, which burst into flame, crackling on the silence, and touched it to the kerosene rags on the end of the pike. As the saturated cloth ignited, he opened the door and took a step inside.

The cavern walls pitched eerily in the flare's red glow. A dozen feet away he saw the oily flicker of a tongue, then two glittering seeds of eyes in a scaly snout as the cobra reared, disturbed and angry, its hood spread. An involuntary shiver streaked through Carr and left a numbing chill in his nerves, and he could remember Kordt saying, "They can smell fear in a human, and the scent makes them angry. . . ."

The flexed hood, which had the shape of a manta ray, hovered on a level with Carr's own head. He raised the torch, and the shadows scattered like party streamers. Again the snake's tongue flashed from its mouth, which was only a black gleaming slit in the chain-mail pattern of the snout, and its hiss sounded like a low growling.

Carr advanced another foot, the burning pike held aloft. In his other hand, the flare spit flame like a pyrotechnic sparkler. The snake's stare was brilliantly fixed on him, and there seemed to be no fear in it, only some bold insolence frozen into the intense scrutiny as the upper body swayed with a vicious, hypnotic grace.

Carr tossed the sizzling flare across the interval, and the red cylinder rolled on the cavern floor and came to rest inches from the snake's pale underbelly. The cobra dropped at once and slid away from the flame in a swift, curving thrust of muscle. Carr slipped quickly down the cavern to the plaited cover blocking the way into the altar pit. It could only be lifted from the other side of the aperture, and he slammed his foot into it until it popped free.

The cobra reared again, provoked, as Carr tried to move around it. The patterned hood was spread wide, the head tensed forward in a belligerent posture. A murderous glee flashed on the two polished beads of eyes as the upper body stiffened to strike. Carr thrust the torch directly at the creature's head, and once more it shied away from the fire. The slithering gleam disappeared in the shadows.

Carr struck a second flare, spilling more light into the crevices and chinks, driving the shadows deeper into the fissures. The hamadryad was as rigidly still as the strata of rock on which it rested, and Carr had a grisly vision of himself, his mouth open on the ground and drooling saliva, his cheek puffed twice its size while his lungs, paralyzed from the neurotoxin, no longer processed oxygen.

Suddenly the cobra jerked into motion. There was no mistaking the menace and vicious purpose in its advance. Carr tossed the second flare into the snake's path and it veered back excitedly. The gliding form moved toward the aperture and Carr lowered the pike, sweeping the fire back and forth across a slow arc. He watched the tail melt out of sight, then set the burning pike down in the opening.

From somewhere on the other side of the fire, a woman's cry of alarm cut through the silence. He was sure it must be the priestess, because she screamed out in Hindustani. A male voice shouted a reply, and from a distance the temple flung back a hollow acoustic of pounding feet.

The hatch cover lay out of reach two feet above his head. Carr got a toehold in the rock and made a lunge for the grooved ledge beneath the cover. He caught it and held on, his legs dangling, and shoved his palm against the trap, but it would not give way. On the other side, someone rattled the locking pin. Carr dropped down and flattened himself in the shadow of the concave rock.

Overhead, the hatch swung open, and a ladder slid down to the floor. The slats creaked under the weight of the man climbing down. A massive foot, strapped into an oversized sandal, descended into view.

Carr clamped his hands around the ankle and drove his shoulder into the ladder. It went over with a crash, the Sikh still on it, his leg trapped between the slats. Carr seized the frame and wrenched it with all his strength and heard the ankle bone pop. The Sikh grunted, but that was his only response to pain as he rolled from his back onto his side. Carr swung the ladder as the other man was pushing to his feet and caught him solidly across the head and shoulders. A slat flew loose, leaving the frame around Ram Singh's neck, and he dropped heavily, stunned. But his legs still moved, like those of a runner in slow motion, a reflex of cold purpose that went on functioning outside the range of brain chemistry that should have powered it.

Carr twisted hard on the ladder, slamming his knee into the Sikh's lower back and locking his arms from behind around the other man's neck in a chokehold. The leverage from Carr's forearm should have closed the windpipe, but the tensed cords in the neck had the strength and thickness of steel cable, and he could feel the swell of blood pushing back against the tension of his own grip. All at once the Sikh exploded like a bull against the sides of a pen. One arm flew out to the side, overturning both Carr and the ladder as if they were nothing.

Carr sprang to his feet and the two men circled. The Sikh made no move toward the double-edged *khanda* at his side. Carr feinted to bring up the other man's hands and drove his fist into the ribs just below the heart, throwing the full weight of his body into the blow. Before he could spin away he felt the huge hands close on him. Even as his feet left the ground he hit the Sikh twice—on the side of the chin and high on the temple—with crisp punches that had no effect and did not even turn the bearded face to one side or the other. Then he was sailing in the air, the wall flying at him, and the impact sent a flash of light into his head like a short circuit that left him dazed and blinking.

Beyond the sizzling brightness of the flare near Carr's head, Ram Singh was advancing gingerly on the broken ankle that had already started to swell above the sandal strap around the Achilles tendon. Carr, whose two hundred pounds were well distributed over a wide-shouldered frame, had been lifted and tossed like a rag doll across the cavern. Without a weapon, it was pointless to try to match the Sikh physically. He scrambled to his feet and fled back into the enclave. Behind him, the Indian limped in pursuit. The oil lamp threw his lurching shadow across the passage, and the bearded face coming toward the light was implacably set and undeterred, like a robot's faceplate bolted in place, unable to register emotion, only calibrations of purpose.

Carr went for the operations room, slamming the plank door and fumbling in the dark to jam the bolt into its iron sleeve. Seconds later, the latch rattled, and fell silent. The stillness reached into Carr's nerves and took hold. Then part of the door exploded in his face. Bits of splintered wood flew past his head, and beyond the cracked sliver of light, the Sikh hovered. Carr eased away from the door, nearly overturning the bucket in which he had soaked the bunting. The kerosene sloshed back and forth in the pail.

He looked up in time to see the heel of the Sikh's powerful fist drawn back. The crashing force of the blow took out a plank and wrenched a hinge loose from the frame. The curled fingers reached through the gap and groped for the bolt.

Carr snatched up the pail and dashed the fuel into the other man's face. The Sikh flinched, his eyes shut, and Carr scraped the head of the last flare against the stone surface and thrust the blazing tip across the side of Ram Singh's massive neck. The drenched fabric around the collar burst into flame, engulfing his beard and face in blue, gaseous petals of fire that slid upward in an instant conflagration, and Carr had a glimpse of the surprise raging on his expression behind the undulating thermal waves before the huge hands were clamped over it.

The Sikh staggered blindly backward, gouts of fire falling away from his burnt flesh, and sank to his knees. Carr was already out the door and past him, bolting for the steps that splashed down from the lamp's glimmer.

26

From the ledge above Vasuki's pit Carr had a glimpse of the priestess gazing up at him. The cowl had slipped back from the ropy blackness of her hair, and the flat hate in the upturned face gave no ground. Then he was past her, up the stairs, into the domed pavilion. Nothing stirred in the sun-shot gloom beneath Shiva's towering relief, and Carr slipped outside among the pillars of the colonnade.

Suddenly he caught sight of the old Brahmin priest, off to the left, thirty meters beyond the spring. The white swatch of his dhoti stood out against the green of the jungle, and he was standing beside a Sikh, armed with a carbine, and pointing his black stick of an arm at Carr.

Carr ducked low and bolted. He heard the crack of the carbine as he dove from the steps into the thick speckling of leaves and loam that broke in a wave of foliage against the stone. The Sikh who had fired from the spring was shouting for help. Carr had already rolled to his feet and was racing along the footpath that twisted back through the jungle away from the ruins. It was the same trail that had first brought him with Kordt and Ram Singh to Nagaraja, and he would not have chosen it for an escape. The steep descent through the gorge would leave his pursuers above him, exposing him to their fire.

From somewhere on the right came a shout from a second man, and the crashing movement in vegetation did not seem too far away. He raced ahead, ducking to avoid the leafy cables strung across the path, and later he halted, gasping for breath, his mouth dry. The voices were well back in the jungle, but moving in his direction. He took several deep breaths and set off at a jog trot.

For more long minutes the shady dappling of the rain forest fled by underfoot, and then the gorge sank into view through the leaves. The cliff on the far side hung in a falling sheet of granite as if to mark a dead end. Directly below, the water spreading into the pool at the foot of the falls had the look of smoke. From this height, the pool was no more than a sky-colored ring. Beyond the mouth of the gorge, the jungle sprawled across the next valley to the crimped green of low ridges, and Carr could see the hamlet, about a kilometer downstream from the falls, where the pack mules must be penned.

Sweat poured off his face, and the blood was blocked up behind his heart, waiting for the lungs to process oxygen. But the cylinders were empty, drawing on the ether of pure adrenalin. Even as he rested, the voices behind him drifted closer.

Carr wiped the moisture from his face and plunged downhill, digging his heels into the embankment to brake his descent. The trail fell away, twisting through the jungle cover, and each patch of sunlight seemed to invite a bullet from above.

The sound of water tumbling over rocks drew near. He stopped once more to catch his breath, his heart slugging, and looked up through the leaves and saw two quick flashes on the rim like a glint of sunlight off a shard of glass. He swallowed another breath and was off again.

Halfway down, the soaring cliff bathed the gorge in shade. Here the stream was a roaring torrent beyond the black leaves, close enough for Carr to feel the cool spray on his face. Now, even if shots had rung out from above he could not have heard them, but the gloomy thatch of the rain forest in the shadow of the cliff gave good concealment, and the valley came up fast.

Above the falls, he caught sight of three figures loping up the trail from the hamlet. A pair of dogs bounded ahead of them. They looked to be about eight hundred meters from the gorge, and wasting no time. Now the mirror flashes from the rim that had puzzled him became clear. The men were coming up to close the back door.

Carr rested on one knee in the shade beside the clear sheen of water where the falls spilled over a flat ledge. It was a thirty-foot drop into the pool that was hollowed out like a basin, and he could see the smooth bottom, slightly distorted where the water lifted in a hydrostatic swirl from the force of the falls. He looked for the men on the trail from the hamlet, but the jungle had taken them out of sight.

Carr sprang from the ledge, his arms spread for balance, the white pony tail of the falls racing behind him as he dropped, crashing into the water and opening a slash of bubbles all the way to the bottom. His feet dislodged a cloudy spurt of sand, and the parcels of marine light rippled in bands about his head and shoulders as he surfaced. He swam to the side of the falls and worked his way behind the ropy cataract into the cavernous dark, gripping a chink in the wetly shining rock.

Beyond the flashing veil of water, the dogs raced into view first, their barking muffled by the noise of the falls. Behind them came the three men and Carr saw the glint of curved blades, used for cutting cane and bamboo, and one of the men carried his ancestral bow and a thatched quiver of arrows. They passed quickly out of sight, leaving only the spray mists boiling off the water.

It would only be a minute or two before they joined the armed men coming down from the rim. Carr did not believe the dogs could pick up his scent. His mind began to calculate the odds of one man out of five thinking to search behind the falls. But already he was feeling the first warm glimmer of gambler's luck. He was sure that Old Mahabaleshwar could not lie very far to the south. If his luck held, he might reach it before dark and get a call through to Sterns in Bombay.

27

"You're certain those were the grids?" Sterns said, the thin mouth spitting out the words as if they had a bad taste.

"I copied them down," Carr said.

"Yes. On the cipher log. But that was left behind. Are you quite sure the coordinates you gave us are the same ones you jotted down? Couldn't you have made a mistake?"

Carr lit a cigarette and said, "No."

"How can you be so damned positive?"

"Because I have a memory for numbers."

"You're not counting cards in a casino game," Sterns insisted.

"What difference does it make," Carr said, "as long as the figures are accurate?"

The colonel glanced down at his own fists on the desk top, his eyes red-rimmed and tired and not altogether focused, like some nocturnal creature dazzled by daylight.

"That's just it," he snapped. "The numbers you brought out don't mean a thing. We plotted the coordinates a dozen times over. Wasted half the night on it."

"Are you sure you had the proper map?"

"We used the reference you provided. Standard military grid. Tell him, Paine."

After a night without sleep, Paine's pink bulk in the short trousers and knee-length khaki stockings lacked its usual chipper energy. He said, "If the grids are correct, then the ordnance depots for China Blue are scattered across Tibet and Nepal, and two of them fall into the Arabian Sea around the tropic of Cancer."

156

The three of them, Carr, Sterns, and Paine, were in a high-ceilinged room in Government House at the tip of Malabar Point. Large open windows let in a stream of morning sunlight and there was a fine view, beyond the tops of the trees, of the sea running in toward Colaba. The salt breeze off the water had died to a few humid drafts of air, which the paddle fan dispersed in short ration.

Carr said, "What's the situation at Imphal?"

"We've airlifted a full division up from Arakan to reinforce the front—troops, artillery, mules, and jeeps."

"From what Kordt had to say, you can bet your last shilling Bose will turn up in Bengal if Imphal falls."

On the other side of a sunny patch of floor, Paine remarked, "Never any doubt of that, was there, sir? I mean, it's his bloody motto, isn't it? *Chalo Delhi*. On to Delhi. . . ."

Carr said to Sterns, "How long can you fly in supplies and reinforcements?"

"Not long, I should think. It was Mountbatten's doing. Diverted aircraft from the Hump operation. I expect the Americans will jolly well give him a rocket for that. Then, there's the monsoon."

A rap of knuckles sounded at the door and an orderly carried in tea on a tray with fruit and pastry, and left. A hot bath and a few hours' sleep had brought Carr back from a deadly fatigue, and now he was hungry. He brushed a fly from a flake of brittle icing and washed down a bite of stale pastry with a swallow of tea.

"See here, sir," Paine said. "Perhaps the grids were only a decoy to throw whoever discovered them off the track."

"Or a coded set of numbers," Carr said.

"I've got some lads working on that theory," Sterns said, "but without a key it's not likely they'll turn up anything."

"Kordt was coming to Bombay," Carr said, "to take charge of the spare parts shipped in from Berbera."

"The parts are still on a pallet in a warehouse at Prince's Dock."

"If I were you," Carr said, "I'd check on that."

"They're in banded crates labeled as machine parts for the Vora plantation. The cargo's under surveillance."

"Has anyone looked inside the crates since they came off the ship?"

Carr saw the rash of color rising on Stern's neck above his collar. The thin mouth clamped down into an ever harder line so that the words had to force themselves past the lips. "Have someone see to it, Paine."

"Very good, sir," Paine said, and stepped out.

"Well, then," Carr said cheerfully, "you've got about twelve hours to stop China Blue."

"And how would you propose I start? Perhaps an amphibian reconnaissance along the tropic of Cancer?"

"I wouldn't dream of offering you advice on a military matter."

Sterns was tapping a dummy cartridge on the desk top. "A platoon from Wilson Point was ordered out at daybreak to Nagaraja. I should think they've reached the objective by now. With a spot of luck, they may find something."

"I wouldn't let my hopes soar too wildly," Carr said. "When Kordt finds out what's happened, he'll likely head for the caves where I saw the lorries and supplies."

"You said last night that you doubted you could find it again." The weary eyes rammed into Carr with new interest.

"Kordt doesn't know that. He can't very well take the risk. If I were a tout, I'd give you odds he'll try to move some of it."

"Could you recognize the site if you saw it from the air?"

"You'd never get a plane into those ravines. They're too narrow, and the caves can't be spotted from above." Carr glanced out the window at the blue flash of the sea, then frowned as his mind superimposed a different scene over it. "Come to think of it," he said, "there was a high point of rock, like a conning tower. I might know it if I saw it."

Sterns stopped tapping the dud, as if it had suddenly become a live cartridge. "I'll have Paine call out to the aerodrome," he said, "for a pilot."

28

At about the time Carr was speculating on Kordt's next move, the German was on a Norton motorbike hurtling toward Wai on the road that looped up through the jungle country of Mahabaleshwar. Word of Carr's escape had reached him the night before at the Vora residence on Malabar Hill. Ashley, going quite pale, had murmured, "But surely it's a mistake."

"No," Kordt said. "Our bird's flown. Straight back to British intelligence, I should think."

Devar said, "What effect will it have on China Blue?"

Kordt was silent. Already, his mind was working out a damage assessment.

"He knows two of our sites," the German said finally. "In one case, it is simply a matter of moving documents and the wireless. Ram Singh will know what to do. The caverns are a different problem. . . ."

"Can't the stores be moved?" Devar said.

"There's another cave site about ten kilometers from the present one," Kordt said, "but it's inaccessible by vehicle. The arms and explosives can be packed out by mule. That leaves the lorries and petrol."

"How many vehicles?" Devar asked.

"Five Bedfords, two jeeps, and a pair of motorbikes."

Ashley said, "It was dark when he was there. Are you quite sure he could find it again?"

"No," Kordt said, "but we have to act on that assumption. We'll load the petrol cans aboard the lorries and disperse them in the jungle. If no British patrols come snooping, we can move things

159

back after a bit." His gaze came back to Ashley. "I'll need your Norton for transport. Can you have it round the other side of Doongarwadi before daybreak?"

"Yes, but do you think it's safe to travel in the open?"

"There's no time to make other arrangements."

"The army has been putting up checkpoints on the main road. You should keep to the back trails. Suppose you're stopped? You'll need some identification."

"Stuff a few bloody books into the saddlebag. I'll be a professor of English from Elphimstone College—on my way to visit a colleague at Poona."

Devar said, "What can I do to help?"

"Stay safe," Kordt replied. "We can hardly afford to lose you, now."

"I rather wonder," Devar said sadly, "why he bothered to save my life?"

"To gain our trust," Kordt said, and looked at Ashley. "It appears he succeeded rather well."

"Trust." Devar nodded slowly, as if the word made sense only in its relation to betrayal.

Kordt smiled, like a player conceding a point in a game, and said, "He's become a devil of a pest."

The Norton was a 480cc International from the late thirties, low slung, with girder forks and a sprung saddle, and it roared along smoothly. Kordt wore a light windbreaker, and goggles, and the lower legs of his trousers were tied with cord to keep them from flapping.

The mountains vaulting back from the sea flung their ridges across the sky, lit by the first blue of the day. In the long valleys he made good time, ducking forward into the wind while the Norton lifted a plume of dust. There was little traffic in the countryside, only a few bullock carts and horse-drawn tongas and villagers who stepped off to one side as he sped past. The roads worsened as he climbed higher into the mountains, and the ride grew rough. He had hoped to get through to Wai without being stopped, but outside Panchgani a roadblock was up. Two sepoys manned the barricade, and Kordt throttled down the Norton. Parked off the road under a big silver oak was a jeep, its canvas top mottled in shade. A young lieutenant stood, leaning against the frame, drinking tea brewed on a burner fueled by sterno. Probably he was there, Kordt thought, to deal with British civilians who might resent being stopped by Indian soldiers. Now the officer left his mess cup on the fender of the jeep and stepped over to the checkpoint.

"Sorry for the inconvenience, sir. I've orders to have a look at all vehicles coming through."

"Trouble?" Kordt smiled and raised his goggles.

"Chaps at headquarters are worried about terrorist activity. I expect it has to do with a wog prisoner who was taken from a train last week. He's still at large. Coming from Bombay, are you, sir?"

"Elphimstone College." Kordt nodded. "Going up to Poona to give some lectures."

"Would you mind awfully opening the saddlebags, sir? I'm required to check, you see."

"Not at all." Kordt unbuckled the straps and raised the side flaps.

The lieutenant lifted out one of the books and opened the cover.

"Chaucer," Kordt said, smiling. "A form of terrorism, I suppose, if you happen to be an undergraduate."

"Been a victim of him, myself." The lieutenant chuckled and handed back the volume. "Sorry about the delay, sir."

"Sorry to spoil your tea. Is the road safe, by the way?"

"Quite safe, as long as one isn't mucking about after dark."

"Cheerio, then." Kordt fitted his goggles into place.

"Have a good trip, sir." The lieutenant saluted by way of farewell. As the Norton rattled off, he thought, *Pleasant bloke*.

Near Wai, Kordt turned off the road onto a footpath that twisted down through the trees to the west fork of the *Krishna*. For a few kilometers the trail clung close to the riverbank, and the flash of water was never far off in the leaves. At last it angled away, climbing over rough, rocky terrain patched with scrub jungle, and the Norton slowed to a crawl, snarling each time the throttle opened and closed.

At noon, Kordt wheeled the bike into a jungle swale where the slump of leaves smothered its outline. From the handlebars he lifted a binocular case and canvas-jacketed water bottle, which had been slung above the fork. These he draped around his neck. Then he followed the rocky bed of a dry watercourse up the hillside in the trees. The canteen banged against his chest as he climbed, the water sloshing inside the tin, and the leaves drifted past at a steeper angle, falling away behind him. Twice he stopped to rest, sweating hard from the climb, and finally the rimrock broke into view on the sky above him. The cavern where the lorries were lay in a deep ravine on the other side, and he had decided to approach it from above on the odd chance that a British patrol had already found it.

At the top, he crawled out into a chink of shade on the crown and took the binoculars from their case. The country streamed silently through them, green distances broken here and there by the far-off floating face of a cliff. He saw no sign of his men in any of the positions where a security lookout would normally have been posted, and their absence troubled him. Finally, he slanted the glasses down into the ravine and the crescent shadow at the mouth of the cavern jumped into the eyepieces. The dark smudge gave up nothing more than a dull gleam of metal and a motionless shape that could have been part of a man's leg, but they were like objects that had been painted over on a canvas.

Kordt worked his way down into a lower fissure in the rocks. Once more he trained the binoculars on the cavern, and the dark interior rushed up at him as if he were only a few meters from it, and this time he saw Ram Singh sitting with his back against the wall, a Sten Mark I across his lap, and the glasses picked up the shine of the double-edged *khanda* on the ground beside his leg, and the religious bracelet, the iron *kara*, on his thick wrist. The Sikh's head turned slightly out of the deeper shadow, and Kordt murmured, "My God."

In the cavern, he knelt beside the other man and took the Sten gun from the burnt hands wrapped in strips of cloth. The Sikh's eyes were puffed to slits, his beard and brows had been singed away, and the lips were blistered and swollen to twice their size. Bits of blackened skin clung grotesquely to the margins of raw suppurating flesh that had split open like the skin of a sausage made to swell and burst when held too long over a fire. His chest was scorched, and patches of charred clothing were congealed to the ulcerated surface where a yellow slick of pus was forming.

Kordt poured water into the canteen cup, held it up to the blistered lips, and said, "Drink some of this."

The Sikh tried to swallow and the water spilled down his chin.

Kordt said in Panjabi, "Where are the others?"

"Moving munitions and guns," Ram Singh replied, his voice no more than a painful rasp of sound. "Two trips with mules during the night. This morning . . . sleep. Return here later . . . in small groups."

"How many stores left?"

"Grenades . . . some cartridge boxes . . . and the detonators."

"What happened at Nagaraja?"

A fit of coughing overwhelmed the Sikh, and he would have collapsed on his side if Kordt had not caught him.

"Never mind," the German said, and could feel the fever burning up into his own hands where they grasped the other man at the shoulders. The fever, Kordt thought, could stem from the secondary infection in the burns, or it might be caused by swollen alveoli in lungs blistered and seared from the inhalation of fiery vapors. That would be the worst luck of all, for the lungs and chest cavity would fill quickly with fluid and prurient matter, and he would die. Kordt did not want to believe it, but he knew it was true.

"You need proper medical attention," he said.

"No," Ram Singh whispered, his words halting, as if they struggled up from a center of congested pain. "The True Master . . . who governs the world with wisdom . . . will decide what is to be. It is the teaching . . . of the prophet, Nanak."

"The burns need cleaning."

Kordt brewed tea and, after it had cooled, made a compress from a cotton cloth steeped in the tannic fluid and bathed the burns. By midafternoon, the men had begun to drift back in pairs and Kordt, worried about patrols, deployed a security force to high ground outside the cavern. The others he set to work loading jerry cans of fuel into the lorries, lashing down the cargo, and reconnecting battery cables so the vehicles would be ready to roll. There was nothing more to do, and he stayed with Ram Singh, changing the tannic compresses and listening to the hollow din of activity, and then he dusted the burns with sulfa powder from a medical packet, though he knew it would make no difference. Probably Ram Singh knew it, too.

For a while the Sikh slept fitfully. His fever had soared, and in his delirium he ground his teeth, and uttered a few phrases in Panjabi, and Kordt could feel the latent power in the heavy hands when he tried to hold them down. Then the resistance went out of them, and the puffed slits of eyes stared up at him.

"What did you dream?" he asked.

"That I was a boy again . . . in the temple. I could not remember . . . the answers to the questions . . . and so . . . I was not given the cup of water . . . or the sweet cake . . . that is the ritual of initiation."

"Sometimes a fever plays tricks with dreams."

Kordt had trouble finding a pulse. It ran, weak and fast, against the touch of his fingers, and the Sikh's breathing had grown shallower in the constricted air space where the fluid and mucous rattled with each expiration.

"I would like to see the Golden Temple . . . one last time . . . the procession at evening . . . on the footbridge . . . over the Pool of Immortality . . . the torchlight on the water . . . when the holy book is placed among the swords . . . of ancient kings." He paused, pain twisting across his face, and some feverish vision burned on his stare. "One last time," he breathed, "to pray . . . and cast rice to the doves. But it is too far . . . too far."

"Perhaps you'll go there in one of your dreams," Kordt said.

The Sikh's blistered lips did not quite form a smile. "I think," he rasped, "that death . . . is only an awakening . . . into a dream."

Just then, Kordt heard the plane. He slipped to the mouth of the cavern and stood in the shadow of the rock and searched the sky above the ravine. The throbbing drone seemed quite close, and suddenly the aircraft crawled into view at about five thousand feet, and Kordt saw the glint of the sun against the silver body of the twin-engined Dakota that was like a floating toy on the blue channel. The drone weakened as the steel shape, skimming sideways in a diagonal of flight, melted to half its size, dragging the sound of its motors away in its passing. It banked out of sight, but after a few moments Kordt heard it circling back, the slow throb sliding in and out on the sunny distance, and the hum of the motors mounted steadily into a reverberating roar. This time it flew in low, at about eight hundred feet, and he could see the round spinning brilliance of the propellers on either side of the cockpit as the aircraft swept past in a sudden, full-throttled hammering of the Pratt and Whitney Twin Wasp engines that split the air.

Kordt was sure now that the site had been compromised, if only from some landmark on the terrain that Carr could have recognized. By morning, British patrols would be combing the landscape. The lorries would have to move out at first dark. He watched the Dakota gaining altitude on the sky above the nearest ridge, the winged sphere shrinking until it was only a silver speck courting the sun, and once more he thought: *A devil of a pest*.

When he stepped back into the cavern, he found that Ram Singh was dead.

29

The Dakota touched down at dusk and taxied to the parking ramp, where Paine waited beside a military sedan. He saluted and held the door open for Sterns and Carr.

"Did you get my signal?" Sterns said.

"Yes, sir," Paine replied. "I put through a call to Wilson Point. They're getting up a second patrol."

"Any word from Nagaraja?" Carr said.

"As of two hours ago," Paine said, "our lads still couldn't get below to the area you described. It's crawling with bloody reptiles."

"Well, then—at least we know the ark of Manu is safe."

"That's not all of it, I'm afraid." Paine hesitated, as if not sure how to break the news. "We checked on those crates at Prince's Dock, the ones labeled machine parts. It seems that's what they contain—machine parts."

"Blast it," Sterns muttered irritably. He had taken off his peaked cap, and now he slapped the cloth crown angrily against his leg.

"Yes, sir," Paine said.

"So he slipped it past you, after all," Carr said, maintaining a serious expression only with a supreme effort of will.

They drove toward the city, the windows down to steal a breeze from the warm, windless evening. Slums stretched away under the blue darkness, and the headlights of the sedan picked out the backs and buttocks of figures squatting alongside the road to defecate.

At Mahim Creek the stench of raw sewage rose from the black gleaming mud exposed by low tide, and Carr had a glimpse of half-naked children scavenging for offal dumped into the creek bed from the slaughterhouse on the bank.

He said to Sterns, "How long will it take to get troops out to those caverns?"

The pitted lower face of the senior officer had taken on a sallow cast, as if from the backed-up bile of his anger. "They'll have to prepare a patrol order, pick the men for the job, and rehearse them on the drill. With any luck, we might have a force out by daybreak."

"Then it's too late to stop China Blue," Carr said.

"If the information you brought back is reliable, I dare say you're right. In any case, we'll know before morning, won't we? The best we can hope for now is to turn up something at those caverns, or Nagaraja, to put us on to his supply sites. He can damn well commence the operation, but he can't sustain it without his logistics."

"Suppose you *don't* turn up anything?" Carr said.

"Then the sod's got us by the crisp hairs, hasn't he? We've alerted General Slim's headquarters to expect trouble, but there's not a lot the field commanders can do without specific knowledge of enemy targets. Our supply routes to the Imphal front stretch for nine hundred kilometers. How do you protect that against a guerilla force?"

"What about Bombay?" Carr said. "Kordt mentioned the port as a target."

"I've already spoken with Colonel Sadler, the Port Authority. He's tightening security. Putting up additional checkpoints."

Beyond the open windows of the sedan the Mahim slum drifted past, the tin-roofed hovels crowding in on each other like a blight. The glimmer of paraffin lamps and candles broke the dark skyline, and even the din of voices seemed compressed into too little space.

From the driver's seat, Paine spoke to their reflections in the mirror above his head. "I forgot to mention that Mrs. Vora left the city this morning and went up to the tea plantation. The word is her husband passed away."

The news seemed to lift Sterns's mood, like the report of an enemy casualty.

"Bringing the body back, is she," he said, "for a proper Parsi send-off?"

"Couldn't say, sir," Paine replied.

Carr lit a cigarette and said nothing. He frowned across the streamer of smoke, trying to recall Ashley's words that night on the porch of the *chawl* in the tenement quarter. They came to him finally, across the passing flicker of the slum against the long pall of darkness. *The two most common things you will find in Bombay are beauty and death.*

Her marriage had been a vital link to the Indian identity she had created for herself. Now her husband's death would annul some part of the illusion. The truth was, she would never be altogether accepted into either world, British or Indian, but that was the larger reality, concealed in small ironies, still to be confronted. The biological passport of a half-caste could not be invalidated, or even surrendered. It could only be stamped for travel, and the psychological visa issued with it would always have an expiration date. It was the same world in which Carr had existed for years. The difference was, it did not matter to him, and for that reason, he felt badly for her.

At five in the morning, the phone beside his bed jangled him awake. Paine was on the line.

"Colonel's sending a jeep for you, sir."

"Don't you people ever sleep?" Carr asked groggily.

Paine's voice dropped a decibel, as if on the other end of the wire he were cupping the mouthpiece. "Not Bloody Albert, sir. He's up all night, like a blooming vampire."

"What pressing problem is it now?"

After a pause, which Carr interpreted as not wanting to say any more over the phone, Paine replied, "China Blue. It got underway three hours ago."

The slender coconut palms were sliding out of the first gray light as the jeep ground to a stop in the drive below Government House, the blackout curtains still drawn across the windows. Paine met him on the steps, and the two men went upstairs to the office room where Sterns slouched tiredly at the oversized desk, as if he himself had grown too small for the problems cluttered there. The eyes staring across the glare of the lamp were bloodshot and beaten.

"You look as if you've had a run of bad luck," Carr said.

"At 0200 this morning," Sterns said in a flat emotionless voice, "a team of sappers infiltrated onto the allied airfield at Chabua. Destroyed seven cargo aircraft and blew up a petrol storage site. They managed to get clear in the confusion and fade into the country." The officer sucked in a breath and let it out. "The rail lines running between Dacca and Nowgong into Silchar were cut in a half-dozen places. Three barges sunk on the Kusiyara River. Damage reports still coming in. He must have a damned battalion in the field."

"That's General Slim's problem now, isn't it?" Carr said.

"The spare parts for the Brens and Enfields were my responsibility. Now they're missing—like Devar."

"Don't worry," Carr said. "They'll turn up together if the Japanese can get Bose in Bengal."

"I suppose you have no idea," Sterns said, "where we might find them in the meantime?"

Carr lit a cigarette and shrugged. "Somewhere in Bombay," he said. "That's all I know."

Sterns had been squeezing a pencil between his fingers, and the cylinder snapped. He let the pieces drop, and his voice was little more than a hoarse growl.

"Those damned supply depots—they're the key."

"Maybe your patrols will turn up something," Carr said.

But by midafternoon, the news from Wilson Point was negative. Neither patrol had recovered anything of value. Both were returning to the jungle warfare center. The need for sleep had finally overtaken Sterns, who said he would be at his bungalow. Carr asked for a jeep and told the driver to drop him at the Taj Restaurant.

On the drive across town, he tried to put Ashley out of his mind. But she was like a reel of film running in his head, and the projector would not shut down. It would only switch to stop-action, forcing him to look at explicit frames as if they were exhibits in his own prosecution. He thought irritably that it was time for him to get out of Bombay. China Blue was a problem for the army and Sterns—not a professional cheat whose game was compromised.

The jeep had cruised past the barrage balloons tethered to the Oval, and now the spires and domes of the Prince of Wales Muse-

um loomed ahead on the afternoon's blue brilliance. Perhaps it was
the image of Ashley buried in his stare that unlocked the memory
from some neglected recess, as remote as Juhu's starry darkness
where she had spoken of Kordt's activities in India before the war.
Some of his work is still represented. . . and Carr murmured the rest of
it aloud, ". . . in the Prince of Wales Museum."

"How's that, sir?" the driver said.

"Nothing," Carr said. "I'll drop off here."

Miss Percival, assistant to the curator, was slight and spare
with a pinched, spinsterish look, and red marks on her nose from a
pince-nez. A sexual rose, Carr thought, never plucked, and now
withered on the branch.

"I shall turn you over to Miss Percival," the curator had said.
"She's been here for twenty-eight years and knows every artifact
and document in existence."

Carr was sure it must be true. Miss Percival struck him as one
of Freud's anal personalities who would hold on to everything—
from useless bric-a-brac to her own virginity.

"Yes, a German." She nodded. "I remember him. He was keen
on Indian civilization. I believe he arrived here about 1933. He was
carrying a letter of introduction from the British Museum in London. They'd given him some sort of grant. He spent the next several years poking about old ruins in the eastern provinces, then came
back to Bombay. Some of the objects he collected are still on display. Would you care to see?"

Carr followed her across the great hall into a dusty alcove. In a
case under glass lay several pieces of stone sculpture identified by
cards as the deities of early Hindu cults.

"Of course, this is only a small sample of what he brought
back. The best part of it was shipped off to London. These pieces
were taken from sites along the Brahmaputra in Bengal."

"I was rather hoping there might be some documents that
described his operations," Carr said. "A report of findings."

Miss Percival frowned, her mouth pinched forward as if she
were waiting to be kissed. "Yes," she replied after a long silence. "I
do believe you're right. It used to be under glass, as well." She
pointed into the deeper shadows of the alcove. "Over there."

On a ledge, several meters apart, were matching busts of Victoria and Albert. The display case stood just beneath the Prince Consort, and Carr could recall Kordt's half-amused reference to the grids for China Blue: *The irony is, they've been right under Bloody Albert's nose all along.*

"The museum ran short of room," said Miss Percival. "We did some rearranging four years ago."

The words hit like a blow from a blunt instrument. Even the pain was real.

"You mean it was thrown out?"

She had been fingering the pince-nez that hung on a chain against her flat chest, and now she gave him an arch look of reproval. "Of course not. It would be in a box in the archives. Nothing is thrown away here."

30

By the time Carr arrived at Sterns's bungalow in Colaba, the twilight was draining out to sea. The orderly who opened the door had a fresh smear of boot polish on his uniform.

"The colonel-sahib is sleeping," he said.

"Wake him up," Carr said with a certain vengeful pleasure. "Tell him it's important."

"Wait, please," the orderly said, and left Carr alone in the parlor.

On the wall behind a bamboo bar was a panel of photographs under glass—Sandhurst, polo ponies, a hiking trip into Nepal, a tiger hunt. Apart from the graying quills of hair, the plaster-of-Paris face had changed little over the years. India might change around him, but not Sterns, or his conception of what India should be.

The shadows drifted on the wall, and Carr turned to find the colonel tying the sash of his bathrobe.

"What is it that's so urgent?"

"I thought you might like to have the proper grids to those supply depots."

The hands on the sash stopped moving. "Is this a blasted joke?"

"Isn't everything, these days?"

The orderly brought whiskey, ice, and soda water on a tray and put it on the bar. Sterns waited for him to leave, then snapped, "Well? Out with it, man!"

"Do you mind if I help myself to a whiskey and soda?"

"For God sake, do," the officer said impatiently.

Carr poured whiskey into a glass of cracked ice and siphoned in soda water. "What do you intend to do with Mrs. Vora?" he said.

"Arrest her, of course, as soon as we've searched her house and the plantation."

"I'm afraid that won't do." Carr shook his head.

"What the devil are you saying?"

"No arrest," Carr replied. "I want your word on it."

Sterns frowned across the silence. His mind could not altogether process the new information. "Have you forgotten which bloody side you're on?" he said.

"Not for a minute."

"Then what the blazes do you think you're doing?"

"Offering you information," Carr said, "for a small favor."

"For blackmail, you mean."

"It's only fair, isn't it? I was blackmailed into this thing in the first place."

"In God's name, man—"

"Spare me your unprincipled blackguard speech. Mrs. Vora is the topic."

Sterns stepped to the bar, poured a whiskey and soda, and downed half of it in one swallow. He glared at Carr. "I can't promise what you ask. She's guilty of sedition, maybe worse. She would have been in prison long ago, except for this China Blue business."

"That's your answer?" Carr said.

"Did you expect any other?"

"Right. I'll be off, then. I've got some travel arrangements to make."

Sterns slammed down his glass, rattling the ice. "Damn it," he growled in a hoarse voice. "*Why?*"

"Because I owe her that," Carr said. "In any case, what's she guilty of? She loves India. There are worse crimes."

Sterns moved to the window, where evening was hatching on the panes. A bit of sea glimmered on the glass as a breath of air stirred the leaves in the garden.

"That's not an exclusive sentiment, you know," the officer said. "I was born here, as was my father. Except for Sandhurst, I've never known anything else. This is my country, too. The British made India what she is. I don't propose to stand about doing nothing while a few damned militant wogs try to dismantle four hundred years overnight. I'd rather take a bashing."

"Your choice," Carr said. "I expect the Japanese vision of India may differ a bit from Lord Clive's."

"Thanks in no small part to you."

"And China Blue," Carr said.

Livid, Sterns said nothing. Once more he gazed sadly out past the leaves at the descending pall of evening.

Carr put down his glass and started to leave. From the long shadows, Sterns's voice cut off his retreat.

"I shall still have to search her house, and the plantation."

"But no arrest?" Carr turned.

Sterns drew a deep breath, let it out, and nodded.

"Your word on it?" Carr pressed him.

"You have it," the officer said. He might have been surrendering his sword to be broken in two. "Now, those grids . . ."

"They're scattered across Bengal, along the Brahmaputra River, and in the Khasi Hills in Assam. He set up his own grid system years ago. He can't know it's been compromised. If you mount a coordinated strike, you should be able to eliminate his base of supply. And China Blue."

Sterns shook his head. "He's given us quite a run—the bastard."

"Hasn't he?" Carr smiled. "All you have to do now is catch him."

31

On a wet morning in Potsdam, not long afterward, Adm. Wilhelm Canaris, now head of the high command's Department of Economic Welfare, was eating breakfast at a cafe tucked out of sight in a courtyard behind a grille gate. Across the table from him sat an old friend, Dr. Fritz Ewers, from the psychiatric division of the Charité Hospital in Berlin.

Animated and dapper with a spit curl and hairline moustache, Ewers could have passed for a stage comic in one of the dingy, prewar cabarets on the Kurfürstendamm. He was ostensibly on his way back to Berlin from a staff inspection of a state psychiatric unit. In fact, he had arranged his trip to meet with Canaris on behalf of the new head of German intelligence, Col. Georg Hansen. A former aide to Canaris, Hansen was still loyal to the deposed Abwehr chief—a dangerous game under Himmler's nose—and it had been his practice in the first six weeks of his assignment to keep Canaris informed of key events. One of his links was Dr. Ewers. On this gray morning, the news from Tirpitz Ufer was as dismal as the weather that drove the rain in gusts against the fogged pane of glass beyond the white tablecloth.

Dr. Ewers flashed a chipper grin, as if the two men were recalling old times. "China Blue," he said, "is finished."

"How?" Canaris said.

"The bases were compromised. Georg said you would understand."

Canaris nodded, prodding the sweet pastry on his plate as if it were a corpse. His face had gone sallower, the pouched flesh under his eyes more puffed. The collapse of his apparatus in Argentina

175

and Spain, followed by the defection of two Abwehr agents to the British in Istanbul, had led to his summary dismissal by Hitler in February. The admiral had hoped that a success in India might restore him to his former position. Now that possibility was ended for him. His disappointment had less to do with vanity than the realities of power—for he was actively involved with a group of senior military officers in a conspiracy to assassinate Hitler, and he imagined he could best serve the coming putsch as chief of the Abwehr.

"What was China Blue?" Ewers said.

Canaris stared out the steamed glass at the rain beating on the black cobbles in the courtyard. "A grand scheme," he said, "that might have given us the brightest jewel in the British crown."

As they were finishing their coffee, a cold draft blew in from the front of the cafe. A tall man in a dripping slicker and woolen scarf had come in the door. His red nose was running from the wet chill of the day and he put a handkerchief to it. Canaris was sure he must be one of Himmler's SD men sent to keep a watch on him. But there could be nothing treasonable about a breakfast with an old friend.

"Georg wanted your view of the situation," Ewers said. "About pulling people out."

"I should like to have only one brought out," Canaris replied, "as soon as possible. Hauptmann Kordt. Then, it would be convenient if a transfer for him could be arranged to my staff here in Potsdam. Tell Georg I would be most grateful."

Now that the SD man was seated, it pleased Canaris to leave him behind. He called the waitress for the bill and paid it. On his way out, he paused at the coatrack within earshot of the tall figure and said to Ewers, "Give my regards to De Crinis, will you, Fritz?"

De Crinis was the head of the psychiatric service at the Charité, and an ardent Nazi. Let Himmler stew over that.

Outside, a thin mush of sleet lay on the pavement beyond the courtyard wall. Canaris climbed into his staff car and settled back as the driver pulled away in the downpour, windshield blades thumping. The sedan crept past the resplendent dome of Sans Souchi, where Frederick the Great had once entertained Voltaire, and he saw the park and fountain in the rain.

He hoped Georg would act swiftly to pull Kordt out of India. Kordt was too valuable to throw away. Persuading him to join the putsch should not be difficult. Kordt came from an aristocratic family with an older concept of honor. For Canaris, the assassination of Hitler was a simple necessity of power politics. The war was lost. The Abwehr, which the admiral himself had built from nothing, was lost—given over to the whims of a chicken farmer. It was time to move to the winning side. For Kordt, it must be made a matter of principle, a way of undoing a monstrous wrong. Canaris had no doubt he could convince the younger officer where his duty lay.

32

On the evening of the twelfth, Carr met Paine for a drink at the bar of the Taj. They rolled dice out of a leather cup to see who would pay, and Carr said, "Did Sterns get off to Delhi?"

"This afternoon. Flying up to brief the big boys on China Blue."

"Have any of those Brens and Enfields turned up?"

"Not yet," Paine said. "But that's a small cut of the pie, isn't it?"

"Thirteen sites." Carr frowned. "You hit them all, but no Brens and Enfields. That would point to a fourteenth site—one that wasn't marked on any map."

"Or the weapons could be scattered by now."

"Kordt said they were going to stay in Bombay. The last phase of China Blue involved an assault on the port."

"He'd be a bloody fool to try it now," Paine said.

"Give you something to work on."

"Work," Paine grumbled. "Look, sir. That's what you give the sergeant major. A proper officer comes in at ten to have a look round, see how things are going. Then break off straightway for lunch. Drop back about two. Sign some papers. Tell sergeant major where you'll be, and pop away to a pint of wallop. That's the correct way to soldier."

"Just in uniform for the war, are you?"

"That's it, sir. When it's done, I'm for Brighton. Take out a license and open a pub. Regular hours and no nonsense."

The barman told Paine there was a phone call. The officer rolled his eyes in weary disgust and went off. At this hour, there was not much of a crowd in the taproom that was cool and dim under the creaking of the paddle fans. In less than a minute, Paine strode back in. "Can you believe it?" he complained. "Bloody Albert not off the ground four hours, and they've spotted our birds."

"Kordt?"

"And Devar, they think."

"Where?"

"Near Doongarwadi."

"Are you going?"

"I suppose there's no way out of it." Paine sighed.

"I'll ride along with you."

"Right," Paine said. "We'll come back here for a jar when it's over."

They drove out the sweeping curve of Marine Drive, where the bay was only a whisper in the dusk beyond the sea wall, and turned onto Malabar Hill. The city fell away as they climbed into the woods, and Carr recognized the stretch of road from his first meeting with Kordt.

Ahead, a policeman signaled with a torch, and Paine braked to a stop. Several vehicles were parked under the trees near the high stone wall of Doongarwadi. An armed sepoy crouched on a low bluff above a jeep that had blown a tire and skidded into the embankment. A havildar caught sight of Paine, trotted over, and saluted.

They had spotted the vehicle, the havildar said, when it ran a checkpoint. His patrol had sped in pursuit, a looping chase up Malabar Hill, and had come suddenly on the abandoned jeep. The driver and passenger had fled on foot, probably over the wall into Doongarwadi.

"Did you order up a search?" Paine said.

"No, Lieutenant-Sahib. It is the holy place of the Parsis. I did not want to enter the grounds without the proper authorization."

Already, Carr's mind was locking into a memory—the wind-blown shadows of the dakhma, Kordt's sudden appearance out of nowhere . . . The more the scenario reconstructed itself, the more uncertain he grew about what he had actually seen. Kordt might have been a stage magician dematerializing in a trick cabinet.

Carr drew Paine aside, and said, "One of the *dakhmas* isn't used anymore. I think you ought to have a look at it."

"The havildar's right," Paine said. "I should think we'd require someone's permission to set foot in there. One of their priests, maybe."

"Did Kordt consult the clergy?"

"If I order a search party in, the wogs will make it out to be a bloody invasion."

"Suppose it were just the two of us," Carr said. "Who would have to know?"

Paine hesitated, staring uphill at the woods, dark above the wall. "It wouldn't do to get caught," he murmured.

"You could always say you acted under military necessity."

Carr waited by the jeep while Paine spoke to the havildar. The officer came back, gripping a carbine and torch, and nodded to Carr. "We'd better have these along, just in case."

The two men set off in the dark, tramping uphill. When they were out of sight of the others, Paine gave Carr a leg up to the top of the wall. Carr stretched down a hand to help the other man over, and they dropped down into Doongarwadi.

"Can you find it again?" Paine said softly.

"Shouldn't be hard to spot."

They climbed into the thick vegetation, where shadows nested among the falling cascades of vine and leaf. Carr could feel the slow pull of the grade in his legs even as the tension worked itself into a knot in his chest. Ahead, the weathered stone of the dakhma took shape in the slumping leaves.

As they drew close, Carr could make out the dull gleam of the iron door under the portal arch. He half expected to find it locked, but it swung open, hinges whining. Both men mounted the steps in the tunnel passage to the main enclave. Overhead, the rim of the dakhma cut a circle of stars from the sky. Tonight, no vultures hunched there in a death vigil. Perhaps they had been disappointed here once too often.

The cobbled deck sank away in shadow to the central pit. Carr slipped quietly down to it, flattened himself on the edge, and ran his hand along the interior. The smooth surface gave way to a foothold cut into the stone. He peered down and could make out a second notch before the blackness welled up.

"Steps," he murmured.

"How deep does it go?"

"I'll drop down for a look."

"Careful you don't slip."

Carr worked his way down, probing with his toe for each new foothold. His shoulders dropped below the edge of the pit, and the shadows closed over his head. The ring of stars, telescoped above him, receded with each step. When he glanced up again, Paine's silhouette was high above him on the sky.

The charcoal bed of the pit came up suddenly in the pitch-black gloom, and he explored it gingerly with one foot before putting his full weight on it. Something slid under his shoe and he thought he could make out the gleam of a bone. Squatting, he groped along the curved base of the pit until his fingers found the hole knocked from the mortar. He called softly up to Paine to come down and waited while the other man descended.

"There's a tunnel off here," Carr said.

Paine knelt on the cinders and ran his hand along the arched recess. "I'm damned," he murmured.

"Give me the carbine," Carr said. "I'll crawl in for a look."

"That's my blooming job, sir, not yours. Mark you, I'm not keen about it."

"Nor I," Carr said.

"I suppose it's no good risking the torch."

"Why spoil the surprise?"

"Right. Stay close, then. We don't want to lose touch. If there's shooting, get out fast. I'll cover you. Understood?"

"Yes."

Paine went in on his belly, gripping the carbine by the sling near the upper swivel. Carr squirmed in after him. Buttressed by timbers, the tunnel ran straight on. They had crawled about thirty meters when Paine froze. "Did you hear it?" he whispered.

In the dark, Carr was dead still, hardly breathing. At first he heard nothing. Then his ears picked up a sound, a far-off murmur of voices that fell like a shaving off the silence. "Ahead of us," he replied tonelessly.

They crept on until the shaft angled sharply, and suddenly the glimmer of a distant candle gave shape to the support timbers that stretched like vertebrae along the passage, tall enough now for a man to walk at a crouch. They got to their feet, stooping low to avoid the crossbeams. A side chamber floated out of the shadows, and they caught sight of the weapons crates stacked in long tiers.

"Your Brens and Enfields," Carr whispered.

"The Parsis may have some explaining to do," Paine whispered back.

"Vora, probably. But you can't prosecute the dead."

"Listen." Paine put a finger to his lips.

The voices drifting into the passage sounded nearer. Carr heard the soft click of metal as Paine released the safety on the carbine.

They eased forward, their backs pressed to the side of the shaft that lay out of the light. Suddenly, Kordt and Devar were in plain view where the tunnel ran to a side chamber—a billet with cots and bedrolls and a table where the candle flickered.

Kordt wore a British uniform, pistol belt, and sidearm and was leaning forward on the table with both hands. The candle threw its glint across his face as he looked up. On the near side of the table Devar stood with his back to them.

"Hands up," Paine called out.

Kordt swept the candle from the table, blacking out the chamber. In the dark, Paine fired his carbine from the hip. At close range, the hammering burst left Carr's ears ringing. Again Paine fired, the muzzle spurting flame as it climbed from the recoil of the automatic cycle. The table had gone over with a crash, and there was a sound of splintering wood as bullets chewed across a plank.

Carr hugged the ground. In the muzzle flash of the carbine Paine's bulky shape flickered on the darkness a few feet away. From across the chamber came a muffled thud, and Paine fired at the sound. This time Kordt's revolver answered with a single shot that tore a low cry from Paine as if he had suffered a minor annoyance.

"Are you hit?" Carr murmured, but got no answer.

On the far side of the chamber the darkness gave up an impression of movement, a darting shape. Carr crawled to Paine, who was slumped, half-sitting, against a timber, his cheek and shoulder resting against the wall. The carbine was still loosely gripped as if he meant to fire it. Carr took the weapon and felt his way in the dark along the side of the tunnel.

At the end of the passage, iron rungs had been driven into the embankment for steps. They rose ten feet to a trap that lay open on a square of floating darkness.

Carr climbed to the trap and peered out across the floor of a lattice pavilion. No breeze stirred, and the silence was lashed down on the night. Beyond the arbor of dark leaves a moon was up, and he recognized instantly the hedgerows and garden and the Victorian house where he had once sat, sipping tea, with Ashley and her invalid husband. There was no sign of Kordt.

Carr dropped back into the shaft and groped his way to Paine. "Easy, Paine," he murmured. "We'll get you out of here to hospital."

But there was no need. Curled against the wall, Paine hadn't moved. The match flaring in Carr's fingers left no doubt. Paine's eyes were open, their stare narrowed and fixed along a few inches of the wall, as if puzzled. Blood had spread in the shape of a rose on his breast pocket where the bullet had pierced the heart. Probably he was dead before he hit the ground.

A groan from the chamber made him drop the match and snatch up the carbine. No more sounds drifted across the silence. He groped for Paine's torch and shone it. The beam swept across Devar on the ground beside the overturned table.

Carr went over to him. Devar lay on his side, a Walther PPK service pistol clutched in his hand, but he was beyond using it. Carr lifted it out of his fingers and stuck it into his own waistband. Blood had soaked through the front of Devar's shirt. Carr started to peel the dirt-caked fabric away from the wound, and frowned. A burst from the carbine had ripped through the lower abdominal cavity, and the light from the torch picked out the bloody shine of an intestine.

The dark eyes looked up at him. They saw the carbine slung over his shoulder, and the stare filled with an odd disappointment. Before Carr could say anything, the life sank out of the pupils in a single heartbeat, leaving only the dilations of betrayal.

33

When Kordt saw the British officer pointing the carbine he reacted on pure reflex, sweeping away the candle and diving from the line of fire. Flying splinters from the table stung his cheek, and he rolled twice and saw that the muzzle flash of the carbine did not shift. He had the Webley out and cocked, and in the dark he sailed his peaked cap off to the left. It thumped against a timber and drew a third burst of fire. Kordt squeezed off a round and heard the Britisher cry out. He knew there was a second man, though he hadn't gotten a clear glimpse of him. Probably they were part of a patrol combing the area. Either he must break off and withdraw, or risk having his retreat cut off. He pushed to his feet and slipped back to the trap cover. Moments later, he was darting along the hedgerows of the garden.

He was sure the house was empty. The cook and bearer were with Ashley at the plantation. The two hamals, who swept and dusted, did not live in, and the chauffeur, Baji, usually slept by the limousine.

A blackout curtain was pulled across the window of the stone garage. Kordt tapped on the pane twice. He was about to force the latch when the curtain jerked aside, and he saw Baji's black, shining face on the other side of the glass. The Madrassi driver, half-naked and rotund as ever in a cotton dhoti, brandished a socket wrench. He recognized Kordt at once, slid the locking bolt out of its sleeve, and pushed open the window. Kordt swung quickly over the sill, secured the window behind him, and drew the curtain.

"Don't put on a light," he said. "I was followed into Doongarwadi. The British are in the tunnel. They'll be finding their way out any minute. Is there petrol in the Norton?"

"I filling tank this morning, but headlight is missing blackout sleeve."

"I won't be using the lamp."

"Oh, dear me, Sahib. British oppressors are everywhere having up roadblocks. Two of them are now this house watching."

"When will you see Mrs. Vora?"

"I driving the memsahib back here tomorrow."

"Then listen carefully, Baji. Tell her I had to leave her brother behind in the tunnel. I'm afraid the British may have him."

"Dear me." Baji wrung his hands nervously, shifting his weight from one foot to another. "These are terrible doings."

"Tell the memsahib I've been ordered out. A U-boat will be off the coast in seventy-two hours. There will be a diversionary attack at the port on the fourteenth. Can you remember all this?"

"Yes." The chauffeur still dithered with his fingers. "But where will the sahib be himself going?"

"Kanheri," Kordt replied. "There is an old *sadhu* at the caves. If there's a need for contact, you can get in touch with me through him."

"I telling memsahib about all of these doings."

Kordt nodded, and a sad smile fell from his mouth. *"Jai Hind,"* he murmured.

Wheeling the Norton out, he had a final glimpse of the pudgy figure, the dhoti passing between his legs and gathered about his plump hips.

"Careful, sahib," Baji whispered, his eyes popping. "British oppressors are being armed and most dangerous."

The gravel crunched softly under the tires as he rolled the bike down the drive in the leafy darkness. The surveillance unit, Baji had said, was parked across the road from the iron gates. Kordt saw the gleam of the sedan in the trees. He did not think they had spotted him yet, and it would take them a few seconds to react once they did. He had no doubt he could get past them, but the sedan would have a wireless to radio his position to other mobile units.

He straddled the machine and kicked the starter. The engine roared, snarling as he twisted the throttle and shot from the drive.

The road streamed upward behind him in the rearview mirror and he saw the blackout lights of the sedan flick on as it pulled out in pursuit. A curve swept the vehicle from sight. Kordt gunned the bike, leaning into each loop of moonlit paving, which flashed under the wheels. The city rose quickly, shifting on the dark axis of each banking motion, and the winding descent soon lengthened his lead over the sedan.

Around a bend, the road uncoiled into a straight stretch, and two jeeps were parked across it. Even as he locked into a back-wheel skid, dragging a foot to keep the Norton from going over, a spotlight came on and caught him in its beam. From behind the lens came a warning shout to halt. The bike had spun half around, and Kordt twisted the throttle and sped off in the direction from which he had come.

"He's doubling back!" The voice from the roadblock crackled over the wireless receiver in the sedan. Both men wore mufti, the driver gripping the wheel with two hands and hunched forward, straining to see the road in the thin parcels of light from the black-out filters. They rounded a curve and the second man pointed. "There!"

The figure on the motorbike was less than two hundred meters out, bent low over the handlebars and silhouetted in the spotlight. Suddenly, the headlamp of the Norton flashed on and the machine swerved into their lane.

"Bloody fool's coming at us head-on," the driver cried.

"He's bluffing."

The man on the bike had gone invisible behind the glaring disc of the headlamp, and at high speed the candlepower seemed to swell all at once to a blinding incandescence. Dazzled, the driver of the sedan flung up a hand, jerking the wheel as he hit the brake. The tires squealed even as the light exploded past them, flinging back the roar of the Norton. The sedan slewed to a stop in fumes of burnt rubber, and the driver snarled, "Crazy bugger! He would have rammed us."

On the far side of Malabar Hill, Kordt hit the second roadblock. It was the same jeep that had pursued him earlier into Doongarwa-di, and the havildar stood beside it in the road, his carbine at the ready. The Norton fishtailed as Kordt braked hard. He was sure the sedan could not be far behind. He wrenched the handlebars into a full turn and gunned the bike, and the havildar fired a warning burst into the air. Kordt throttled down, sliding into a sharp turn with his foot, and had a glimpse of the havildar and his two sepoys running toward him. The ground flew from under the wheels as the German opened the throttle and went for a culvert in the trees off the road. More shots from the havildar's carbine clipped the leaves overhead, but Kordt was sure the soldiers must have orders to take him alive, if possible.

The culvert ran alongside a property wall—a trench cut for drainage during the monsoon—and it dropped steeply in the shad-ow of the trees high up along the bank. He could see only patches of ground, but dared not risk the headlamp. Each rut nearly tore the handlebars from his grasp while his spine absorbed the shock, and the bike bounced and bucked, careening from side to side. Suddenly, there was no ditch at all under the spinning wheels, only the weight of the machine in the free-fall of gravity and darkness. He had gone over a bluff, and he knew it first in the pit of his stomach even as his mind no longer counted seconds but raced through a time warp of light years that seemed to fall with him on the sky. The rear wheel struck first, the impact like a blow between his shoulders that snapped his head back, and the front wheel seemed to take an interminable time coming down. It slammed into the soft embankment, and this time the handlebars flew from his grasp, and he pitched from the saddle.

The impact knocked the wind from him and snapped through his brain like a power surge that left the circuits black. Dimly, his perceptions came back, as from an overload, and he could see the flash of tall grass on the sky above his head. Then he heard the Norton, still snarling, stall out in the dark below him.

The bluff jackknifed outward, and he staggered to his feet and stumbled downhill to the bike. Torches bobbed in the woods above, the leaves racing in the beams. Below, the glimmer of a squatters' colony seeped into the larger darkness. Kordt mounted the Norton, kicked the starter, and chugged downhill toward the sprawl of shanties.

While the havildar and his sepoys searched the wood with their torches, the two men who had given chase in the sedan gazed down from the bluff at the squatters' colony. It stretched away in the dark at the bottom of the hill where the water flowing down from the monsoon rains would wash away half the hovels in their own mud and sewage. The gleam of oil lamps melted from cracks onto bits of tin and tattered canvas and picked out the dull shine of refuse heaps where the lanes bled away in shadows. The motorbike had faded to a far-off whine, lost on the dark distances of the night.

"Ruddy sod," the driver murmured. "Never find him down there."

"Hell of a drop." The other frowned. "How did he manage it without breaking his neck?"

At midnight, the stars were jammed together in a bright blaze over Kanheri as Kordt cruised down the long valley toward the wooded hill honeycombed with ancient Buddhist caves. The moonlight turned the plume of dust behind the Norton to silver that settled softly on the landscape. The country beyond the caves ran to ravines and forests where one man could easily evade an army of trackers.

In two more nights, a U-boat would be lying off the coast below the Koli village of Versova. Before he slipped out to it, he had a small payment-in-kind for the British—an act of reciprocity for China Blue.

He throttled down, slipped the bike into neutral, and, balancing with one foot on the ground, stared at the stars spilling off the horizon. One day, with a bit of luck, he'd come home to India. He would go first to Amritsar to the soaring, gilt-copper domes of the Golden Temple and take rice, for Ram Singh, to scatter to the doves. He would offer a flower in the Sikh's name to the priest to be pressed to the sacred book, and then he would set the blossom afloat in the Pool of Immortality and pray that his friend's spirit would be released there.

34

On the afternoon of the fourteenth Kordt was waiting in the shade of a signal box beside a spur track that ran from the freight yards to the restricted area of the harbor. The short trousers and knee-length khaki stockings gave small relief from the sweltering heat, and the drill shirt, sporting the insignia of a major on the shoulder loops, had streaks of perspiration in the faded fabric.

A switch engine pulling three empty boxcars chugged slowly around a curve of track under a distant gantry, and Kordt unsnapped the flap of his holster. He could see the banded boiler and cab, slightly distorted in the mirage waves of heat and billows of steam. Then it was coming straight on, swelling all the time above the track and still thermally bent on the distance. At last it drew close, shaking the ground with its ponderous trampling, and Kordt grasped the hand rods and swung up into the cab.

A burly fireman in sandals and shorts was shoveling coal into the firebox and Kordt brought the butt of the revolver down hard on his skull. The shovel clanged as it dropped from the man's grasp, and he lay on the footplate.

"What the devil do you . . ." The engineer on the jump seat broke off his protest as he gazed down at the barrel of the Webley thrust into his side. He was an Anglo-Indian of middle age, and sudden fear widened the stare in his brown face that was slick with sweaty grime above the bandanna knotted about his neck.

"Do as you're told," Kordt said, "and you'll get out of this alive. Have you any more crew aboard?"

After a moment, the engineer nodded. "One man, for switching and coupling."

"We're going on in," Kordt said.

"Don't you know there is a military checkpoint, mister? All traffic going in is stopped and searched."

"I've watched them," Kordt said. "They look in the boxcars and gondolas. They don't come up into the cab. You give them a thumbs-up. That means no trouble. If you don't give it when the sentry flags you on, that's your code for duress."

On the footplate, the fireman stirred and pushed up on his hands. Blood tracked down the side of his face from a deep gash in his scalp. Kordt pointed toward the coal tender and gestured with the revolver. The Indian staggered to his feet and lurched across the shifting plates where the engine and tender were coupled. He squatted on the bank of coal, holding his head in both hands and glaring straight ahead.

Kordt glanced through the narrow forward window beyond the jump seat and saw the checkpoint sliding toward them on the glass against a backdrop of warehouses and big dock cranes. He stood just behind the engineer, who wore no shirt under the high overalls soiled with soot and grease.

"Mind you give a proper thumbs-up," Kordt said, and crouched beside the firebox door.

The engineer closed the regulator, forcing a plume of steam from the safety valve as the locomotive ground to a halt. Two sentries manned the post and Kordt had a glimpse of one, rifle slung across his shoulder, moving back to have a look at the empty boxcars. They would be shunted off to warehouses inside the restricted zone, and the switch engine would then couple on to other standing cars, already loaded and padlocked, and pull them back to the yards for hookup to a train.

After a few moments the engineer, who was leaning out the side window with his head craned to the rear, gave a thumbs-up. The sentry would be flagging him on. He shot Kordt a nervous look, tugged once on the whistle cord above his head, and opened the regulator. The ground was sliding past again, the click of the rails slow and measured.

Kordt spotted a track looping off the main spur into a shallow culvert on the blind side of a low warehouse. On the other side stood a fenced power station. The rails ended in a pile of ballast.

"Pull in there," Kordt shouted.

"That spur isn't maintained," the engineer said. "The fishplates are probably loose."

"Take a chance."

"The switch will be closed," the engineer protested.

"Open it."

"Well, it is probably padlocked, besides."

"Find out."

They halted at the switch pit and the engineer leaned out on the hand rods and called to the crewman in the rear. A young Hindu in dhoti and dirty turban came up at a jog trot. He looked surprised at the order. "But track is not being used," he protested.

"Just do as you're bloody told, Baboo, and don't argue!" the engineer exploded.

Baboo stepped at once to the pit and heaved on the lever, opening the side track. He waited until the last car had cleared the main spur, then closed the switch.

The train crawled and creaked to the railhead, grating to a stop, its dark iron sweating under the slow clank of a steam valve.

"Off," Kordt said. "Both of you."

The engineer had taken off the bandanna, which left a light ring in the coal dust caking his neck. He shook a finger and said, "You will be in serious trouble for this, mister, I can tell you."

"Right." Kordt lifted the clipboard from the peg by the jump seat. "Off, now. Double quick."

The fireman climbed down first, followed by the engineer, and then Kordt. The German had holstered the Webley, but kept his hand on the grip. Baboo hurried toward them in the trench beside the ballast. The sliding doors of the first coach gaped open, and Kordt said, "Up you go—the lot of you."

"You bloody well can't . . ." the engineer stammered.

"I can," Kordt said. "Don't make a sound unless you want things to get more unpleasant than they are. I won't be far away."

They slid the door shut on its rollers and Kordt snapped the padlock. He ducked under the boxcar, secured the other side, and moved toward the docks.

The eight-thousand-ton, Canadian-built liberty ship lay moored fore and aft alongside the pier. A Royal Indian Navy guard stood watch below the gangplank. Kordt returned his salute and asked if the captain were on the bridge. The guard called up to the deck through his cupped hands. After a few moments, an officer leaned out over the rail and signaled Kordt to come aboard.

Climbing, he had a view of the harbor sprawling away. Tractors towing strings of flatcars crawled in and out of sheds and warehouses along the quay. Dockers swarmed around pallets lifted off ships by the tall cranes. The creak of block and tackle in the next berth down was lost on the screech of gulls and steady hoot of tugboats on the water.

At the top of the gangplank, a wire-thin Britisher waited.

"My name's Dowling." He smiled out of a wind-burnt face. "First Officer. Captain Bradwell's ashore. Should be back, presently."

"Major Locke." Kordt flashed his identity card. "Bombay Port Trust of Docks and Railways. Colonel Sadler's staff. I've a requirement to check the holds of all vessels docking with explosives prior to unloading."

"Can't say we were aware of that procedure, Major."

"New drill, I'm afraid. There was a fire aboard an American ammunition ship the other day. Careless storage of inflammables. Could have been quite serious, actually."

"Bloody Yanks," Dowling said. "You might know it."

"You're carrying explosives, I believe. . . ."

"Amatol." Dowling nodded. "Three hundred tons of the bloody stuff."

"What else?"

"Cotton. Scrap metal. Gold bullion, and a bit of timber."

"If you can give me an escort, we'll have a look," Kordt said. "Shouldn't take long."

"I'll take you below, myself," Dowling said.

"Better still," Kordt said.

In the hold, the steel ribs of the inner hull curved upward in the dank gloom. The canisters of amatol were packed in crates labeled HIGH EXPLOSIVE and lashed down in the forward bay. The gold bullion was stored aft behind a thin bulkhead near the bilges.

"One hundred and fifty-five bars," Dowling said. "Worth millions, that lot. I suppose they thought if we took a torpedo the stern might break off and the gold could be salvaged. Stupid, of course. If that much amatol had gone up, there wouldn't have been a rivet left."

"Quite a packet," Kordt said.

"It seems there's a war to finance in Assam."

In the center bay they worked their way past the bins of scrap metal, and the banded timber. Bales of cotton under cargo nets towered above their heads. Pen and clipboard in hand, Kordt glanced down one of the narrow avenues between the pallets and said, "I'll just have a look in there, and we can be done with it."

He slipped between the stacked bales, stepping over the canvas straps of the pallets into another dark defile. He had already twisted the cap of the fountain pen one full turn, arming the incendiary, and he thrust the device between two bales where it could not be seen.

Topside, Kordt shook hands with the first officer.

"I'll call in your clearance," he said. "I expect you're anxious to proceed with unloading."

"Not much danger of a torpedo here," Dowling said.

"Right." Kordt winked. "None at all."

At Government House, Sterns was sitting down to a cup of tea when the call came from the harbor. On the line was Lt. Col. J. R. Sadler, general manager of the Bombay Port Trust of Docks and Railways.

"Something odd going on. I thought you ought to be brought in on it."

"Yes?" Sterns lifted his tea for a sip.

"Some bloke in a major's uniform jumped aboard a switch engine from the yards and forced the engineer at gunpoint to take him through the checkpoint into the harbor. Once they'd got inside, the engine and cars were shunted off onto a piece of track that's not presently used. The engineer and his crew were locked into a boxcar, and the fellow vanished. The worst of it is, he fits the description you gave us of the German chap impersonating a British officer."

Sterns slopped a bit of tea over the rim as he fumbled the cup back into the saucer. "How long ago did it happen?" He tried to keep the hoarse excitement in his tone under control, but it, too, spilled over, like the tea.

"Little over an hour," Sadler replied. "Someone heard the crew shouting and banging for help."

"You mean to say he's been loose for an hour in an area of ammunition stores and explosives?"

"I'm afraid so. I've alerted our security people. We're doubling up surveillance."

"I should triple it, if I were you," Sterns said. "I'm coming over."

Halfway down the gangplank, Kordt saw two jeeploads of armed sepoys weaving in and out of traffic along the quay. They were spotting troops at various storage sites in the area. It was enough to convince him that the engineer and his crew must have been discovered. The incendiary device was primed to ignite thirty minutes after its activator cap had been twisted. He looked at his watch. Twenty-three minutes left.

He crossed to a warehouse storing grain, paint, and paper. It was not likely that a guard would be posted at the facility since it presented no target for sabotage. A dozen small offices divided by glass partitions ran along a wall. He slipped into one that was unoccupied and picked up the telephone.

"Get me Memorial Hospital, please," he told the operator. "Emergency."

In the next cubicle, a clerk stared at him. Kordt gave him a stern look, and the man immediately busied himself with papers on his desk. The hospital came on the line.

"This is Major Locke at the harbor," he said. "One of my civilian crew just took a nasty spill off a scaffolding. Knocked him cold. We can't seem to bring him round. From the look of him, he may have a broken backbone as well. Can you dispatch an ambulance? Let me give you the location. . . ."

Outside, Kordt pressed back against a wall in the shade and did not move. Another jeepload of security forces skirted the pier, dropping a sepoy on the L-shaped dock across the slot of water where two more cargo ships were berthed. He was too far off to be a threat. Kordt wondered where the ambulance was. It should have arrived. He couldn't wait much longer. Once the fire broke out, the pier would be swarming with fire brigades and security forces.

It seemed an interminable time before the singsong bleat of the siren came out of the distance. He looked at his watch. Three more minutes.

The ambulance swung onto the ramp and cut its siren. Kordt could make out three figures in the cab—the driver, a second man, and an Anglo-Indian nurse. As the vehicle wheeled to a stop, Kordt trotted out to it. The nurse was standing by the running board, and the two attendants were hurrying round to the rear doors to bring out the litter.

"I'm terribly sorry," Kordt said to the nurse. "We tried to call back a few minutes ago, but the lines were tied up. The lad who was hurt regained consciousness. When the ambulance didn't come, we packed him off to the hospital in a motorcar. He's got a nasty swelling above the temple, and he's quite unsteady."

The nurse's unpainted features were rather pretty in a plain sort of way, though a bit too solemn. "You should not have moved him," she said.

His nerves absorbed the passing seconds like blows. "We were anxious to get him medical attention."

"Moving him like that could make the condition worse," she said. "Besides, the hospital is terribly busy just now. The ambulance could have been dispatched for other cases."

"I know," Kordt said. "It's quite inexcusable. I can't tell you how sorry I am."

Some of his contrition seemed to work through her icy disapproval.

"I suppose it is not your fault."

Kordt smiled, and said, "Look here, Miss. I wonder if I could impose on you for a lift back to the hospital. I should like to chat with the doctor after he's examined the patient."

She hesitated, but then he saw the resistance on her brown pupils burn up in the atmosphere of his concern.

"You can ride in the back if you wish."

"That's jolly decent of you," Kordt said. "By the way, you may want to use your siren. It can be slow going in here with all the noise and traffic and dockers moving about."

Inside the ambulance, Kordt checked the time. The incendiary device should have ignited in the hold thirty seconds ago. He could see no sign of smoke as the ship receded on the panel of glass in the rear door.

Before they reached the checkpoint, he heard the thunderous clang of the first fire engine passing from the other direction. The ambulance driver turned on his own siren to clear a path. With any luck, in the mounting confusion, the sentries at the checkpoint would wave them through.

Twenty minutes later, Kordt was astride the saddle of the Norton, kicking the engine to life. He had slipped out of the ambulance when it slowed to a crawl in heavy traffic, and made his way on foot through the crowds to Victoria Terminus, where he had left the motorbike chained. Now, as he picked his way past the trolleys, cars, and bullock carts that crammed Cruikshank Road, he could see the column of black smoke swirling up from the harbor beyond the gothic towers of the railway station. A dozen sirens played toward it across the blue distances of the day.

35

On a street not far from the smoke and sirens, Carr stood in an alcove and watched the hearse bending out of the distant thermal waves in the traffic. It came straight on and rolled to a stop near the wall of a burning ghat where the Hindus cremated their dead. A limousine bearing Ashley and a small funeral party pulled up behind it.

Carr remained out of sight where a stone arch purged its shade into the alcove. The bearers drew the litter with the white-shrouded corpse from the hearse and put the poles to their shoulders. They carried it in through the open gates to a shallow trench filled with sandalwood. Ashley stepped from the limousine, a fold of the black sari drawn over the top of her head and around her lower face, and followed them. There would be no procession through the streets for Jai, no musicians playing a dirge on *tarai* trumpets and horns, no public outpouring of grief. The British had released the remains on the condition that cremation be private.

The bearers lifted away the shroud as they placed the body on the pyre, and Carr saw that the thumbs were bound together, the forehead marked with ash, the mouth stuffed with betel nut—as for a caste Hindu. He wondered if the priest knew that Devar was not a true Sudra. Or perhaps the Vora wealth had relaxed his interpretation of doctrine. Either way, the flames could make no orthodox distinctions and would consume the mistake.

After prayers had been chanted, and the pyre purified with holy water, the priest handed Ashley a torch, which she touched to each of the four corners of resin-scented wood. Flames slid upward, engulfing the dead man. The cotton shroud, which had been draped once more over the corpse, burned like damp paper, and Carr had a final glimpse of Jai's face before the flesh began to swell and peel. Smoke swirled above the rim of the ghat, but it was only a smudge compared to the dark ribbon trailing skyward from the harbor.

Later, the priest and bearers drifted out, leaving Ashley alone at the pyre. She stood motionless for a long time, her head bent. Carr came up quietly from behind, and said, "If I could change places with him, I would."

The words had the sound of a forgery, but there was no way to authenticate a sentiment.

He wasn't sure what he expected from her—tears, turmoil, outrage at his presence. But her eyes were dry when she turned, as if she had passed beyond the range of her own emotions into some larger emptiness. Pain, hate, and sorrow did not extend there.

"Why have you come here?" she said dispassionately.

"There were things to say," he replied. "Saying them in the presence of the dead may give them some credibility."

"If you had never set foot in India," she murmured, "he might be alive, still."

"Or dead that night at the train," Carr said. "Dying is all part of karma, isn't it? Ordained from birth? That's what he believed."

Over the harbor, the column of smoke had turned white. It streamed high, and the afternoon sun lit it to creamy brilliance.

"That's a convenient logic," she said, "for avoiding guilt."

"Only if you believe it yourself," Carr said.

"Is that what you came here to say?"

"No." Carr shook his head. "I thought it might ease your mind to know that the British aren't going to arrest you. Sterns gave me his word on it. Unfortunately, his spirit of amnesty doesn't extend into the future. If you keep on with this business you'll go to prison."

"Then I shall go to prison," Ashley said.

"I have several friends who went to prison. None of them liked it."

"It has to do with a principle. Something you wouldn't understand."

"Probably not. But do you really believe the Japanese intend to hand the country over to Bose? They're using him. Not that it matters, because without China Blue they'll never pull it off. Look, I know a bad gamble when I see one. You've bet on the losing side. The stupid part is that independence is coming anyhow. The British are fed up, except for a few diehards like Sterns who can't tell Gandhi from Gunga Din. The longer the war goes on, the longer India waits for freedom. It's that—"

Carr didn't finish. An orange bubble swelled above the docks as an explosion tore across the city in a thunderous shock wave of sound. Fiery debris shot into the sky on rocket trails of smoke that streamed outward in arcs. Carr threw Ashley to the ground against the wall and covered her body with his own. The shower of white-hot steel seemed to go on forever. Even before it subsided, Carr could hear women screaming across the district, and the far-off wail of another fire truck.

Above the harbor, black smoke boiled up into the stratosphere. Already the monstrous cloud dimmed the sun. The priest and one of the bearers stumbled into the ghat and jabbered wildly in Marathi. They wanted Ashley to leave with them. When it was clear she would not, they fled back into the street, and Carr heard the limousine pull away.

"They think it's a Japanese attack," she said. "They're afraid to be near the harbor."

"And you?"

"I'm a doctor," she said. "I can help."

"There's bound to be panic down there. I'll go with you."

"That won't be necessary."

"We can talk about that later," Carr said.

They drove toward the smoke until their taxi, caught in the snarl of traffic and swarming people, could go no farther.

"We'll have to make it the rest of the way on foot," Carr said.

The crowd surged in all directions. Above the blare of horns and shriek of sirens, people shouted to be heard. The blast had taken out most of the shop windows. Broken glass and smoking debris lay in the road, and small gouts of fire still burned.

At a checkpoint behind the docks a police inspector stood on the fender of his jeep and used a loud hailer to turn back the crowd.

"What's happened?" Carr shouted up at him.

"Fire aboard a liberty ship. Cargo of explosives. She blew up. Seven bloody fire engines and their crews went up with it. Whole blocks knocked flat. Can't get the fires under control."

"I'm a doctor," Ashley said. "Where are they bringing out the injured?"

"That way." The inspector pointed. "You'll see the ambulances coming in. But keep clear of the fires."

They crossed the cordon and hurried along a spur track. Beyond the twisted wreckage of dock cranes, half a dozen more ships were burning. Clouds of smoke rolled across the charred ramp where sailors of the Royal Indian Navy and British troops dragged fire hoses to fight the flames.

At the casualty area a doctor was separating the critical cases from the less serious for evacuation to the hospital. Before Ashley could join him, the docks shook and rocked under a second explosion. The force of the blast knocked those who were standing to the ground. Carr's ears felt as if they were packed with shot and ringing on the inside where the sound could not get out. He raised his head and saw birds slanting wildly on the air. A thousand feet above their streaking shapes a column of black smoke erupted into a huge ball while bursting shells and runaway tracers filled the sky with streamers. He glanced at Ashley, but her own gaze held fast to the snaking contrails overhead, and for once the dark pupils were rounded in some confusion of self-doubt.

Carr joined a rescue team doubling back to the scene. Along the quay, the badly injured were being borne out on litters. Other survivors limped along with help. Each time the smoky vapors shifted he could see hawsers of water shooting up from hoses where men with wet handkerchiefs tied about their lower faces fought the blaze.

A dock worker who looked to be no more than fourteen lay on the warped planking beside a slip. One arm had been blown away at the shoulder, and blood from the stump drenched his shirt. Beneath the kerchief tied about his skull, the eyes in the smooth face stared vacantly. Carr broke away from the others and lifted the boy in a fireman's carry. Below, in the slip, corpses floated in oily scum. He looked away and hurried back to the casualty point.

"This one's in a bad way," he said to Ashley.

"Put him down."

She pressed her fingers to the carotid, then forced open an eyelid and released it. "He's dead," she murmured.

He stared at her and replied, "In the cause of Jai Hind, I suppose."

They stood up slowly. Smoke left a shiny grime on her face and arms, and she had torn part of her sari to tie a sling for someone.

"We don't know if it was sabotage." Her protest sounded almost like a plea. "It could have been an accident."

Carr nodded toward the other burned and bloodied casualties on the ramp. "Either way, they'll pick up the bill, won't they?"

Her eyes brimmed momentarily, a reflex of contrition. Or was it only despair? Carr wasn't sure, though the distinction would hardly matter to the dead youth lying at their feet.

"They need me at hospital," Ashley said.

She would have turned from him, but he gripped her wrist. From the center of the disaster, fires stretched more than a mile.

"If it was Kordt," Carr said, "he'll try it again. Are you sure that's what you want?"

In the distance a fire brigade, no bigger than ants, suddenly scattered back from the burning shell of a warehouse. A wall toppled, covering two of the running figures in fiery rubble, and the searing updraft from the collapse swept a sheet of flame before it. The far-off shouts of the men and distant sound of whistles were lost in a windy blast of heat.

"He's been ordered out," Ashley replied in a low voice. "Back to Germany. He'll be gone in a few hours."

"By U-boat?" Carr said.

Her dark stare shifted slowly away from the conflagration. The conflict he had seen in the pupils a few moments before was gone, along with the familiar violence—buried in the terrible sorrow of the moment.

"Please don't ask me to betray him," she murmured.

Carr let go of her wrist. She moved toward one of the ambulances and did not look back. He watched the vehicle pull away, its lights burning in the pall of smoke that had already turned afternoon into night. He was thinking that she needn't have worried about betrayal. He knew with almost a blind certainty where Kordt would be.

36

The taxi dropped Carr a few kilometers above Juhu, and as soon as it had rattled off he slipped away from the road to the beach. The German service pistol he had taken from Devar made a comfortable weight taped to his leg below the bulge of the calf muscle. A salt breeze blew off the sea under a star-stung sky, but over Bombay fires cast an eerie glow on the smoke surging upward in black billows. Farther up the coast, the Koli village of Versova glimmered on the blue darkness.

He was sure the hut where he had been taken under blindfold to meet Kordt must lie somewhere between Ashley's bungalow and Versova. His memory gave up impressions like tagged evidence—the creak of coconut palms, the faint soughing of the sea, a stench of rotting fish—and he could remember the damp shine of Kordt's dark clothing in the candlelight, as if the German had been out in a dinghy. It would be the ideal spot for a U-boat to lie off the coast, Carr thought, remote and unlit, where the Koli fishermen kept to themselves in a few villages scattered along the shore.

He set out toward the pinprick of light that marked Versova. Small, brittle waves curled in, breaking against the wet slant of beach, the water flashing up with silver deposits of foam. The moon put a pearl luster on the palms, and the frond shadows swayed on the sand. Now and then a bungalow squatted in the trees that stretched out to the coast road, but the windows were shuttered and dark, and except for the windy silences that courted the night, he was alone.

The stars were another hour down the horizon before he stumbled onto the spot. It took shape suddenly on the balmy darkness as if it had stolen into his nerves—three mud-and-cane huts clumped together under massive palms. Down the beach, poles were lashed together on tall posts sunk into the sand. The frames were bare now, but tomorrow they would sag under the weight of several hundred bombil hung to dry in the sun and wind. Smaller fish had been left to rot at the base of the racks, and the decaying reek hung on the air.

Beyond the empty poles, a fishing dhow was aground in an inlet where the water at low tide did not reach. Its mast and hull were tilted to one side, and a large eye, painted on the prow under the bowsprit, glared at Carr as if it sensed his intrusion. A few skiffs had been dragged onto the beach above it, and nets with cork floats were stretched between them.

The huts looked to be abandoned. The thatched roof was gone from one, the cane siding breached on another, but the mud walls of the third stood intact. Carr approached it from its blind side. He ducked under the projecting thatch of the roof, worked his way around to the window slot, and peered in through the bamboo bars. Nothing stirred in the darkness. He checked the other two shells, then slipped back into the leafy scrub and spear grass and settled down in the dark to wait.

Around midnight he heard the whine of a motorbike on the road out of Versova. The sound drew near, throttling down before the engine was cut, and he could hear the crack of dry brush as the driver wheeled the machine into the scrub. The night fell silent again. Whoever had brought the bike must be waiting, too.

Carr untaped the pistol and hefted it in his hand. The tide was washing in, floating the dhow. The mast no longer tipped at a steep angle, and the water made a hollow splash against the hull.

Later, he heard voices from the beach. Beyond the thatch of spear grass, two Koli fishermen came into view. They were bent under the weight of a sail furled around a spar across their shoulders. Carr watched them struggle to get it across the thwarts of the dhow. One of the Kolis stayed with the boat to unlash the canvas. The other tramped up the beach to the huts, a bundle of clothing under his arm.

A third figure stepped from the cane shell of the second hut. There was no mistaking Kordt in the short trousers and drill shirt of a

British officer, the shoulder strap of the pistol belt gleaming in the windblown shadows of the palms. He spoke briefly to the Koli who handed him the clothing roll. The Indian went back down to the tidal inlet, and Kordt ducked back in under the thatched roof of the hut.

Carr crawled through the scrub to the first hut, flattened himself against the wall, and slipped around to the other side. The cocked pistol pointed at the ground, the trigger snug against the first joint of his finger. Enough moonlight seeped through the cane siding onto the clay floor to give a clear view of Kordt, stripped to the waist, buttoning on a pair of tight navy dungarees. The drill shirt and shorts lay in the dirt at his feet. The pistol belt hung within reach on a peg by the window slot, the butt of the Webley visible under the flap of the holster. Now the German pulled on a dark, long-necked seaman's sweater.

"Don't turn around just yet," Carr said, "unless you fancy a bullet in the liver."

The German froze, yet Carr could feel his mind racing. The blonde head turned slightly, no more than a millimeter, and remained fixed on the Webley slung on the peg.

"Don't be silly," Carr said. "You'll be dead before you reach it."

Kordt was silent. Carr stepped forward, lifted the pistol belt away, and looped it over his shoulder. "Turn around," he said, "but be a sport and keep your hands where I can see them."

Kordt stared out the window, watching the men at the dhow, or perhaps gazing past them out to sea. Probably he was thinking how close escape was, lying just off the skyline—a low steel shape on the water. Finally he turned, the edge of his mouth pulled down in a smile. "I rather hoped we'd seen the last of you," he said.

"Some people turn up like bad pfennigs."

"Always at the wrong time. Bloody inconsiderate of you."

"I'll try to work on it. You've left a nasty mess behind in Bombay. Quite a number dead. Indian as well as British."

"The ammunition stores would have been moved east. Some of them would have killed Indian troops fighting on our side. That's the nature of war, isn't it? Someone generally dies so someone else can live."

"I'll ask Clausewitz about that when I see him."

"He'll tell you that war is nothing more than a duel on an extensive scale."

"Or a gamble," Carr said.

"I should like to think it is more honorable than that."

"Wasn't China Blue a gamble? You nearly pulled it off."

"It might have turned the war our way. For a time, at least. But history loves success. It only flirts with failure."

"The unkindest cut of all," Carr said. "In cards, of course."

Kordt glanced out the window toward the tidal inlet. The dhow floated free on the water, its mast rocking gently on the stars as the swells washed against the hull.

"Were you planning to fish for bombil?" Carr smiled.

"Perhaps."

"Pity to spoil your trip."

"You've spoiled quite a few plans, lately. One more shouldn't make much difference."

"All in all, it seems a fair exchange. I expect you would have given me a bullet behind the ear at Nagaraja."

"Fortunes of war." Kordt shrugged.

"It might even have been the one that's in the chamber now," Carr said.

"They kill quite impartially," Kordt said.

"Someone has to pull the trigger first."

"That only takes a small effort."

"And no skill," Carr said, "at this range."

"Then you won't have to cheat."

"Did you think I planned to?"

"Please yourself," Kordt said. "You've got the pistol. It only takes one if you do it properly."

"Unless you prefer a rope on a British gallows."

"Are you offering a choice?"

"Think of it as a gamble. You might convince a court that you weren't here as a spy. Preposterous, of course, but it would gain time for you. There's always the chance of a careless guard, or a venal one. You might even escape. Consider the odds."

Kordt glanced out to sea once more where a U-boat waited beneath the phosphorescent sparkle like a promise. The melancholy smile came once more into his mouth, and he shook his head. "Then I'll gamble on a bullet."

"Why?" Carr said.

"I prefer the odds."

"There *are* no odds with a bullet."

"That's why I prefer one."

Kordt's gray stare came up, level with Carr's. Then it seemed to pass through Carr into the distant past, as if locked into a vision.

Carr raised the pistol until the front sight was trained on an axis between Kordt's eyes, which did not flinch at all, even as Carr's finger took up the slack of the trigger. He could feel the steel shape itself like a half smile against the whorled ridges of skin as he squeezed the sear into disengagement. The hammer fell with a dull click against the firing pin.

"Bang!" Carr gave a low chuckle. "You lose."

For once, the German seemed unable to comprehend. Behind the puzzled frown, his mind would not unlock from the idea of his own execution.

"If you expect to go out on the tide," Carr said, "you'd better get moving."

He slipped the Sam Browne belt with the Webley from his shoulder and tossed it back to Kordt. The German caught it, but did not move.

"Why?" he whispered finally.

"Call it a gambler's debt." Carr shrugged. "You saved my life at the train, remember?"

"No," Kordt said. "That's not the reason."

Carr nodded, thinking of Devar and Ashley, and replied, "Then let's say I owed someone else a life."

"Who?" Kordt pressed him.

"India," Carr murmured.

After a moment, Kordt nodded. India was something he could understand. "The British won't likely give you a Victoria Cross for this," he said.

"They got China Blue out of it. That's as far as our contract extended."

"Suppose I had made the other choice just now?"

"I would have packed you off to the nearest British gaol, of course."

"And I would have killed you if I'd got the chance," Kordt said. "You took a silly risk with an empty pistol."

"But you thought it was loaded." Carr laughed again. "Preconception is the best basis of all for a bluff. Sound advice. Try to remember it."

The two Koli fishermen were waiting in the stern of the dhow with long poles to push off. By now, Carr thought, they must be wondering what had happened to the German.

Kordt started out, but from the doorway he glanced over his shoulder at Carr. "It was always just a game with you, wasn't it?" he said.

"The rule for a cheat," Carr said, "is never to win too much. After you've won, lose a little back. Then quit."

Kordt smiled again from the shadows, and said, "You're a bloody puzzle, Carr, do you know it?" Then he was gone, the doorway empty.

Later, on the beach, Carr looked out to sea where the single-masted dhow, its sail shaped to a triangle of breeze-filled canvas, inched across the watery sparkle lit to full brilliance by the moon. For awhile the boat slipped in and out of the blinding gleam, like spangles hurled down on the water, and then it was gone off the skyline.

37

"You'll be going out at noon, tomorrow," Sterns said. "HMS *Phlox*. She's lying off Timber Bunder. Anything you need, meantime?"

"Some transport," Carr said, "if you can spare it."

"I could let you have a jeep till then," Sterns said, "if you promise not to flog it."

"Don't worry," Carr said. "Jeeps aren't moving well these days in the Thieves' Market."

Ashley was not at her home on Malabar Hill. Carr checked the hospital and found that she had worked thirty-six hours into the disaster, then left. He had a fair idea where she would be and drove out the coast road toward Juhu. It was now four days since the explosion of the liberty ship in the harbor, and a few fires still smoldered among the charred ruins that stretched several miles along the waterfront. The pall of smoke on the sky over the docks hung for a long time in the side mirror of the jeep.

Twilight was sliding out to sea when he turned into the trees below the bungalow. He parked the jeep and followed the footpath in the bending grass out to the beach. The sea gave its glimmer to a few swirls of stranded dusk in the last light, and he saw Ashley a short distance down the sandy strand. She sat against one of the slanting palms, one knee uplifted in the flaring jodhpurs where her hand rested with her father's riding crop. A sweater top, open at the throat, held the round swell of her breasts tightly confined, and the breeze off the water gave a gleam of black movement to her hair, unbound and spilling heavily down.

For what seemed an interminable time Carr himself did not move, gazing at her. After awhile she seemed to grow aware of his stare, as if it exerted some gravitational pull, and her head turned slowly.

Carr went straight to her in the cool darkness, dropped to one knee, and dipped his fingers into her hair. Neither of them said a word, and he could feel the peaceful, clinging surrender of her mouth under his long before the lips stirred apart in the heat of sexual response.

Once, during the night, Carr woke and found her gone, the bed still warm. He sprang up silently and caught sight of her, naked, where the French doors lay open to let in the breeze. Beyond her nude figure the sky soared out to the horizon and a line of clouds, white and stainless as the floes of ice in snow water. Her cheek was pressed reflectively against her hands, which were flattened on the frame, and there was something outrageously female and attractive in the curve of her hips and the glaze of her bare flesh against the brightness of the clouds.

Carr went over to her and put his arms around her from behind. Her breasts were still warm, the tips engorged from the intensity of lovemaking. He bent and kissed her neck at the shoulder. Ashley closed her eyes, leaning back against him and holding his hands to her breasts.

"What were you thinking about?" he asked.

Her reply was a long time in coming, as if she were still unsure. "I was trying to decide who I am," she said, "and where I belong."

"We're both outcasts of a sort," Carr said. "You because you're half English, and me because I prefer to be. We don't fit into the two worlds we were born into. It forces you to invent a new one. You might enjoy it there. Why don't you come along with me and find out?"

"Where?" Ashley smiled. "To a gambling casino?"

"Try to think of the casinos as an international banking trust. A place to keep your money. A withdrawal is no more complicated than pulling a card out of a shoe, or your sleeve. It's quite safe as long as you know which card is coming up."

"Suppose it's not the card you expected?"

"Then you call for a new deck, and start over."

"You never think of it as cheating?"

"The house cheats with the odds," Carr said. "I'm only squaring things."

"A form of retribution?" Ashley smiled.

"Exactly." Carr chuckled. "Come back to Lisbon with me. I've got some affairs to settle. From there we could go on to Rio and take a villa above Botafogo Beach. You can get used to being yourself in tropical surroundings."

"Myself." She shook her head. "I'm not sure who that is."

"A fascinating woman," Carr said. "Beautiful. Passionate. Enormously complex. I wouldn't change anything about her."

She stared silently at the dark gleam of the sea under the stunning brightness of the clouds ablaze on the horizon. "I can't leave India," she said finally.

"What's to prevent you?"

"Obligation," Ashley said. "If not to myself, at least to Jai."

"When independence comes—and it *will* after the bloody war—do you think the new government will feel any obligation to an Anglo-Indian?"

Once again her glossy black hair grazed his chest as her head shook in the tiniest negation of movement. "Perhaps not," she murmured. "If it turns out that way, maybe I'll be ready to leave."

Carr drew her around by the shoulders, away from the silver distances of the sea, and took her face in both his hands.

"Then I suppose I'll have to come back for you," he said. "Will you be here?"

She did not reply, but the glimmer of a tear lost itself swiftly on the translucent blackness of her stare, and it was answer enough.

At the north tip of the harbor, Sterns was waiting in a military sedan as Carr drove up in the jeep. The senior officer opened the door and stepped out into the sun. "You were late the first time we met," he said. "I should have expected that you would uphold the tradition."

"What kind of a sentimental farewell is that?" Carr clapped him on the shoulder.

"Another five minutes and you would have missed your ship."

"I can see you're anxious to be rid of me."

Sterns squinted hard at the shadow of the mainland across the harbor. He was a man who neither gave nor accepted praise easily. "I expect that might have been true, once," he said, as if he were pinning the words on Carr like a minor decoration. "What do you propose to do with yourself?"

"I suppose now that you people have got me into it, I might as well stay around for the end of the game."

"Join the fight?" Sterns gave him an incredulous look. "*You?*"

"We all have a patriotic duty to get it over with as soon as possible," Carr said. "The allies will be invading any day. How can I rest with Monte Carlo in German hands? Besides, if I help in the liberation, it's bound to insure my welcome after the war. They couldn't very well post the photo at the *salle d'entree* of the man who delivered them from the Nazi yoke, could they?"

"Or the chap who cheated the Germans out of China Blue," Sterns said. "The dinghy's waiting to take you out. I'll see you off."

HMS *Phlox*, one of the aging corvettes of the Flower Class, lay at her mooring in the harbor. After six months of escort service between Bombay and Suez, she was bound for Liverpool by way of Alexandria and Gibraltar.

On deck, a sublieutenant led Carr down the companionway ladder, through a cramped wardroom, into a two-man berth.

"We're shy one officer," he said. "Ever been to sea on a corvette, sir?"

"No."

"The ship rolls a bit, even in calm weather. Better have the lower berth. Makes it easier if you're seasick."

Carr smiled, knowing the officer meant easier for the man above.

"We were scheduled to be in port ten days," the lieutenant went on, "but with the docks gone, they're turning us out early. Pity. The lads were looking to celebrate."

"The voyage home?"

"Didn't you hear it ashore?" The officer looked surprised. "*Phlox* got a U-boat. Four nights ago, on the way in."

Gripping a bulkhead, Carr had ducked low for a look at the berth. He stopped moving, and said, "Where?"

"Bit north of here. Not so usual to find one operating in these waters. Probably belonged to the group at Penang."

Carr straightened, gazing at the young officer who reminded him of Paine. "Were there any survivors?"

"None, sir. As soon as the asdic pinged her, she dove. The best guess is a depth charge cracked her open on the bottom."

"How can you be sure?"

"Quite a massive oil slick, and large amounts of flotsam. Of course, the Admiralty will classify it as a probable kill, but there's not much doubt we finished her."

"Bad luck for the sub." Carr shrugged.

"I've got to get topside, sir. You might want to stay below until we're underway. Lots of activity on deck, and not much room. Once we're out of heavy traffic, I'll show you round the ship."

Later, the throb of the engines settled into Carr's head. He climbed the ladder to the fo'c'sle, and leaned on the starboard rail below the four-inch gun. Across the sparkle of the water, the blackened ruin of the docks streamed away, but beyond it Bombay lay sun-washed and clean on the blue brilliance of the day. He watched it shrink and fade until it was only a dim impression on the distance, lifting and falling off the horizon like a lovely mystery. Probably it had looked that way to Kordt on the deck of another ship steaming toward it years earlier.

A fleck of spray from the bow wave touched Carr's face, and he thought, *I wonder if he made it?*

HISTORICAL AFTERWORD
AND ACKNOWLEDGMENTS

I n the last days of the war, Subhas Bose decided to seek asylum in the USSR. He hoped to exploit the deteriorating relations between Stalin and the West to gain entry. Word of the Soviet declaration of war against Japan reached him on August 11, 1945. He knew he could not stay allied with the Japanese and expect to be received by Stalin. The situation forced him to act.

On August 17, Bose and his chief of staff, Lt. Col Habib-ur-Rehman, flew out of Saigon aboard a Japanese aircraft bound for Tokyo via Dairen in Manchuria. In Dairen it would be possible to place themselves under Russian protection. The flight touched down at Taihoku on Formosa for refueling. On takeoff, it crashed and caught fire. Severely burned, Bose was rushed to a Japanese military hospital where, conscious, he survived for six hours. According to Habib-ur-Rehman, the remains were cremated and the ashes flown to Tokyo.

Since independence in 1947, the Indian government has conducted a number of inquiries into Bose's death because of persistent rumors that he did not die in a plane crash. One scenario purports that he reached the Soviet Union, where he was imprisoned with the secret consent of the British. Since Stalin had now joined in the war against Japan, he could not very well grant asylum to Bose, who was still technically allied with Tokyo. The British did not want him either, for they would have been compelled to execute him for treason, inciting a new crisis.

The mystery took a bizarre twist some years later when Bose was allegedly sighted in a Siberian prison camp by a visiting Indian official. This took place at a time when India was politically aligned

with the USSR and receiving Soviet aid. Public release of the information would have caused a rupture between the two powers. So
goes the story.

There are still many who believe that Bose faked his death and
reached Moscow. It was, after all, his intention. But it is always
a controversial hero who passes so swiftly into myth in the minds
of men.

Literary debts are easily incurred, and impossible to repay, so
the author can only sign IOUs to: Indian poet and writer Dom
Moraes of Bombay; John Masters, D. S. O. and O. B. E., who fought
with the Chindits in Burma and wrote novels about India—no one
ever wrote them better; and finally Frank Collier, Lt. Col, USAF
(ret), who fought in the India-Burma Theater and helped in the
research of this book.